Red, White, and Scotch
An O Line Mystery

M. Saylor Billings

A Billibatt Production

ISBN: 0985859718
ISBN-13: 978-0-9858597-1-8

For my family.

Library of Congress Catalog Card Number: 2013912062
ISBN: 0985859717
ISBN 13: 9780985859718
Billibatt Productions
www.billibatt.com
www.olinemysteries.com

CONTENTS

ACKNOWLEDGMENTS

As this is the last book of this series I need to once again thank all the people who worked on The O Line Mystery Shorts. Especially Beth and Nina who brought Lorna and Annie to life in ways I could never have imagined. Thanks to all of you.

A special thanks to my wife, who endured five years of the series in all it's forms. Thank you to my "writing partners", Claude and Boudreaux.

And many thanks to my sister for reading over my shoulder.

PROLOGUE

Jones Barrett took another long, controlled stride and quietly sounded out the word, "confidence". He was in management now, this is the National Security Agency and there are standards expected of him. Which is why he wore these slightly ill fitting and uncomfortable slacks. Regaining his balance, he took another step forward and murmured, "competence". He should have chosen a different shade of navy. These slacks were too dark. They look black to him. And with the next carefully placed step he said, "control". Using the length of the conference room his mantra grew quicker with each long stiff knee stride becoming shorter until he was stabbing the bristled carpet with his heels; confidence, competence, control, confidence, competence. Turn. Control. On the final lap he eyed the beverage caddy laden with a teapot, a coffee pot, a water pitcher, and coffee cups he himself cleaned. Competence. He recounted the file folders, containing his forthcoming inter-agency alliance meeting's agenda, neatly stacked in the middle of the long conference table. Control.

He stopped in front of the glass-framed certificate of occupancy, dated September 1985, squatted down slightly and checked his nose hairs in the glass reflection. A blue fluorescent beam bounced off his brown lacquered hair helmet and he caught himself, suddenly remembering this wood paneled room was a surveilled room, and tried to cover for his uncouth behavior by rubbing his temples, doing facial exercises, then capping it off by shrugging his shoulders with a couple of over exaggerated deep breaths. His dark eyes jetted about as he left the room, closed the door, and locked it from the outside.

"Buzz me when they get settled in." He tapped Chris' desk a couple of times as he strode past.

"Sure." Chris responded without looking up. She had heard his deliberate, arrogant gait echoing through the hall and declined him the eye contact a subordinate customarily yields to their superiors. After all, she was a good fifteen years older than him.

Christiana Cook had just turned fifty years old, but still had the body of a fit thirty year old. The gray hair that she refused to dye back to its chestnut hue gave her age away. Unlike the wisdom whiskers she plucked daily from her chin, she honored her gray hair. She had worked in this NSA office, tucked inside the shell corporation of Pearson Imports in downtown San Francisco, for 23 years. No promotion, but no lay off's either. She kept her head down, spoke only when spoken too, and had only concealed information once. But, then, she was acting under orders.

She had weathered at least six "bosses", so far. One died, which was unfortunate considering that he had only been two years older than she was now. And his dispirited replacement retired a couple of years later. The *most* unfortunate, in her opinion, was the one who took early retirement. (Read: He had a nervous breakdown.)

That poor man was definitely a cut above the rest simply by being considerate and levelheaded, but then again, he did end up wearing tube socks over his hands in those last days. A few others came through during the big pot stirring that happened just after September 11, 2001. But this last one, a woman no less, seemed to have done a bunk and was on the lam. Chris considered this for a moment; it was vey strange behavior for Agent Karen Bernard, who had seemed so docile.

No one seems to be asking the question, why. Why would a woman with both CIA and NSA experience steal a satellite device like this one? They're treating it as if she woke up one morning and said, "Fuck it. Fuck 20 something years of work, fuck the retirement fund, and fuck the mortgage. My whole career has gone tits up and I'm outta here!" Chris pulled herself out of her revelry and clicked on her computer.

So the pot had been stirred again and she ended up with this, do si do, with the two last names and she couldn't tell if she should hyphenate it or if his first name was Jones, and his last name Barrett.

What she *did* know, not that she'd share this with anyone, was that this little mister with the two last names rise through the ranks from the general office staff in "the pit" to a managerial Under Division Chief could only be called meteoric. In her own personal estimation, not that anyone would ask, Van Elder, the Division Chief had made a critical management error in promoting Mr. Two Last Names. It should have been Donny or that woman from downstairs, the one who came up with that closed network computer thing. She's a sharp one, Chris thought to herself, and doesn't wear tube socks.

Chris watched the elevator doors slide open from her hallway alcove as two men, one trim and one fat, stepped into the small waiting area and looked expectantly at her.

Chris gave a begrudging grin, Federal Bureau of Investigation and Homeland Security, obviously. Then a short, scruffy looking man stepped out from behind them. Now *this* should be interesting, Chris thought. Who invited the Central Intelligence Agency?

Chris slid her hand into her desk drawer and pulled out a set of keys. "Follow me," she said to them.

Jones let a few supercilious minutes lapse before joining his guests. "My apologies," he said hurriedly as he swept into the conference room. He looked up and realized there was a third man at the table, an uninvited man. "Oh." Then he recovered and stood up slightly reaching his hand across the table. "Jones Barrett."

The man stood and offered his hand but not his name.

"Jones!" The Homeland Agent, Patrick Hudson's, booming voice bounced off the hard surfaces of the room and stopped Jones mid squat back into his seat. "Considering the possible international expanse of this mission we felt it necessary to read in the CIA."

"I'm sorry I don't have enough file folders-uh-We? Who decided this?"

"Don't worry about it." The CIA agent bit off his sentence like he was savoring a bitter lemon sandwich.

"The Director," Patrick referred to his boss in Homeland Security.

"Van Elder said nothing to me about it," Jones protested.

"The *National* Intelligence Director," Patrick corrected him with growing disdain. "But I'd like to thank you for hosting the meeting today. Generally, it's Homeland that has to do the catering." Patrick glared at the pitiful beverage cart.

Confidence, competence, control. Jones eyeballed the FBI agent, Sunil. Sunil looked down as he laced his fingers together.

"Now, tell me," Patrick spoke deliberately at the wood paneled walls, "just as a reference, how exactly does the NSA lose the most valuable piece of TECH-INT (technical intelligence) known to clandestine services since the Enigma?" Patrick grinned and chortled, expanding his already expansive gut.

Jones jumped up and quickly slid the folders over to each person, except the unkempt CIA man. "I've arranged the memo's here for you. Basically it amounts to a rogue agent taking advantage of some corporate espionage that took place about a month ago."

"A MONTH!" the CIA agent bellowed.

Jones held up his hands, gesturing agreement. "Before I got here."

The CIA agent and Patrick exchanged a knowing look.

"Well, promoted to this position, I mean. We don't have any indication that the Aurora has left the country. Personally, I feel like this could be retaliation. "

"So what is this? A retrieval mission?" the CIA agent asked.

FBI agent, Sunil, was skimming through pages in the folder, looking at the dates and names on the memos. "A slow train wreck," He murmured aloud.

"Pardon?" Jones asked Sunil. "It's a retrieval mission." Jones scoffed indignantly at Sunil's obvious lack of actual mission experience.

"This is a slow train wreck. First, the FBI needs to know that all domestic options have been exhausted. Are you certain, and what proof do you have, that your agent did not go on a retrieval mission on her own for this Aurora and get herself killed? What you're saying is one *lone* agent pulled this off from underneath the entire NSA's nose." Sunil shrugged. "If so then you have two issues, a missing agent and a missing object. Are they related? And secondly, in order to prosecute we need the proof of fraud between Spectorgies and The Hayward. Actually, memo's," Sunil shut the folder and slid it back to the center of the table, "are not going to cut it." Sunil leaned back in his chair and fell silent again.

"Good." Patrick slid his file folder over to the CIA agent, who didn't bother with it and slid it toward the center of the table. "This Barbara Rutledge, I'm guessing was called Bobbie at one point."

Jones was staring regrettably at his file folder.

"You know her as Karen Bernard, or the Nurse." The CIA agent directed the comment at Jones.

"Yeah," Jones answered the CIA agent fractiously. "Look, I'm just curious-"

Patrick cut him off. "Let's hold your questions until we get this all out on the table."

Outside the conference room, Chris watched Donny, who wielded a mop and scuttle around the corner, playfully hopping over to her desk. Chris rolled her eyes at him. Donny had worked with Agent Bernard on this very case and she wondered why he wasn't in on this meeting as well.

"What are you doing?" Chris asked.

Donny smiled menacingly. "I heard Homeland was here. I'm just here for the clean up."

Chris laughed and raised an eyebrow at him. "You're no good, you know that?"

"How's the yoga going?" Donny asked.

"I'll outlive all of you."

"That doesn't worry you in the least, does it?"

"Nope."

"Have you heard anything?" he asked with a cagey grin.

"Nope."

Donny got serious for a moment. "Agent Bernard got a raw deal, you know. I only hope she's safe, somewhere." He leaned on the mop and nodded. "We've got a missing agent and they're probably in there treating this like a treason case." Donny shook his head with regret. He would get no reaction from this secretary who, no doubt, had seen and heard everything. But Chris was like petrified oak, he thought, unbreakable.

Chris desperately wanted to tell this young man to keep his head down, work his assignments and stay out of the fires but instead she said, "I hope all our agents are safe. But you know, we all make choices, it seems Agent Bernard made hers, I'm afraid."

"Yeah," Donny agreed wondering just how much Chris knew. "Did you ever think you'd live to see an actual inter-agency alliance meeting?"

Chris gave him a closed mouth grin and slowly shook her head at him before returning her gaze to her computer monitor.

"Let me know if you need anything?" he added backing away.

Chris guffawed at his offer. "Oh yeah, you'll be the first person I call."

Donny walked away laughing. "You don't know what you're missing."

Chris answered him in the same singsong tone, "Because I don't watch horror movies."

The meeting of the inter-agency alliance seemed to be winding down now that Jones had finally been able to take his turn at leading the discussion. Without using the economy of the FBI agent, nor the command of the Homeland Security, nor the confidence of the CIA agent, his words fell on deaf ears.

The CIA agent flipped languidly though the file folder as Jones spoke then slid it back to the center of the table for the fourth time. "We're not using our cyber assets here," he said.

"As you can see," Jones began pointing out one specific memo he had arranged.

"No."

Jones gave his own begrudging chortle. "In the light of the cooperation we can afford one another here..."

The CIA agent scratched his cheek stubble. "Yeah, yeah, listen. Van Elder should never have hired a fly-by-night contractor like The Hayward in the first place. We're not offering up *any* assets to you. This is strictly a retrieval mission. We don't care about any personnel issues you have going on here. And I'm gonna need your billing codes for this, before we go out there. This isn't going on our books."

"Just let us know what you'll need and we'll provide it for you."

The CIA agent flexed his hands out in frustration and enunciated each word. "I'll need the billing codes before I leave here."

Sunil, who had been sent into the inter-agency alliance meeting in place of his boss, watched with fascination. Sunil was at least three rungs down the ladder in agency hierarchy from these guys, but they didn't know that. And he was congratulating himself that he had covered for his boss without anyone being the wiser. And now, after experiencing this devolution of "inter-agency animosity" himself, he was more sympathetic to his boss's suffering from what he secretly believed to be a white man's disease, irritable bowel syndrome.

"I'll pass it by Van Elder," replied Jones.

Patrick, Sunil, and the CIA agent remained seated as Jones pushed his chair back from the table and stood. "Thank you guys for coming in," Jones said.

Sunil began to push back from the table too but

stopped himself and pretended to resettle himself back into his chair in defiance.

Patrick and the CIA agent didn't budge but looked up at Jones. "Where are you going?" Patrick asked. "We're using Homeland protocol here. This is just the beginning; you haven't even reached out to local authorities."

Jones realized his mistake and covered for himself. "Help yourself to some drinks. I'll be back in a few minutes. Restrooms are down the hall to the right."

Sunil stretched his legs again and stood up. He walked over to the beverage cart and poured himself a cup of water.

"We could all use one of those, I think." Patrick directed his comment to Sunil.

Sunil realized his mistake. With Jones out of the room now, he felt the weight and heat of a large red target being placed firmly on his own back. Sunil replaced his cup back on the tray and purposefully strode out of the room and turned right without closing the door behind him.

Jones scurried down the hall to Chris' desk. "I need Van Elder and billing codes."

"For what?"

"Why are you so fucking difficult, *woman*? Get me Van Elder. You know what? Forget it. I'll do it myself, since it's just *so* tedious and mundane for you to use a fucking phone." Jones continued raging as he slammed the door to his office behind him.

Chris muttered into her tea, "Let the good times roll."

CHAPTER 1

Sally Thompson locked the back door of the 1930's Craftsman bungalow, the home she shared with her partner, and pocketed the key. She took a deep breath of the sweet lilac and honeysuckle aroma. Briefly glancing around the high fence that enclosed the backyard she walked over to the bike stand and pulled out the red single speed cruiser. Her partner, Lorna, had bought the bike three years ago when they first moved from New York City to Ohlone Island. Sally pulled the helmet and yellow fluorescent vest out of the wicker basket and laid them on the ground before mounting and kicking off.

The cold murky waters of the San Francisco Bay surround Ohlone Island like an industrial waste moat. The island does not lay due north to south or east to west. But the northwest tip of the island, where the aborted military base lay rotting in the salt air, sits inside the San Francisco County line. And the furthest southeast point then lays three miles away, well inside the Alameda County line right next to the Oakland airport. As a matter of fact, the same bottom muck that was dredged up from the canal between Ohlone and the adjacent Oakland Port was used to build up the land where the vacated military base sat upon and was also partly used to build the Oakland airport runways on. It is an uninteresting and little known fact, but a fact that made many industrialists very wealthy. Perhaps it is only a matter of time before the same type of thinking and progress happens in the sky above us. This wayward thought brought Sally to a halt at the first stop sign.

The mile and a half bike ride from her house to the Auld Alliance Cafe stretched across the island on a main avenue where tall palm trees and Coastal Live Oaks stretched into the sky. Despite the decades of industrial waste much of the island was built upon, the floral scent was the first thing visitors noticed; wild rosemary, fennel, and rose bushes grew in manicured front lawns of well preserved Victorian homes. Law enforcement and motorists take their bike lanes, which are well marked out, seriously. And it's safe to say that almost everyone, able bodied or not, on the island rides a bike and that can sometimes make the bike lanes congested. But not today, thankfully. No - it's been *four* years, not three, since they moved here because Lorna visited the island, met Annie, and found the apartment they had rented during the same trip in August. That's right, and they moved here in September. Four years this month.

Sally cruised past memories starting with the car mechanics garage where Lorna had discovered an illegal poker game. There, Lorna felt the need to extricate her buddy, who worked at the hardware store, from the clutches of men who prayed upon his addiction and consequently she ran afoul of the local law enforcement.

The Victorian mansion on a perpendicular street to this main avenue was where Lorna and her best friend, Annie, had volunteered at the Victorian Homes Tour and stumbled on a dead body. Well technically, Annie had quite literally stumbled on the dead body, but it was Lorna who finally pointed the police detective to the actual killer. Annie and Lorna had gotten themselves mixed up in so many altercations with local murderers and fraudsters; it really was only a matter of time before Lorna got shot.

Perhaps this whole situation they are in now had been building around them ever since they moved here. Seeping into their lives like a fog, intermittent and slow but absolute. Sally cruised past a small dog park deep in thought. There isn't even a name for what has happened this last year but it - whatever you'd call it, a situation, maybe - was like a lie told in seven steps. On one end you have the truth, she and Lorna moved from the frenetic world of New York City to settle down and enjoy life each second a minutes worth. Then, on the other end Lorna, escaped a killer's mark by a hair's breadth. Sally stared into the dark windows of the Auld Alliance Cafe searching for those five other steps that held the gears, and mechanisms of that final lie. The sign taped to the inside door of the Auld Alliance Cafe read: *Closed for kitchen renovations.*

~~~

Michael Chan knitted his expressive eyebrows together and paused briefly before climbing the wooden spiral staircase. He winced and gazed up as the first step wheezed belligerently beneath the weight of his foot. The entire Auld Alliance Cafe was dark but the office door at the top of the stairs, where a safety light usually shone, was particularly dark. He didn't have much time, he just needed to climb this scary dark staircase, go into the office, grab the deed, and leave. He's been in hundreds of scarier situations. You are a trained FBI agent, he reassured himself. Well, maybe not hundreds, but at least ten, maybe eleven. The prickly hairs on the back of his neck were troubling him. He took a deep breath, dashed up the stairs and threw open the heavy oak door to the office.

He slapped on the light switch and watched the bare bulb swing back and forth ever so gently. The room was crowded, part storage and part office space. A stack of plastic storage bins sat precariously atop a stack of unfolded cardboard to-go containers defying gravity as it leaned away from one wall. An old metal four-drawer filing cabinet stood sentinel next to an expansive antique desk. A modern metal kitchen-shelving unit filled with kitchen equipment took up the far wall and a large black leather four-person couch took up the wall to his right. He looked first at the couch, then the desk, and then back at the relatively small door jam he stood in and the spiral staircase he had just climbed and thought, how?

He would have to figure out the dynamics later. The owners of the Auld Alliance, Lek and Ivy Souceck, (most recently known as Wallace and Eunice Baumgarten or Tom and Rose Kautz among other aliases) were not here and he was running out of time. He lingered in the doorway for a moment, on second thought - he walked into the cramped office space and felt around on the walls giving each wall a knock with his fist. He crawled under the desk and banged on the wall.

"Mmm Hmm." He uttered aloud to himself. He pulled off the panel and saw a hole big enough for a two-foot square safe. He lifted out the envelope off the bottom and pushed himself back on the black leather couch and rubbed the base of his palm back and forth across his brow.

"You don't think -" A voice emitted from the walls.

Michael shot off the couch, a shudder past through him as Sally Thompson stirred out from behind the plastic storage bins and cardboard containers.

"It's you!" Michael grabbed his chest and exhaled as he collapsed on the couch again.

"You don't actually think my parents would leave anything behind for you, do you?" Sally finished.

Michael fought to compose himself. "No, of course not. What are you doing here? I was going to meet you at the safe house."

"Same thing as you. My parents are old and their disappearance acts are legendary, but it's just a matter of time before they slip up."

"Who are you, exactly?" Sally maneuvered her lanky frame over in front of the desk and towered over Michael, who remained seated on the couch.

Michael looked up at her. "My name is Michael Chan. I work for Elliot, well, before he died, I work in Elliot's FBI division. But I was recruited," Michael waffled, "I'm just an IT guy - I was recruited."

Unmoving, Sally considered him. Chinese heritage, smooth hands, slightly flabby, nervous, so he's a geek. He's visibly jumpy, so he's had almost no field training.

"I thought you'd meet me at the safe house but this is fine. I was running late." He continued letting out an exaggerated puff of air. "You make a hell of an entrance."

"Wait till you see my exit." Sally said flatly but her wide dark eyes sparkled. "Your note said above the Lemon Suds, how was I to know that was your safe house?"

But how did she beat him here, he speculated, but dropped it. "Right. Well, I'm sure you're wondering what happened to your parents."

"No. I'm not."

Michael looked up at Sally again, he really wished she'd sit down and stop hovering. "I know who shot Lorna. I know who killed Tim. How's the code book coming? Have you cracked it yet?"

Sally didn't budge. He gave her a minute to react but nothing, she didn't even blink. Finally, she rolled her eyes at him, gave a sigh of disgust, and moved toward the door.

"Hold on," Michael croaked out desperately.

"Take it to the police." Sally tossed over her shoulder as she walked out the door.

Michael followed Sally down the spiral staircase. "Wait a minute, I've got information for you."

Sally stopped and turned around. "Really? How do you know the information that I need? Because I'm pretty sure you don't even know my questions. What kind of damage has Lorna's heart taken? Will she have any weird memory loss? Is someone else going to make an attempt on her life? And most of all, *really*, how the *hell* am I gonna make it through the next month of my life? Do you have those answers? Have you been bestowed with some higher power and can tell me all that?"

"I'm sorry." Michael whispered. "I'm really, really, sorry. Those are your priorities, now I understand that. I just want to help."

"No you don't. Who the hell do you think you're talking to? If you wanted to help you'd be at the police station or at the hospital."

Michael took a furious glance around the deserted cafe. The wood polish on the dark wall paneling glistened from the street lamps shining in through the storefront, the smell of pastries and coffee, and the silence was normal. He determined they were safe to talk in here. He felt the flop sweat trickle down the back of his neck and down his rib cage. He had no other options left and even though she didn't know it, Sally didn't either. They had both been inexplicably drug down into this thing. He began again. "Please. I'm sorry. Let me start again. Let's just have a seat and we'll start again." Michael grabbed a chair off a cafe table and placed it on the floor for Sally and quickly grabbed the other chair and sat down. "Tell me how can I help you." Obviously, Sally had her mothers Chinese heritage with her straight black, almost blue, hair but her height bespoke of a father with Caucasian ancestry.

Sally looked at the chair before sitting down. "You asked me to meet you. Why don't you just tell me what it is you want? Do *not* try to bullshit me either."

"You know who I am?"

"Yes, you *Putz*! Damn it! I'm not playing this cloak and dagger bullshit with you. Got that? Not playing. Not buying it. You, my parents, the entire intelligence apparatus need to FUCK OFF. I'm done! So you tell whomever to back off."

Michael nodded but frowned and offered earnestly, "You know that's not going to happen, Sally." He continued quietly, "They are going to keep coming. The more people find out about the Aurora the harder they will come at you and they won't stop. And not just the intelligence services - private contractors, foreign agencies, the justice department, and God knows whom else. Right now and for a small amount of time, we can control this. We can find it and turn it over and be done with it. I'm being honest with you. That's all I've got left, you're all I got left and unfortunately for you..." Michael trailed off. "But I'm going to need your help here."

Sally shook her head and looked down at the floor. Her whole adult life she's been running from this very situation. And now, after she worked so hard to build a family, a career, and a good life for herself to have her worst possible imaginings laid at her doorstep like this was an absolute crushing blow. Michael looked out of the storefront windows into the shadows of the street lamps, giving Sally a moment to adjust to this new reality. If there were such a thing as clandestine royalty, she was it. Her grandfather had been an establishing figure of the intelligence services. The operations her father and mother executed were legendary and even taught at Quantico.

Michael continued. "I'm very worried about Annie. I'm worried he's going to strike at her next. We need a plan. Look, I sent your parents away. They're in Prague. They think they're going to rendezvous with some agents. But really, I just needed them to be safely away somewhere."

For the first time, Sally looked at Michael approvingly. "That was smart, you know they had very lucrative careers in the CIA. God only knows what they would have done to get their hands on and sell the Aurora to the highest bidder."

"Yes. But, ya' know, Elliot pulled them in on this. He must have trusted them somewhat. He told me it was your father who pulled him out of that burning car in Belgrade back in the day."

"I know the story." Sally, in no mood to reminisce, cut him off.

"That was some serious cold war shit, Dude. I mean, your Grandfather helped set up the CIA from the OSS and your mom is a legend - everyone who does any work on China knows, we even studied your mom's embassy work, Dude. Why-" Michael stopped himself. This wasn't his business. "I'm sorry, off topic, I know. Okay, I got a line on Lorna's shooter; he's a hired assassin. I know where he's staying and I've got a tracker on his car.

What do you want me to do?"

Sally was incredulous. "Why are you asking me? Why haven't you taken him out?"

"I can take him out at the drop of a hat. But if you want to try and put him through the system, have him arrested, we can go that route too."

Sally's face contorted into disbelief. Two things occurred to her at once. First, this neophyte, however misinformed, was telling her the truth. She knows this because it was her mother who had previously mentioned Elliot's name as well. And if her mother was telling the truth about that then this is the young man who had botched the Aurora retrieval that got Tim killed. Secondly, this woefully agent before her has no idea about the Nurse, which means she is acting on her own and not with the NSA. But Sally, always one to play her cards close to her chest didn't show her hand here. "I can't believe you guys. You've got the CIA, the FBI, and the NSA working together and you guys can't figure out what to do with a hired gun? This isn't on me. Seriously, you people are the most feckless - no wonder everyone's hiring these independent contractors."

Michael rocked back and forth excitedly, "Wait, what? The CIA? Who's working with the CIA? Elliot brought your parents out of retirement as just hired hands. We didn't bring in the other FBI divisions, either. Who told you otherwise?"

"You *are* the FBI! What are you saying?"

"No wait, go back. Who told you all this?"

"The Nurse. Karen Bernard with the NSA. I was told this had become an inter-agency alliance for the purposes of recovering the Aurora."

Michael's eyes grew wide as he let out a long, low moan and leaned back in his chair. "No. There's no interagency nothing. She told you this? What else?"

Sally leaned back in her chair and paused. Her eyes narrowed. "Why don't you tell me what it is *you* know?"

Michael looked at his watch. "Hold on."

Sally watched as Michael began muttering to him self and gesticulating as if he were typing on a keyboard.

"Okay, okay, let me just put it in order." Michael lapsed into his own bubble for a moment.

Sally folded her arms across her chest, "I've got all the time in the world."

He mentally came back into the room, took a deep breath and met Sally's hard gaze, "Okay wait, let me explain this component first."

"Okay."

"Of course you don't know this, why would you? Listen, back in the Johnson, Kennedy, Nixon era -"

"Oh God." Sally slapped her forehead.

"Just listen. Hoover, J. Edgar, right? He was getting old -"

Sally shook her head in frustration.

"Please." Michael pleaded. "I know he was a power hungry troll. But! He believed he was really doing the best thing for the people of his country."

"Oh sure," Sally mocked, "his motives were *pure*."

"And as a Chinese American I agree with you but, because of all the political infighting and how the politicians were using the intelligence services for their own parties benefits he foresaw a lot of the problems that were coming down the road. So he set up this division within a division of the FBI. See, I work for the fraud division but I work specifically in the *special* fraud division out of Virginia." Michael rippled with excitement. "Our ops are seen as income generating *and* classified. Only to be overseen by the *special* director. It would literally take an act of Congress to open up our division and they can't do that because of the classified nature of the work. This thing is *solar*. Hoover handpicked Elliot to lead the division and Elliot handpicked his successor. Anyway, our job has nothing to do with fraud cases. Well, some do but it's not the goal. Basically, the nature of our division is disinformation and to keep an eye on espionage activities, you know, corporate or not because the government relies so much on the corporate sectors. Sometimes we just report on their operations, sometimes we throw a wrench in their work, and we've had to sabotage a couple. If someone is developing specific weapons in this country to be used solely in another country, well, that's a big no-no. Nine times out of ten that stuff is used on their own populations."

Sally nodded as they made eye contact.

"Anyway, about a year ago, wait, scratch that, a little more actually, I was summoned to a boat over there across the estuary. Apparently I was summarily relieved of my dream job as an IT guy with the FBI into a special fraud division, of all things. Not for nothing, but like you, that IT job was something I too had worked my whole adult life for."

Sally nodded again at his meaningful eye contact.

"Just as I'm getting a handle on what my career holds for me, the boat blows up taking my trainer with it. Detective Keeling and Sergeant Fitzgerald fish me out of the estuary and the next thing I know I'm on a plane headed for the east coast where I receive the shortest training session known to the FBI."

"Roberta? Roberta Fitzgerald?"

"Yeah. She knows just about everything that's been happening. She hates me by the way."

"Does she now?" Sally nodded. Of course Roberta hated him. Roberta had been in the Afghanistan war prior to working for the Ohlone police department. And due to Lorna and Annie's frequent sojourns with the local law enforcement, she had become somewhat of a friend.

Michael nodded qualmishly and took a deep breath, "Then, I meet up with Tim, because he's been working with my former trainer on this Aurora project. At the time all we knew was that The Hayward was building satellite-cloaking software for the NSA. But then, my trainer got suspicious when The Hayward hired Spectorgies to handle their human resources, and that's where Tim fit in. He became our inside man at Spectorgies on this."

"So, Tim was in your division?" Sally interjected.

"No," Michael corrected her, "The Hayward outsourced their human resources to Spectorgies. Before that Tim had just been an informer to my trainer on general things Spectorgies got up to. Tim was never fully employed by the FBI but he was an informant, as it turns out, a very valuable informant."

"Okay then if Tim was doing The Hayward's human resources, how'd he end up with the Aurora?"

"We had a guy from our division actually working on the Aurora project at the Hayward, Sunil, but it was so under lock and key we had to get him out but he told Tim there were two Aurora projects, one for the NSA and the other was being sold to Spectorgies."

Sally dropped her head down in understanding. "And Tim built a fake one and replaced it with the original that was being sold to Spectorgies. I see."

"And that's where everything went lopsided. But let me stop here and say something and I've thought about this and I think you need to hear it. This whole thing, as it relates to you, is a fluke. There you are just living this life you'd built for yourself and out of the blue your partner's best friend has a husband who is an informant for us. I mean, what's the likelihood? It's like getting blamed for a train wreck because your grandfather designed the train."

"Hold up, Michael. No, it's not. That's a horrible analogy. Tim was killed because he took something that didn't belong to him, and secondly he shouldn't have been put in that position. My partner was shot because she was inadvertently in this crazy man's way. And both of these incidents have their root causes in your division, you are the link. Do you see my point of view here? I don't blame myself. I blame you."

Michael swallowed hard.

"But the question is, who hired the assassin to kill Tim? Spectorgies or the NSA?"

"Does it matter? They exchange employees like library books. There is no inter-agency working here. It's just me. But obviously the NSA has gotten wind of this and whoever approached you is trying to recover the second Aurora. As well as trying to cover their ass."

"Or make some big money. What is it? 30 million?"

"Pfft, on the black market, to a hostile nation or maybe China? Try 60 or more. The Aurora Shield is one of a kind. It's the only piece of equipment that can shield a satellite from everyone else up there. I can't even fathom the ramifications of such a thing. They could spy on anything, gather whatever intelligence they wanted, and start selling off the information bit by bit. And no one would ever know."

"So, Karen Bernard, we called her the Nurse back when I was in training in Bosnia-"

"You trained in Bosnia?" Michael was aghast.

"Look, it's a long story. I was supposed to, or I thought I was doing aid and relief work before law school, my Grandmother set it up. Anyway, I did not join the CIA as I was surreptitiously being groomed to do, but I had worked with the Nurse there and she approached me recently at a bus stop." Sally rolled her eyes. "From what I understand from her now is that she worked at the CIA but then moved over to the NSA at some point. I gather they are trying to recover the second Aurora as well."

Michael's fingers began twitching again he was searching his memory for something. "Karen Bernard. The Nurse, that sounds familiar to me. I can't put my finger on it." Michael rubbed his eyes before continuing. "Anyway. Okay, the way I figure it is we have only two things to accomplish. Find the Aurora and then hand it over."

Sally squinted and held out her arms. "But, that thing has got to be huge."

"No, well, the hardware is of course but that actual software is encased in a box a little smaller than a shoe box. That's what we're looking for."

"And this assassin? Doesn't your little sub-agency have contingency plans for these things?"

Michael blinked. "No, actually, as a matter of fact we don't do violence. But frankly, I have no problem with eliminating the issue all together." He said haughtily.

Sally snarled at him. "Have you ever eliminated anything, Agent Chan?"

"You have to start sometime." Michael said flatly.

"Oh and you're going to start with a cold blooded chameleon like an assassin? You won't get within a hundred feet of him."

"And you have a better plan, *Not An Agent* Thompson, or should I say Soucek?" Michael teased.

"It's pronounced Sue-check. But it's Counselor Thompson, for the record. And yes, I do. Right now the Nurse thinks I'm helping her out, I doubt she even knows about you or your division. Now, with Lorna getting shot, I can demand she deliver that assassin in return. For all we know at this point she could be in league with him or whoever hired him."

"But what are you going to deliver to her?"

"The Aurora. It belongs to the NSA anyway." Sally searched Michael's face for a reaction. "Unless you think it should be in the hands of your outfit with the FBI. Finders keepers?"

"No. I hadn't thought that far ahead."

Sally scoffed and placed a defiant hand on her hip.

Michael continued, "I hadn't. Cut me some slack will ya'? This has been hard for me too. I lost a good friend in this as well. But yes, now that we're talking about it, I do think the Aurora would be safest in our hands."

The ringing in Sally's ears preceded her outburst by milliseconds. "Cut you some slack? Sure Michael. Gosh ya' know the first thing on my list this morning was to cut *you* some slack. By all means we should all just pause right now and think, 'What does Michael need in all this'. You are absolutely inept."

Michael jumped to his feet. His demeanor lifted, he grinned, and then he gripped her shoulders. "That's it! That's why Elliot brought your parents here. That's why - " Michael stopped and released Sally from his grip. "*That's* why I was teamed up with my trainer originally. I'm IT and he's espionage."

Sally gave him a dubious frown.

"You're right. I'm unfit for this job. Look at me. I'm a techie, an IT guy. Right down to my Star Wars underwear. That's why I was teamed up with my trainer. Listen, Elliot had been talking about a coming cyber war. He wasn't obsessed with it but he did mention it quite a bit. Now that's something my trainer had said too, before he was blown to kingdom come. And you know Elliot probably foresaw all this, so yes, yes I do want that Aurora. It's the only way to level the playing field."

Sally sat down on a barstool. The shadow of a late night passerby flickered across the floor.

"It's like a veil has been lifted. I finally get it. I'm having my ah-ha experience. And you," Michael pointed at Sally, "Elliot was so totally right, you're the perfect counterpart. 'Cause you already have the field training *and* you have a government job already."

"Hold on. I'm an attorney for Housing and Urban Development, that has nothing to do with the FBI."

"Sure it does. So I'm in a," Michael made air quotes, ""special fraud", division of the FBI and my cover for the *actual* fraud division is I ferret out fraud cases and turn them over to my cover boss. But in reality I answer to Elliot, or I did. But I haven't been doing that good of a job bringing in my cover cases. So what does Elliot do? He sends your parents in and they open this place."

"Why would he do that?"

"Because we're self-funded." It was Michael's turn to look exasperated at Sally, "I don't want to be rude, but I've got to meet Sunil, he said it was urgent."

"What do you mean?"

"Follow the money trail. How do most of these white-collar criminals get caught in fraud cases? You follow the money trail and Elliot didn't want anyone in the lower ranks knowing about our division so he didn't leave one. We get money from these fraud cases we bring in but we also can't exactly account for a lot of what we do with the informants and bribes. It's a cash system, right?"

"Forgive me, I need a little more. What do you mean, cash system?"

"The fraud cases." Michael paused for a moment letting it sink in.

A light bulb went off in Sally's eyes. "Oh, you steal from the thieves. I always wondered about the money from those cases."

"Right. And who investigates fraud for HUD?"

"The FBI." Sally eyeballed Michael. "Boy, it's really sink or swim for you isn't it?"

"Bingo." Michael slammed himself down onto a wooden bar stool and slowly twirled it around. "Man, I see my mission so clearly right now. I've just been waffling around here for a year. Having control of the Aurora would be like having our own digital panzer tank division. Elliot was building his arsenal for what's to come. That's why he insisted that everything be done analog." Michael looked around getting lost in his thoughts. "That's why they gave me everything to succeed. We have got to deliver the Aurora Shield."

Sally leaned forward gripping Michael's knee to stop the twirling. "*You* have to deliver the Aurora Shield. There is no *we* here, Robin Hood. I'm not your Little John. All I want is that assassin."

Michael smiled. "Do you know what Auld Alliance means?"

"Did you hear what I said?"

"It was an alliance between Scotland and France, ya' know, back in King Arthur's day, that if anyone attacked one of their countries the other one had their back. Your parents are clever. See? We're FBI and they were CIA, basically frenemies, but -"

"So, what do you want from me, why am I here?"

"I'm not asking you to join the FBI. My job is to keep the players honest. That's where the disinformation jobs come in."

Sally put her hand out to stop him. "Can you hear yourself?"

But Michael continued. "There's no justice for

companies like Spectorgies and the Hayward. Our government has become reliant on them and their technologies. You think they give a shit that Lorna was shot? Tim was killed? They don't. But I do. I'm asking you for an alliance. We'll handle the assassin and then make the Aurora Shield disappear."

"I want a contract. I'm a lawyer, I need it in writing."

"I've got cash."

"I'm not that kind of lawyer."

"How about I make sure, after this, you're never bothered again."

"Oh, you think you can control other people and their motives now?"

"No, but after this I can take you off the radar, make sure no one can track you. Keep you safe, and Lorna."

"What about Annie?"

Michael nodded. "I owe it to Tim."

Sally took a deep breath and sat back down. He was right about one thing. This thing was not going away. She thought about Lorna, lying under sedation in the hospital and nodded.

Tim bounced back up from his seat and checked his watch. But sat back down with the same enthusiasm. "You know what, I'll just reschedule with Sunil. This is more important, right?"

Sally arched an eyebrow at him.

"Right. First things first, let's sketch out a plan."

"No. First we backtrack -" Sally rubbed her hands up and down her face, "Look, we both know that the Aurora must be in Annie's house, right?"

"Maybe. Tim could have hidden it anywhere. Did you decode that notebook I delivered?"

"I haven't exactly had the time."

"Well, we should look into that, like it should be one of the first things we do."

"No. Sorry, no. The first thing we do is to eliminate our obstacles."

Michael swallowed hard again, but nodded in regrettable agreement.

CHAPTER 2

The Nurse sat in the white four-door sedan slowly flexing individual muscles. Being able to sit without moving conspicuously for long periods of time was a skill that took practice and she was feeling very out of practice just now. The white wire from the earpiece crept down the brown skin of her sleek neck, across her long arm, and attached itself to the portable police scanner that rested in a beverage holder in the center console. Her eyes never left the parking lot and paid particular heed to the small hedge lined passage that led down to the marina. The shared parking lot where she sat, between the Ohlone Inn and the Ohlone Yacht Club, was never empty and never full. Despite the late hour, people shuffled in and out of the parking lot. A long finger tapped the Velcro strip that covered two very small L.E.D. sensors, red and green, and two corresponding buttons. It was a handmade remote device made with electronic bits picked up at the local hardware store. Her eyes scanned across the shrubbery in her rearview mirrors, people didn't linger here, no troublesome youths, no late night lurking, and no sight of her prey.

Dead men tell no tales. That was a mistake Agent Nelson had made all those years ago, he let his hit man live. Nelson, she hadn't thought of that vacuous asshole in years. She shook her head unconsciously. What kind of agent hires a hit man and allows himself to then be blackmailed by the same hit man? Everything comes full circle and frankly she was glad she could give an old acquaintance some closure. This whole thing has been snowballing every since Van Elder contracted The Hayward. But the trick here is to just step aside and let the snowball do the work. If she had known this little trick ten years ago, while she was still with the CIA she wouldn't have left for the NSA. She made a tiny circular motion with her left ankle. Maybe she made a mistake going AWOL from the NSA. She slowly flexed her knee up and down. No, Van Elder was making moves to exclude her from the line of accession. It was clear to her when that ninny Bartlett started withholding information from her and Van Elder awarded his effort with this mission.

Focus. She told her self. This was quid pro quo. By giving Sally what she needed, Sally was doing her, the Nurse, a favor. She had been there for Sally's first kill and now she could be here for her last. It's too bad she couldn't get to Sally's parents, as they could act as her broker to sell second Aurora. The Nurse lost herself in this thought for a moment but yanked back to the present and checked her mirrors and the passage. On the other side of the parking lot she saw a plumbers van rock gently from side to side. Honestly, she thought indignantly, there's a motel right in front of your van. Stay in the present, she told herself, just a little longer. But she was having a change of heart. Maybe she wasn't done with Sally after tonight maybe there was still a way to get to her parents. She was entering no man's maze and who better to guide her through than two notorious non-entities.

~~~

"How does she do that?" Michael said aloud. He looked at his watch. That woman hasn't moved a muscle in, like, two hours. He squinted into his monocular, maybe she's dead, he thought. No. Nope, her head just flinched. I could never be a sharp shooter, he thought, those guys sit like Buddha's for days, man. He put the monocular down and stretched. He really needed to pee. He looked around for a vessel to deposit his golden stream and chuckled to himself. "Okay, now I'm punchy." He said and reached across the van to pick up a fountain cup from the floor and slipped off his chair.

~~~

Perched in a couching position on top of the seating bench within the Cabin Cruiser Sally stared into the unforgiving gloom. For two hours she breathed through the cramps in her legs that came and went as she listened to the waves slapping against the hull of the boat. Slap. Slap. Slap. The painter's coverall's, plastic gloves, and goggles had long since drained her body of moisture, leaving her soggy and cold. She slowly put the 9-millimeter that had been fitted with a "hush puppy" sound suppressor down and stretched her hand out, snapping several stiff finger joints, before lifting the heavy gun back into place. She glanced down at the black band on her arm and lifted the Velcro strap, a small red light blinked twice. She took a deep breath and slowly let her shoulders relax. Careful not to grip the gun too tight, Sally took another breath and focused her mind. She slowly began counting to herself as she aimed the gun at the staircase leading down to the cabin. The mental counting stopped as she followed the sound of shuffling feet across the deck above her, then lights came on in the cabin nearly blinding her for a moment. Sally braced her back against the cupboard next to the small galley; she looked up at the latch as it creaked open. Finally, she saw thick and hairy male feet, calves, knees, the cuff of denim shorts, and a blue clad wide back. Thwack! Thwack!

His body slammed first against the ladder and then crumbled to the deck of the cabin. Sally jumped up and before she could get a good look at his face she put a bullet in his forehead. The Nurse had insisted she wear an adult diaper and at this moment she was grateful. She hovered over the lifeless body to get a better look at his face. White male, mid-40's, medium build, scruffy beard, and his recently shaved head had a few weeks light stubble growing back. No noticeable scars or moles. Hazel eyes.

She reached over and flipped a switch and the cabin was dark again. She looked back down at the black band and pressed the green button twice. She took a paranoid glance around the cabin once more. The green light from the band on her arm flashed twice. Sally pulled off her goggles and pocketed them. She pulled out a floppy sun hat from the coveralls and placed it over the hood. She tucked the gun back in her belt and zipped the coveralls back up before mounting the stairs to the deck and latched the cabin door lock.

Sally pulled off and pocketed the plastic gloves as she walked quietly and casually off the marina's wooden dock and climbed into the waiting sedan.

"You good?" The Nurse asked while eyeballing Sally for a moment.

"Yep." Sally said, flinging off the floppy sunhat and dropping it in the backseat.

The Nurse saw Sally's chest heaving quick and shallow breathes. "Feel like running fifty miles at top speed, until you collapse?"

"Yep."

"Nauseous?"

"Yep."

The Nurse put the car in gear and slowly pulled out of the parking lot. "Ahhrighty. Where to?"

Sally stared out the window as they passed by the quiet houses on the quiet streets on this quiet island. 'The worst is over. Stick with the plan.' She mentally chanted to herself over and over. The Nurse was still talking. 'The worst is over. Stick with the plan.'

"Sally?"

"What?"

"Don't slip into shock now. Come on, how'd it go?"

"Flawless. It was a good plan. Well executed."

"Look, you did yourself and the world a favor. That's hard to hear right now, I know. But it's still true."

"That's self justification for an unjustifiable act."

"Unjustified? He tried to kill your wife! It was self-defense. You think he was going to stop there? Sally, guys like him - look, he probably saw the fact that Lorna did not die as a failure. Someone or some entity has paid him to recover that Aurora and he was not going to stop with Lorna and Tim, for that matter. Obviously, whoever sent him is not on the right side of the law here. You think they'd let him stand trial for those crimes? Huh uh. You got to fight fire with fire."

Sally began to shiver, "Where are we going?"

"I'm just driving. Do you want to go home?"

Sally moved her head side-to-side. "Home, I guess."

This disjointed answer caused the Nurse to steal a glance at a now very pale-faced Sally. The Nurse slowed to a stop sign and looked carefully at Sally's flesh colored lips and realized Sally was slipping into shock. "No way. You've got Lorna's family still there don't you? Let's get you out of orbit first. I've got a room over in Oakland and they've got an all night diner downstairs. We'll stop by, get you cleaned up and grab a bite or some coffee, or tea, whatever." She reached into her pocket and pulled out a peppermint candy and held it out. "Here. Eat this."

Sally took the peppermint and unrolled it into her mouth.

The white sedan made a right hand turn onto Warner and the tunnel to Oakland loomed ahead; its dim yellow fluorescent lights flickered fitfully. The Warner tunnel enveloped them and the muted sounds whooshed by as they raced through to the other side. Sally rolled the window down. She needed some fresh cool night air.

~~~

The stale odor of decomposing carpet was partially masked by the eye watering ammonia fumes that lingered about the nostrils like a bad memory. The charmless pastel color pallet from the mid-1980's further impaired the aged hotel room. The bathroom, however, was downright disreputable from the water stained ceiling to the mold stained and cracked shower tiles all the way down to the threadbare shag carpeting. Sally stood with her back to the mirror, her stiff fingers made deliberate attempts at unwrapping the small soap cake from its wax paper covering. She was finally able to scratch loose a corner, grasped the tip, and gave it a sharp fling. The soap cake landed behind her in the sink.

Sally grimaced at the ghostly reflection in the mirror. Her eyes focused on a small red speck of blood on the arm of her white coveralls. She unzipped and disrobed, stuffing the offending materials into the plastic bin liner from under the sink and started the shower.

Bobbie Rutledge, aka Karen Bernard, aka the Nurse, sat at the foot of the bed and stared at the blank television screen. She had her hand in the jacket pocket that held the hush puppy silencer. She was thinking but the jolting sound of the shower turning on focused her attention back to the moment. Although she was sitting three feet from the television "on" button, she reached up and over to the nightstand, grabbed the remote control, and gave the remote wand a flourish.

Now that this is over she needed to glean some information. Sally's parents' bakery had been closed for a few days with the "Closed for Kitchen Renovations" sign in the window. Where were they? And how could she find out, without revealing that she, the Nurse, knew about the FBI using the bakery as a front? She took a moment and mentally played through a scenario where she could meet with Donny, who still worked at the NSA, once more and possibly buy some more information from him. Even if there were only rumors going around, Donny would have heard them. But no, it was too dangerous. And who's to say he would even believe the version of events she would give him. And there was no way Sally would allow her too close to Lorna or the rest of that family. If Sally knows where the Aurora is, and doesn't want anything more to do with this mission, then why doesn't she simply turn it over?

The Nurse flicked through the stations mindlessly. Maybe it would have been better to force Sally's hand first and make her turn over the Aurora then eliminate the assassin. The Nurse absently shook her head at the television - no it had to be this way. He was a psychopathic killer and he had to be removed from the equation. Maybe, though, it was time to change tactics. She pulled her hand out of her pocket as she heard the bathroom door open.

Carrying the now filled trashcan bag, Sally stepped out of the bathroom. The Nurse was staring at the television, remote control held out in front of her pointing at the television. "God, I hate these reality shows. I can just feel my I.Q. drop when I watch them." With a flick of her wand the television turned off and the Nurse turned her attention back to Sally. "Feel better?"

"Much."

"Good, I'm hungry. I was too nervous to eat earlier," The Nurse stood up and held out her hand for the bag. "You should leave that here and we'll put it in the dumpster outside when I take you back."

Sally looked around, "No, I'll hang on to it."

The Nurse shrugged and grabbed her hotel card as they left.

The all night diner was still bumping at midnight. Truck drivers, late shift workers, a few drunks, some students, and some drunken students all filled the tables and booths of the Sunshine Cafe. Waitresses scurried back and forth with food trays like it was a Sunday morning brunch. The Sunshine Cafe's hostess greeted everyone with a smile.

"Two?"

"A booth if you got one." The Nurse requested.

"Right this way."

The smiling hostess presented them with a booth in back near a waitress station and handed them menu's as they sat down. Sally looked around and took in the scene but images the man's bare legs, his short cuffs - what happened next? She asked herself.

The Nurse surreptitiously glanced at Sally's blank face before putting her menu down. "I'm having the fried chicken."

Sally flipped through the pages and put the menu back down.

"You have to eat something," The Nurse implored.

"Waffles."

"That's a good idea. Get some bread to soak up some of that stomach acid. I'll change mine to French Toast."

Sally leaned forward and hissed, "How can you be so casual?"

The Nurse held up a page of her menu and perused it as she softly spoke, "Because, Sally, it was the right thing to do. You know that and so do I. Now, you can torture yourself all you want but I'm not going down that road. We've got a lot to accomplish together and the hard part is over. So let's just get on with it." The Nurse lifted her head up again and smiled as the waitress approached them.

After they ordered Sally leaned back, "I just get the feeling, and maybe it's our shared history, but I get the feeling, somehow, that you're going to screw me over in this."

"How? Why?"

"I don't know."

"Look, if I was going to screw you over somehow, I had the perfect opportunity tonight." The Nurse raised her eyebrows knowingly at Sally.

Sally nodded and shrugged, "Look, I don't know where to turn anymore. I never wanted any of this-"

The Nurse inwardly rolled her eyes. "It's fine. You did fine. Now you just worry about finding," the Nurse paused, "the *tool*. And taking care Lorna. How's she doing by the way?"

"Better, but they're going to try and bring her out of sedation tomorrow or Saturday at the latest. After that, we'll see."

"That's great. That's great news, right? Just one thing at a time, right?"

The waitress came by with their drinks and placed

them on the table.

"Thank you," They said in unison.

"Your food will be out in a minute." The waitress said and hustled away.

"There's something else I need to talk about. Someone else approached me," Sally said conspiratorially.

The Nurse leaned forward.

"He said his name was Sunil, but he didn't look like a Sunil, he was Asian. Like Chinese Asian, or maybe Korean."

"What'd he want?"

"Said he worked with Tim and that he's got buyers lined up for the Aur-," Sally stopped and looked around, "the *tool*."

The Nurse scrambled through her memory for a Sunil, it was a familiar name, perhaps one of the engineers from Hayward who worked on the Aurora. "So he's with Spectorgies? Or maybe the Hayward? Man, those guys don't know when to quit. Actually, I'm surprised you haven't been approached by more people."

"Like who?"

"Whom ever Spectorgies took bids from. Spectorgies themselves. Anyone this has leaked too. Just toe the line, you don't know anything."

"What about this Sunil?" Sally asked.

"He didn't give you any credentials?"

"No."

"Did he set up another meet with you? Give you a phone number?"

"Nothing."

"He's probably just a front man for someone else. Just ignore it." The Nurse said.

"But wait. Wouldn't your guys at the NSA be interested in that?"

The Nurse adjusted herself in the booth, "Yeah, but he could just be a hanger on or looking for low hanging fruit. He approached you, how? And he doesn't give you any other information about himself? That he represents someone else?"

Sally stuck with the story she and Michael had worked out and said, "I was on the bus, two days ago. I had to go into work and check in with my office. He got on here in Oakland and rode into the city. Got off at the depot. He said he'd be in touch. He was kind of casual about it. 'I've got a buyer interested in'-" Sally stopped and lowered her voice, "interested in the *tool*, if you're interested I'll be in touch."

The Nurse pursed her lips together. "Hmm. So he was just seeing if you'd bite. But ya' know that's interesting he didn't give you a hard sell. He may just be a broker. Well, at any rate, if he contacts you again let me know. Have you noticed anyone else? Someone unfamiliar around your block, maybe those little utility vans?"

Sally shook her head.

"If you feel like you need a detail, let me know."

Sally nodded and breathed a faux sigh of relief as the food came to the table. The Nurse never said, 'maybe it was one of ours'. Or that she would take his description in and ask around about possible brokers or foreign agents. Michael was right after all. They had decided to use Sunil's name on purpose, because Sunil was one of the FBI IT agents that had been placed at The Hayward to keep an eye on the Aurora but the Nurse gave no recognition of the name. Clearly, she's working on her own here.

After a few minutes of chewing and swallowing had passed the Nurse said, "Tell you what, we're setting up an office there on the island anyway, until we get this thing. Just to be in the vicinity. If this Sunil contacts you again just go ahead and set up a meeting. Let me know and I'll handle this guy."

Sally gave a warm smile as she choked down a bite of the syrupy waffle, "Thanks."

~~~

Back in the mid-nineties, when Lorna was off in New York City struggling for a foothold in the burgeoning online publishing world, her engineer father, Quill, and Tessa, her adopted and now blind older sister, revolutionized Internet accessibility for the seeing impaired. What had started out as a home computer and an engineering project between Tessa and Quill resulted in a billion dollar audio interface industry. Furthermore, they currently held patents in most micro-device and audio interface technologies. And for this reason, Tessa Tollison, with her untamed kinky red hair, became a rock star in the small but influential world of Geekdom. Quill, only too happy to turn any limelight over to his daughter, played the role of the benevolent patriarch. But in truth, the familial bond between his daughters, their tenacious willfulness that bordered on derangement, coupled with their blood thirsty brawl's scared the bejezus out of him.

So when Sally came along and joined the family, Sally and Lorna's relationship wasn't a question of social morals or genetic predispositions, it was a question of survival. Finally someone who seemed earnest and capable of helping him navigate their miscreant sorority. Even after he found out about Sally's parents, he reassured himself that if Sally had survived that family, surely, she could survive the constant onslaught of terror his daughters committed. The electrocution's, missing eyebrow's, the duct-tape incidents, the narcotized Seeing Eye dogs would all seem normal to a woman who was brought up in half-truths and subterfuge, he told himself.

This was before his youngest daughter had been shot and left for dead at the hand of a hired killer.

The yellow house on Saint Charles Place, which Quill helped renovate for Lorna and Sally, had once been a cheery refuge for the whole family. And yet lately, for Sally at least, the house felt ominous. As if one swift kick onto the foundation would bring the whole thing down around her ears. She let her self into the darkened house and flipped on the entry way light. She was exhausted. Patience and Fortitude, their big yellow tabbies, met her at the door. Fortitude let out a plaintive meow. Sally dropped her bag and sat down on the wood floor. "I'm sorry guy's. I know things have been weird lately." Patience crawled into her lap and turned around a couple of times before plopping down. The familiar hum of the frequency jammer didn't startle her when it was turned on from the darkened house. Sally had become used to Tessa not turning on lights while she was alone in their house. At Tessa's request, the frequency jammer had been installed by Quill when they remodeled the house. Lorna called it Tessa's cone of silence. Ever since Tessa had acquired government contracts for audio interface models she had to beef up her security and an audio frequency jammer, although not foolproof to eavesdroppers, gave her some comfort in speaking freely in their house.

Sally heard Tessa's tentative footsteps approach and thought she better let Tessa know she was sitting on the floor. "Hi. Is Dad still at the hospital?"

"Yeah. How'd it go?" Tessa stopped moving and asked quietly when she entered the entryway clutching an afghan around her shoulders.

"It went."

Sally watched as Tessa crumpled down next to her. "The deed is done?"

Sally paused and contemplated admitting out loud

what she had executed. There would be no going back. "It is."

Tessa let out a long exhalation of air. "Thank you. That was," she paused, "a sacrifice. I mean - are you okay?"

Sally felt oddly comforted with her two tabbies vying for space in her lap. She too exhaled. "Yeah. I guess. I mean. You know, probably not."

"No. I can't imagine. It's horrible. And for-" Tessa tensed up. "I'm not sorry though. He...it was deserved. I think it's safe to look at it as self-defense?"

"No, but I'm going to have to find a way to live with this now."

"Hey, you're not alone, okay? Just keep moving forward, one step at a time. The doctor is going to try and bring Lorna out of sedation tomorrow. Perez is with her tonight, Dad's said he'd be at the hotel for a few hours."

"Did you tell your dad? I mean, has he wondered where I am?"

"He knows you're taking care of business." Tessa said carefully.

"Damn."

"No. It's okay. He'll come around. He'll be okay with it."

Which means, Sally thought, that Quill is now in on it, which means that Perez must also know. Sally shook her head, that's three people too many. But she didn't have much of a choice; she needed Tessa as a plausible alibi. Sally knew full well, this guy had been a government contractor and it would never come to a trial, but that didn't mean her actions tonight didn't exacerbate the situation. Really, what was she supposed to do, wait for him to come after them again? "Where's Annie?"

"Oh, I gave her a sleeping pill. She's still kinda messy."

"And who can blame her?" Sally grimaced. "What time do we need to be at the hospital?"

"Well, if we want good seats we should get there by 5 or 5:30 at the latest."

"5:30? A.M.?"

"Yeah, that doctor makes very early rounds. Plus I think Mrs. Strangler is hitching a ride with Annie. And Annie did mention something about Roberta coming along." Tessa explained.

"You are kidding me, right?"

"What time is it now?"

"Almost 2 a.m."

"Why don't you take a quick nap? I'll wake you up in a little while and we can go." Tessa offered.

Sally lay on the floor and looked around the darkened house. The idea of climbing just one step to the second floor bedrooms exhausted her. "No. I'll just lay here."

~~~

Michael took a cursory glance across the parking lot before jumping out of the rusted out old beater and back into the white van. From the diner, the white sedan carrying the Nurse and Sally had made a left back onto Center, the avenue that would have led to Saint Charles Place. It would then take the Nurse five minutes at the most to make it back here to the marina. He decided he would wait ten minutes, tops, for her then he'd head back to see if she'd crashed at her rat hole.

But he didn't have to wait. Five minutes after he had peeled off on Warner the white sedan parked in the marina lot. The Nurse got out of the sedan and ambled her way over to the passage that led to the docks.

He waited again, feeling the adrenaline coursing through him. Sally had been right about this too. The Nurse was using this as a set up. The Nurse had hired this guy, this assassin, and let Sally to get rid of him. Damn, Michael thought, these people play rotten.

A few minutes later the Nurse came back, got into her car and drove off. Michael watched her tail lights disappear around the bend. He put on an oversized blue jacket and a round pair of glasses without the lenses in them and got out of the van.

The small passage seemed to shrink around him as he made his way down the steps to the docks. He looked across the estuary at the boats that rocked gently with the waves. The third slip in he stepped onto the 30-foot sailing boat and quickly made his way into the cabin.

He dropped down the last three steps of the ladder and looked around with his flashlight. The place had been obviously tossed. He purposefully did not look down at the corpse near his feet for a few moments as he gathered himself. Sally had predicted this whole thing, he thought about what she had said. He needed to look for two pieces of evidence, one obvious - he scanned around with his flashlight until he found it. The gun was sitting on the floor under the table. He picked it up, checked that the safety was on, and placed it in his waist ban. Then he looked for a less obvious piece of evidence. He pulled on a pair of plastic gloves and began randomly picking up books and looking under cushions.

He stopped and looked at the corpse. He nodded his head down and took a deep breath. The body was flexible, to his surprise. For some reason he thought it would be stiff, no it's still too soon, he told himself. He pushed the body over to its side and slid out the man's wallet. He flipped it open and found what he was looking for. Sally and Lorna's home address on a small post it note. He crumpled the note up and put it in his pocket. Was that the second piece of planted evidence or was that an accidental piece?

He stood up and looked around again. If he, Michael, was going to lead someone to the killer what other evidence would he plant? He scratched at the facial stubble on his chin. Not DNA. That would take too long to process. Not clothes, too obvious. But if the gun couldn't be traced to Sally in the first place, then why leave it? You're over thinking, he told himself. The Nurse came in here, threw shit around and tossed the weapon under the table. Except that water glass, he thought looking at the counter. He lifted up the water glass and flashed his light beam on a thumbprint. Michael lifted his head and smiled to himself with relief.

Then his eye caught something blue and shiny from across the cabin. His heart sunk into his stomach and a drop of flop sweat landed in his eye. Had he not seen the exact kind of light the last time he had been on one of these sailing boats? And that time the boat blew up and nearly killed him. Michael took a step closer to the blue light. He moved his flashlight beam following a thin black cord tucked behind a thin wooden wall railing. He followed the railing across the cabin until he saw the black cord poking out again in the corner. He moved a cushion from a corner seat and put his finger in a small hole and lifted up. The wood seat lifted easily and he moved his flashlight beam into the dark niche. There it was.

As he stuffed the water glass, recording equipment from under the seat, and the camera into a plastic shopping bag he took a quick glance around the cabin before departing. I *am* getting better at this, he thought.

CHAPTER 3

Below a jet-black pompadour, a male octogenarian wore oversized surgical scrubs, an oversized lab coat, and oversized square black framed glasses. At exactly five a.m. he shuffled through the Oakland General Hospital corridors poking his head into random rooms and pointing to various hall carts. People of a certain age might ironically mistake him for a teenager wearing a Dick Nixon rubber Halloween mask. But four earnest looking internists, all with dripping wet hair, followed him at a respectable distance. They scratched down notes in their various notepads with deep deliberation. The only sound that could be heard, however, was the shluff, shluff, shluff that Dick Nixon's shoe covers made on the linoleum floor.

Inside the hospital suite 328, Quill Tollison watched his daughter breathe with the same intense consideration the young internists had for the elderly man. At the foot of her hospital bed, on top of a rollaway cot, a stout Hispanic man had fallen into a deep sleep. The door to the hospital suite swept slowly open and Quill stood expectantly as Sally led Tessa into the room. Quill sat back down but searched Sally's face for a sign. It had taken him a good part of the night just to digest what Tessa had told him about Sally's actions. It was all too much and his consternation had grown through the night. Lorna, or Sally, or Tessa, someone had gone too far. Sally met Quill's expectant gaze and she gave him a corroborating nod. Quill lowered his eyes and down to Lorna, his disappointment was palpable.

Tessa, unaware of Quill and Sally's silent exchange, charged into the room and banged her shin on the cot. Her body folded in half, and she did a face plant on top of Perez, her sleeping assistant.

"Aye!"

"Damn!"

Sally scrambled to help Tessa up from the bed as Perez fought to untangle himself from the sheets.

"I'm sorry, Rojo." Perez said.

"Perez, I thought you'd be back at the hotel room by now."

Perez cleared his throat. "I didn't want to miss anything."

Tessa was pointing at the large glass window as she directed Perez. "Well, get that bed out of here then. I think Annie and Roberta are on the way too."

Sally pulled Tessa over to a chair near the window. "Tessa, it's still five o'clock in the morning. I think we should kinda keep the volume down."

Perez busied himself with folding up and rolling the bed out to the hallway, grabbed a brown paper bag from the window ledge, and disappeared into the bathroom.

"The anesthesiologist came by a couple of hours ago and changed her drip. 'said she'd wake up naturally as if she was coming out of a good nights sleep." Quill said almost to himself. All night his mind had been playing tricks on him. He kept thinking back to when Lorna's mother died twenty years ago. It had always been a comfort to him that when Lorna slept she had always looked so much like her mother but now the sight haunted him. The last two weeks had shaved years off his life but he would have given all his remaining ones for his daughter.

"Dad, do you want me to order some breakfast?" Tessa said in her best whisper, which was a little quieter than a train whistle.

"Nothing for me. Let's just wait a bit."

The hospital room door opened again and Annie and Roberta walked in. Roberta's head snapped sideways as Perez suddenly popped through the bathroom door in only a towel, holding a toothbrush in his hand. Then just as quickly, he saw who had entered and leapt back into the bathroom and shut the door.

Roberta looked at Tessa and Sally and said quietly, "Good morning. What's the word?" Prior to joining Ohlone Island police force, Roberta had served in Afghanistan as a medic. So blood and guts never bothered her, but the weird aura she was feeling in the room right now made her skin crawl.

Annie's eyes didn't leave Lorna and she found herself fighting back tears, again. Roberta nodded at Lorna. Detective Keeling, Roberta's mentor on the police force had often used Lorna's penchant for trouble as a solid bellwether for corruption, fraud, and even murder on Ohlone Island. However, when Roberta took over for Keeling she took a different route, keeping Lorna away from the homicide department. In a way, she too blamed herself for Lorna getting shot. Keeling always said of Lorna, "if I had a leash for her, I'd use it." Roberta had always thought Keeling meant it in a derogatory manner. But now she understands it to mean he wanted to keep

Lorna out of harms way. Roberta wondered, with a momentary glance at Quill and then at Sally, if they had gotten more bad news.

"We're just waiting for Sleeping Beauty to wake up." Tessa said.

Annie saw Quill give a disapproving twist of his head.

"She is beautiful." Annie sniffed.

"Annie, darlin', you *have got* to crawl down from that cross. You didn't pull that trigger." Tessa said.

There are too many people in this room, Quill thought. He only wanted to hear his daughter's voice. Why hasn't she woken up yet? He looked at his watch.

"I'm sorry." Annie said meekly.

Quill looked up at Annie and took his glasses off. He rubbed the lenses with the bed sheet and said softly, "Annie."

Annie nodded at him and sniffed.

"If you don't stop feeling sorry for yourself I'm gonna pitch you clean through that window. Okay? Now you come over here and talk to Lorna, I want her to hear loving voices when she wakes up." Quill turned around to the rest of the group. "Do you all understand?"

Everyone nodded.

"Yes sir." Tessa added in an uncharacteristically small voice that drew the attention of both Roberta and Sally.

Annie scurried over to Lorna's bedside and began humming softly. Quill got up and sat next to Tessa. The two of them went into deep mutterings and leaned their heads away from the rest of the room. Roberta wondered if he was giving her the bad news. Perez walked back into the room clean-shaven and smelling like soap, he dropped his bag back on the window ledge and nodded at Roberta and Sally. "Good morning," he said to them hastily.

"Perez, your English has gotten so much better." Roberta said approvingly.

"My English is always good," he said. "And my French is very good," he added huffily. (But it came out, "My eeenglish iz al'a'z goot. And my Freeeench iz berry goot.") He returned to Lorna's bedside and began mumbling his Rosary and worrying his beads.

Roberta locked eyes with Sally and moved over to her side.

"I thought she was given the all clear?" Roberta asked nodding toward Lorna.

"She was. But, well, I think we all had a Come To Jesus moment in our own way ya' know, over the past few weeks. Quill may just be paying up his end of a bargain he made."

"I hope it wasn't Faustian." Roberta muttered.

Sally was genuinely surprised. "Faustian? Well read, Roberta."

Roberta smiled down at her and added faux haughtily, "I am berry well read. Thank you berry much."

Everything stopped as they heard the shluff, shluff, shluff grow ever nearer and nearer to the door. Suddenly the door popped open and Dr. Stallone (pronounced Stallonee) shuffled inside followed by his four minions. "Oh goody! I love a party. How's the guest of honor?"

Quill jumped up and spoke in a demanding tone, "She's still hasn't woken up."

Two of the minions took a step back looking around the large suite in awe.

"That's because we have to wake her up! But, before I do this I want to tell you, she's going to be groggy, possibly quite confused. So let's give her space. Sometimes they wake up confused, sometimes happy, sometimes who knows. But the fact is they wake up and everything works out for the better." Dr. Stallone gave a little nod to his audience. He lifted up the covers from Lorna's feet as if he was about to pull a rabbit out of a hat. He wielded a reflex hammer out of his lab coat and rubbed it up the sole of her right foot. Nothing. He did it again to the left foot and Lorna's foot shifted a little. There was a sigh of relief all over the room. Dr. Stallone rubbed the hammer again, "Wake-y, wake-y."

The two minions who had fell back away from the action were muttering together. Tessa turned an ear just a fraction of an inch in their direction. "Nice room for a shooting victim." She heard a small voice utter.

Tessa stood up and faced the direction of the utterance. "That's because I pay $10,000 dollars a night for it, you whiney little shit. What do you think? I'm running an insurance scam here? That's why you have suites in this hospital. So you can take the big money then turn your holier than thou nose up at us, right?"

Confused eyes shifted from Lorna to Tessa.

The two minions turned to Dr. Stallone, who simply said, "Out."

But Tessa was on a rant and continued at the space they had just vacated, "This is *not* a shooting *victim*, this is a *survivor*. We have deigned to allow you incompetent shits to observe-"

"Tessa!" Quill shouted then added quietly, "They're gone."

Dr. Stallone smiled at the group. "But well said, Madame, she is a survivor this one."

He was still holding his reflex hammer up, ready for another rub on Lorna's foot when they all heard, "Hit me again with that thing and I'm gonna shove it straight up your *asssssssss*!"

From the window to the bedside, Roberta moved into action and deftly shifted Perez out of the way. She placed a firm hand on Lorna's arm that held the tubes in place.

Quill held down the other arm as Lorna profane laced diatribe began, "Fu**youwithyourpieceofshi%*o*ksuck-inmother%u*king*d^amned^itch*ssface!"

"Put her back under!" A minion demanded.

"I'll get help!" Another minion bolted for the door.

"No!" Perez caught the bolting minion's arm. "She's always like that."

Dr. Stallone gave a flat footed hop, "'at a girl!" He gave her foot another rub. This time her leg rose up in a full-fledged kick, missing his chin by an inch.

Lorna's eyes weren't opened yet but her mouth continued, "$hiteatin'bu%%uckin'a**lickin'-"

Sally reached over to hold down one leg, while Annie reached for the other. Perez moved over to Tessa and quietly described the action to her.

"That's my girl, keep fighting Lorna!" Dr. Stallone encouraged her. "Raise her head up, Son." Dr. Stallone instructed Quill, who pushed a button to lift Lorna's head and chest up higher.

"Wake up Lorna!" Sally instructed her. "Patience and Fortitude miss you!" But Lorna had faded away again.

Dr. Stallone was laughing, "Did you see that kick? She almost knocked my block off!" He looked around at the solemn faces. "Well." He pulled the covers back over Lorna's legs and gently rubbed them, "let's give her another minute. That's quite a fighter you have there, Quill."

Quill nodded.

"You should hear her on a bad day," Tessa added.

Roberta snorted a laugh and quickly recovered, "Sorry."

"I like it when they come out swinging." Dr. Stallone chuckled. "She's going to be fine. She's got a long life ahead of her. Have you heard anymore about who shot her?"

Roberta, who was out of uniform, fielded the question and moved back over toward the window. "We're working on that night and day. We just don't have a lot to go on. Hopefully, Lorna can give us a description at some point. At least tell us what happened."

Sally thought she had glimpsed some movement under Lorna's eyelids and replaced Roberta by the bedside, placing her hand in Lorna's.

"You're the Detective?" Dr. Stallone asked.

Roberta nodded.

"How was the crime reported then? Sometimes it's reported by the shooters, they get scared and call for help."

"It was a report of shots fired. We actually got several calls and we tracked all but one because it was a pre-paid cell phone."

As the room's focus turned to the conversation, Sally watched as Lorna's eyes struggled open and gaze about in a private moment. Lorna gave a squeeze to Sally's hand in a silent acknowledgement as they both listened to the conversation.

"Did you get anything off the bullet? Or is that a forensics thing?" Perez asked.

"No, we think we got the whole set up. She had been holding a big thick book at the time, so that's what took the brunt of the shot."

"Really?" Dr. Stallone asked, "which book?"

Annie giggled, "The Complete Works of Jane Austen."

"Why's that funny?" He turned to Annie.

"Because I hate Jane Austen books." Lorna voice scratched out loud enough for everyone to hear.

Everyone's heads jerked back to see Lorna's blue eye's shining. Sally bent down and kissed Lorna's forehead. "Good morning, sunshine."

"Who are you?"

Sally smiled at her partner, "Please don't joke about that."

The hospital door swung open and an elderly voice chimed. "Did I miss it?" Mrs. Strangler, who lives two doors down from Sally and Lorna, stood at the door smiling in her best Chanel, circa 1962, pillbox hat and pearls.

Annie moved to the door. "Come in Mrs. Strangler, I'm just going to step outside for a minute."

Mrs. Strangler locked hard eyes on Lorna and leaned forward slightly. "You okay?"

Lorna nodded.

"I'll be just out here if you need me." Mrs. Strangler said and joined Annie in the hallway.

Lorna looked up at Sally, "You okay?"

"I'm good. How do you feel?"

"Cold."

Perez jumped up and left the room muttering, "Another blanket."

Lorna looked around the room and cobbled together another sentence, "So dramatic, everyone."

"Any pain?" Dr. Stallone asked.

"Breathing."

Dr. Stallone looked over at his minion and nodded. The minion left the room quietly. "We can take the edge off, but I'm afraid if you want to stay conscious you're going to have some discomfort. We'll give you something to take at night so it won't wake you up though."

Lorna touched her throat, "Water."

"Yup," Sally pulled a cup up from a serving tray next to her. "Right here."

"Coffee." Lorna looked at Sally.

"Not for a while." Sally said.

"No, that's coffee."

Sally looked into the cup. "I'm sorry."

Lorna took a tentative sip of the water and then looked over at her fatigued father. "Thank you."

Quill touched her forehead, "I'm so glad-" he began but hunched over in a spasm of emotion.

"Roberta? Come here," Lorna said. Sally and Roberta changed places.

"We shouldn't do this now," Roberta started. "I just wanted to make-"

"Shut up - listen," Lorna scratched out and put her hand to her throat as if to support her voice. "He was completely non-descript. Okay? Like he was in a disguise, wig, shaved eyebrows, all that. But he was medium build 'bout 5'9" and he was right handed. I think he had hazel eyes, but he could have worn contacts."

"Okay." Roberta patted Lorna's hand.

"I can't remember what he said his name was but he pretended to have worked with Tim. He was after something, he said he was after Tim's work."

"Okay."

"Listen, this guy must be desperate," Lorna swallowed hard, "he came in the middle of the day."

Roberta took her hand in her own. "That's enough for now. We'll go over it later, I promise you." Roberta placed Lorna's hand back down. "I'll see you later then, okay?"

Lorna nodded and Roberta left to join Annie and Mrs. Strangler in the hallway.

Finally, Dr. Stallone took his place next to Lorna. They smiled at one another like two old confrere's who share a secret history. "How soon do you want to get out of here?" Dr. Stallone asked her.

"Now," Lorna replied.

"Good. I can't tell you how tired I get of seeing healthy, young, beautiful heart patients on my rounds.

The nurse is going to come by later with a Spiro meter. Once you hit your target you can leave. I mean, uh, once you're able to strengthen those lungs you can leave. So, who do I talk to about wound care and further check up's?" Dr. Stallone looked around the room.

"Me," Sally said.

"Good, come with me."

Dr. Stallone left the room with Sally and one lone minion straggled along. The hallway and nurses station was coming alive with early morning activity. Dr. Stallone shuffled toward the nurse's station as he spoke, "I'm going to prescribe a series of pain relievers, some of them are narcotics. And I'm afraid she's going to have to be weaned off the narcotics as she heals." He stopped and looked up at Sally. "That's not fun. It is imperative that she remains as docile as possible. Except for a book, a remote, or a pencil; no lifting of any kind." He flicked his finger pointedly ahead as he resumed the shuffle. "I mean that, she can *not* tear her stitches. No straining. Your father-in-law said she wouldn't need a visiting nurse care, but I want to pass that by you as well. I recommend it, but what do I know?"

"Well, what does that entail?"

"Monitoring blood pressure, heart rate, drug dosage, activity, dietary needs; a nurse would be more apt to know if she's running into trouble. Look I know he's footing the bill for all this but this is something you should consider. It's a lot to be responsible for as well as to work full time."

"Yeah, of course. How do I get one of those visiting nurses?"

"I'd prescribe it. Do you want one then?"

"Let me discuss it with her family and let you know, they may have something else planned already."

The doctor nodded knowingly. "When they leave, and

it gets too much for you, you'll call me. Okay?"

Sally nodded, "Yes."

"Okay. Let me get all this paperwork together. If she's able, she can leave tonight, which I seriously doubt but what do I know? Otherwise, it will be tomorrow morning. Probably then." Dr. Stallone turned his attention to the nurse station and his minions took the ringside seats pushing Sally aside.

Sally took a deep breath and pushed it out audibly as she looked back down the hall and caught sight of Mrs. Strangler and Roberta sitting in a small lounge area. She passed by them as she walked back to the room. "Roberta, can you hang out a minute more, I need to talk to you. But let me just check something with Tessa and Quill first."

"Where is he?" Mrs. Strangler spouted out.

"Who?"

"The doctor." Mrs. Strangler said fervidly.

"He's at the nurses station," Sally said.

Mrs. Strangler rocked herself up from her seat. "Gotta go," she said as she shuffled off, pulling at her suit.

Roberta rolled her eyes at Sally.

Sally walked quickly back to the room. Quill, Perez, and Annie were standing next to the bed that held a sleeping Lorna. Tessa had stolen the extra blanket and was curled up in a chair.

"Visiting nurse?" She asked the room.

"No." Quill said quietly. "I wanted to talk to you about that."

Sally put her hand up to stop him. "Quill, we have room. You'll stay as long as you want."

"That's not what he's saying." Tessa leaned up and let the blanket fall off her shoulders.

"Obviously," he started, "I think, we think, it may help everyone if we take Lorna home for a while. Until she's healed and things return to normal."

Sally felt her face flush and her heart did a nosedive into her stomach. Her brain shifted into fight or flight mode. She paused and took a deep breath, trying to push away his hurtful response.

Quill continued, "We can provide twenty four hour care for her. And it's just," Quill looked at Annie who was wiping a moist cloth on Lorna's lips. "Safer."

Sally's eyebrows shot up. "I think we both know *now* that's just not true."

Annie's attention was pulled away from her task for a moment.

"That is sort of the point, Sally." Tessa said.

Annie couldn't believe her ears. What was going on? All of the air in the room seemed to have been sucked out. Annie caught Sally's eye, "Shouldn't Lorna have a say in this?" Annie asked as Lorna began to stir again.

Quill gave Annie a pitiful look but turned to Sally, "Let's discuss this in the hallway."

Sally took a step over to the door and opened it up for him. Once out of earshot, Quill turned on his heel and said sternly, "Legally, you don't have a leg to stand on here."

Sally was flabbergasted, "Legally? Quill, how did this go from giving Lorna a place to heal to 'not having a legal leg to stand on'?" She didn't let him answer. "I'll tell you how. You think you're the final say in another person's life. What about what Lorna wants? You're acting like she's brain dead in there, but she's not. I don't care how much money and influence you think you have, right here and right now, you just lost all credibility with me. Everything, years of building trust and making a family, you just flattened with your little bomb you dropped in there. Congratulations."

Quill moved his face inches from Sally's nose and

said accusingly, "You are a *murderer*."

"Yeah, you might want to keep that in mind. But try proving it. You don't actually know a single bit of information about anything. You are only a distraught and frustrated old man." The judicious part of Sally's brain that would normally stop her from saying something she ought not to say was stifled by a more primordial part and she was in full fight mode. She was going to end this battle before it begins. "Oh and by the way, that quick vacation Lorna and I took to Palm Springs last Fall? We eloped and got *legally* married, none of your kumbaya backyard amusement so yes, I do have a legal leg to stand on. We both do. You take her out of this state and it is kidnapping. That's a federal offense, so you think very carefully about your next move."

Winded, Quill took a step back and grunted at the floor.

Sally threw open the door to Lorna's room. Tessa was standing next to Lorna's bed talking to a groggy Lorna. "Annie? Can I talk to you for a minute?"

Annie moved around the bed toward the opened door. "Sure." Annie met Sally just outside the room. "What's going on?"

"What have they promised you?"

"Who?"

"Quill and Tessa, did they offer start up funds for a new business? Have they given you money?"

Annie was put off by Sally's insinuations, "No."

Roberta came down the hallway. "I better head out. Annie, can you catch a ride back to the island?"

"Hang on." Sally said. "I may need your help."

Roberta, who had witnessed the aggressive posturing between Sally and Quill, lifted her hands up. "I don't want to get involved in any family business here. I just saw Quill heading out like his ass was on fire."

"You're not. Just hang on for two minutes, please." Sally turned back to Annie, "Remember, right after Tim died? The first few days?"

Roberta took a step back and looked at her watch.

Annie answered honestly, "Not really. Why?"

"Because I'm asking you to help me, and Lorna's going to need a lot of care. I don't know if I can do it by myself so I'm gonna need some help."

"Good. I had planned on that." Annie agreed. "I don't know what they're talking about in there." Annie looked up at Roberta. "They were talking about taking Lorna back to Atlanta without her approval, like she was twelve years old or something."

Roberta wrinkled her brow and shook her head, "Wow. People do some stupid shit. Are they serious?"

Sally nodded. "They think that guy is going to try and attack again, but that's not going to happen."

Roberta tilted her head, "How do you know?"

"I just know."

Roberta blew out air between her teeth and nodded, "Well, I could handle monitoring her medical needs. But I ain't bathing her. That's on you."

"Yeah, that wouldn't be right. You should have to do that Sally." Annie agreed sincerely.

Sally couldn't help but smile at Annie's candid assessment of the negotiation. "You're right of course. How silly of me. Lorna will be so disappointed."

Annie nodded. "You know how she is."

"No, I'm serious. I've wiped enough ass's in my life," Roberta added.

Just then they all heard raised voices coming from inside Lorna's room.

"Sounds like she broke the news to Lorna already," Annie said.

"You should get back in there, Sally, there's no telling

what they are saying to her," Roberta said.

"Yeah. Annie, I'm going to have to head back to work and talk to my boss today. I need to change out my work schedule and stuff. Can you stay here today, just while I'm away? I don't want to leave hear alone now."

"Sure."

"Roberta, can you go back to our house? Use the hidden front door key; it's under that planter near the garage. I need you to pack up the guest room. It has all of Quill and Tessa's things in it. Just put the suitcases on the porch and keep the key."

Roberta pursed her lips, "Ew, shit. You mean business."

Sally said definitively, "Yes. I do. Unfortunately, Quill just showed me the little man behind the curtain. Annie, I have some business to attend to with the hospital and Tessa right now. You may want to go with Roberta and pick up your car and come back."

Annie put her hand up and interrupted, "Sally listen, you left exhaustion about ten days ago and this is bad. You are making decisions that will divide familial bloodlines now. Are you sure you want to make an enemy of Quill and Tessa?" Annie reasoned.

"No. And I'm sorry that you are in this position but there is no way Lorna would want to be away from her home and the cats right now. If I agree to let them take her, she'll never forgive me and she's the person I have to live with, not them. If I don't fight for her, what does that say?"

It was a persuasive argument and Annie looked at Roberta, who nodded agreement.

Roberta stepped forward, "Do what you have to do then. But you and I need to have a sit down, I think," she nodded at what sounded like a full blown argument coming from behind the closed door, "after this blows over."

"I know, and I owe both of you that conversation. But can I just deal with one disaster at a time?"

"We'll see you later," Roberta said taking a step back.

"I'll try to get back within a couple of hours," Annie said nodding.

~~~

Annie's absence from Lorna's hospital room was mercifully short. But Sally's feeling of urgency made her feel lopsided somehow. And the entire drive from the hospital to her office felt like it was on a curve that she wasn't straightening out from. Sally walked into the sterile Housing and Urban Development offices in downtown San Francisco, past her assistant's desk and into the glass cage that held her desk. Katie, her assistant, followed her and sat down across from Sally's desk. Katie watched for a moment as Sally stared at the neatly arranged piles before she spoke.

Katie tapped the far right pile. "This ones urgent." She waved her hand over to the next pile, "these are for mediations." And hovered her hand over the final pile of manila folders, "and this is the research I gathered for the fair housing policies that are coming up for-"

"Okay." Sally waved her hand interrupting Katie.

But Katie continued. "You have a meeting next week and you'll need to go through this," Katie tapped the last pile of manila folders, "and put together an outline, at least, for the mortgage insurance-"

"I got it. Thank you."

Katie stood up, closed the door, and leaned against it. Her black spiky hair gel shone bright, almost blue, under the fluorescent light. "I don't want to badger or stick my nose in it, but -"

"She woke up this morning but she's gonna need

twenty-four hour care," Sally shook her head slowly in genuine incredulity. "I don't know how I'm gonna do this. I gotta figure something out."

"For how long?"

"A few weeks at least."

"Okay look, that's nothing. That's good news." Katie moved a few steps forward and leaned on the desk. "These sharks around here already smell blood in the water. If it's only for a couple more weeks I think you should just carry on like before. Don't put in for an extended leave. Seriously, don't."

Sally pinched her face at Katie. "What have you heard?"

"Plenty. They are measuring the curtains. 'know what I mean?"

Sally nodded.

"If I can keep your case management to a minimum, right? And if you just work on this substantive stuff, you'll be golden. No one needs to be any wiser for a couple of weeks."

"I still need to check in."

"Sure. But as long as the work is getting done, no one needs to know *when* it gets done. Right? Just tell Scott you'll be on the same schedule working from home."

Sally nodded again and looked at Katie questioningly.

Katie answered the unasked question, "Don't leave me with these back stabbing bitches."

Sally laughed.

Katie nodded in the direction of their boss's office, "And you know he doesn't care as long as you make him look good."

"And in return?" Sally asked.

"Return nothing. If you leave Katherine takes your place and becomes my boss. She is completely incompetent and a turd to boot. This is my own survival

I'm talking about here."
      "Thank you."
      "No, thank you," Katie said smiling.

CHAPTER 4

For all Annie knew, at this point, it could have been her that the gunman was targeting. All of these crazy happenings must have something to do with her house. Before they finished filing the divorce papers Tim had used his savings and a chunk of the trust left to him by his father to pay off this house and then signed it over to Annie. Why would he have done that? And then Tim was murdered in the living room. Then Lorna was shot at the front door.

Annie finished combing her hair and gazed blindly at her reflection. She had moved through her morning routine of feeding the dogs and having her breakfast, walking the dogs and showering with an indifferent air. There just didn't seem to be any answers. It was no wonder that Annie took great pains in the daily care and feeding schedule of her friend Lorna. It was Lorna who had pulled Annie out of the depression she felt about the divorce. Lorna who stood by her when Tim was murdered while everyone else it seemed had turned their backs on her. And really, as immature and shameless as Lorna could be, she was the one person Annie could count on through thick and thin.

So, maybe at first she acted out of guilt. But after a few days of caring to basic life sustaining needs and giving over her constant attention to healing another person, Annie could honestly say she was feeling better emotionally. Finally, she smiled at her reflection and took a gulping breath for the first time in what seemed forever.

Downstairs Annie gave her two Australian shepherds, Burt and Ernie, big hugs and let them into the back yard. "I'll see you two at lunch." She said cheerily as she shut the gate behind her. The early morning fog swirled about her as she made her way across the street.

Watching Annie from the front windows of Lorna and Sally's home, Patience and Fortitude jumped down from their window seat perch and situated themselves in the front entryway and waited. Aside from their other household duties, including but not limited to debugging and mice extermination, welcoming guests was an important part of their day. Examining the contents of the guests shoes and bags always seemed to arouse a certain amount of ire in the guests but it was none the less a duty they upheld. Annie, however, was a special guest to Fortitude. She had such interesting smells about her person and her shoes reeked of predator scents.

After Annie had let herself into the entryway and slipped off her slip-ons, she petted each tabby in turn. Fortitude mounted one of her slip-ons and positioned himself for a pee. "Oh, no you don't Mister, not this time." Annie admonished and gently pushed him off the shoe. She placed the shoes outside the front door and then turned around and checked the collar. "Fortitude," she said to him. "You've got to stop peeing on people's things when they come inside. It's not nice for humans." Patience reached up and tapped the arm that was petting

Fortitude. Annie reached over and gave him some additional attention. "Poor little guys."

"Are you kidding me?" Sally said as she strode past and into the kitchen. "That's like saying, 'Oh poor Prince William and Prince Harry.'"

Annie joined her in the oblong kitchen. "I know, but cat's don't like their schedules interrupted and these two have had their fill lately. I just want to reassure them." She took the cup of coffee Sally handed her, "Is she awake yet?"

"Not yet. Listen, we need to give each other some breaks along the way. I mean, we seem to have gotten a bit of a routine going now."

"Do you need to go into work today?" Annie asked.

"I do, but that's not the point. Look, she's going to be in this narcotic haze for a couple more weeks. I was listening to this podcast last night and they were talking about how people who care for other people are more likely to get run down and sick. Honestly, I think we should," Sally corrected herself, "You should take tomorrow and go to the dog park with Bert and Ernie. You know, go out for lunch or maybe get your hair done."

"Is my hair a mess?"

"No. I just mean recharge your batteries."

"Do you not want me here?"

"No. Annie. Listen to me. I have no ulterior motives here." Sally waved her arms freely about, as if fanning away the ulterior motives in front of her. "I'm only saying, suggesting, that after you've set up this genius food, medicine, bathing, and exercise schedule perhaps you'd like to do something for yourself as well. Wouldn't you like to take Bert and Ernie out for a relaxing day?"

Annie searched Sally's face for a moment, "I guess. Have you made Lorna some breakfast?"

Sally gave Annie a pitying grin. "No. Not yet. So tomorrow you'll take a day for yourself?"

"Let's see how she is today. Maybe." Somewhat disgruntled, Annie put her coffee cup down and reached under a counter to pull out a saucepan, "I thought maybe a little oatmeal this morning. She was complaining about being nauseous yesterday."

Sally rolled her eyes and turned away as a white clad figure caught her peripheral vision. She gasped and dropped the coffee cup before it registered in her conscious that it was Lorna, half leaning and half grasping, onto the doorjamb. "Good God!"

Annie's attention snapped to the doorway, "Lorna!"

Both women raced to the doorjamb in time to catch a sliding Lorna and help her to a kitchen chair.

Lorna looked at them both with unfocused eyes, "I'm not taking another pill until someone tells me what the *fuck* is going on in here!"

"What do you mean?" Annie asked.

"Oh my God honey, what are you thinking coming all the way down here? You can't get out of bed yet."

"Where are Tessa and Dad?" Lorna demanded.

Sally and Annie stopped and looked at each other questioningly.

Sally answered, "You don't remember?"

It looked as if Lorna was trying to focus her eyes on something in the distance for a moment. Finally Sally helped Lorna make the connection, "They went back to Atlanta."

"Why?" Lorna asked.

"They wanted to take you back to Atlanta," Annie started softly. "And Sally said no so they got mad and left."

Lorna leaned her head back. "Ohhh," She drew out. "I thought I dreamed that. Yes. Now I remember," Lorna added generally.

Sally gave Annie a dubious look. "Okay, let us take you upstairs and put you to bed."

When Sally moved forward, Lorna opened her fist up and held out a handful of pills before smacking them down on the table. "I stopped taking these yesterday. So I can tell you two things for certain: one, I'm in a great deal of pain and two, I'm very lucid. Now how about you start telling me the truth."

Annie was aghast, "Oh Lorna. How could you? We've put our whole lives on hold to get you well again and this is how you repay us?"

"Annie, inside, in the back of the refrigerator you'll find an old loaf of bread, hand it to me."

Sally's hand flew up to her forehead with a smack, "Oh my God, I totally forgot about that."

"What is it?" Annie wanted to know.

"Just hand it to me," Lorna snapped.

Annie reached into the refrigerator and in the very back was a half of a loaf of bread. "Ew," She pulled it out and handed the abnormally heavy loaf to Lorna.

"Okay. Just wait. One thing at a time," Sally said pulling the loaf away from Lorna's weak grip. She stood up and reached on top of the refrigerator and pulled down a small key fob and pressed the button. The low hum of the frequency jammer began and Sally sat back down. Sally turning on this sound barrier caught Annie's attention and she watched them in growing anticipation.

Sally sat back down and touched Lorna's hand. "When you got shot, Lorna, everything stopped, ya' know?"

"No. How could it? You haven't moved forward at all?"

Sally shook her head, no.

Lorna looked at Annie with a weak gaze.

"What?" Annie asked.

Sally stared down at the table and slowly shook her head for a moment. "Lorna, can you not give this a couple more days?"

"No."

"I should leave you two alone, I'll go upstairs and-" Annie got up from the table, but Sally caught Annie's forearm and stopped her.

"About a week ago I got some information about the whereabouts of the man who killed Tim and shot you. He was a hired gun. We don't know who hired him, but we know he was definitely the gunman."

Annie looked at the loaf of bread.

"Who are *we*?" Lorna wanted to know.

"Eunice and Wallace," Sally named her parents leaving the Nurse out of the explanation.

"I forgot about them, where are they?" Annie asked, her eyes widening.

"They left. I don't know where they are."

"Did they close Auld Alliance?" Annie wondered.

"Annie, I don't know. Please, just listen."

Lorna was quicker to connect the dots. "So he had to have been CIA. Or maybe they had a connection to him."

"No, I don't know if they *were* the connection though, you see? The thing is, they could have gotten their information from anywhere, or simply gleaned it off of someone."

"Who?" Lorna asked.

Sally shook her head and shrugged. "The thing is, I looked into this myself. And I know for a fact he was the guy."

Annie's mouth dropped open and she exchanged a bewildered glance with Lorna.

"Was?" Annie asked.

Sally nodded soberly.

Lorna locked eyes on Sally, "You mean-" she started and stopped. She finished her sentence by dragging her finger across her throat.

Annie bounced up from her chair, let out a distressed whine, circled the chair, and sat back down. She rubbed her hands up and down the top of her thighs as if to rub out a sore muscle. "But why? Why Sally, why would you do a thing like that? Why not just tell Roberta?"

"There was no legal proof," Lorna answered. "Annie just stop for a minute and think about this. I remember Roberta did say they didn't have anything much to go on except my description. No weapons, no fingerprints, no motives, nothing."

"Yeah, but-" Annie mutely mouthed out the rest of her question, "to take a life?"

"He was coming after you next," Sally said.

"We don't know that," Annie whined.

"Annie, I do," Sally reassured her.

Lorna butted in, "I can't believe in all this you didn't explain more to her."

"Explain what!" Annie demanded.

Sally threw up her hands in exasperation. "Oh. Okay. I see. This is all on me then." She said sarcastically to Lorna, "That's right, I'm the asshole in all this. Got it. I shit on Christmas."

"That's not what I'm saying," Lorna defended.

Just then the doorbell rang out and they all stopped arguing.

"Roberta," Annie whispered as Sally charged out of the room.

Lorna wiped the pills off the table and jammed them into her pocket. She nodded to the key fob, "Shut that off."

"How?" Annie asked urgently.

"Just push the button."

"Act sick," Annie whispered back to Lorna and pushed the button on the key fob as she heard the front door slam shut.

Sally appeared at the doorway again and gave a game show sweep of her arm.

Roberta stopped mid-step. "Get her ass back to bed. What is wrong with you two?"

Lorna let her head drop a little before holding it up, "Good morning Berty. Are you going to look at my boobs again?"

"Don't call me that." Roberta snapped and turned her attention to Annie, "How'd she get down here?"

"Do you remember how you got down here?" Annie asked Lorna.

"I scooted on my bum."

Roberta looked accusingly at Sally.

"I'm sorry, she was just here when we were cleaning up the kitchen," Sally said honestly.

Roberta looked confused. "Sally could you go get my medical bag? I left it in the bedroom."

"Sure," Sally quickly began hopping up the stairs.

"Have you been giving her the meds? From the schedule?" Roberta asked Annie.

"Yes. I have," Annie answered truthfully.

"Well, she shouldn't be lucid enough to take those stairs. She could have very easily fallen. You two," Roberta acquiesced, "I know it was a freak thing, but these are heavy narcotics and if she's walking around, either she needs a heavier dosage or you guys are really going to have to keep a closer eye on her."

"Yes. I agree," Annie looked pointedly at Lorna, who was giving her best fake head bob.

"I'll examine her in here, but we'll need to get her back upstairs before I leave."

After Roberta left, Annie came back upstairs with the loaf of bread and flung it on the bed next to Lorna. "Okay, what's with the decrepit bread?"

"Wait," Lorna was sounding significantly weaker in her demand; a bead of sweat ran across her top lip. "Annie, please tell me how you feel about what Sally told us."

"How I *feel*? I'm freaking out. This whole, whatever it is, this isn't my life. It's like a bad dream. I just feel like I have no control and I can't make the spinning stop."

"I feel exactly the same way," Sally said soberly. "And every time I make a choice, it's somehow the wrong choice."

"Okay. Then we need a plan. But first," the narcotic haze was beginning to cloud Lorna and her speech was slow and slurred. "Sally, that choice you made well, actually you made two choices. The first one we just learned about and then standing up to my Dad and Tessa, they were both correct in my eyes. Maybe not in Annie's and maybe not in uh," Lorna shut her eyes but lifted her eyebrows knowingly, "Roberta's, in her current occupation but they were difficult ones and I will help you carry that burden. Secondly, I'm about to pass out from the pain so can you fill Annie in on the rest? I'm sorry I scared you guys and got you into trouble with Roberta. It hurts to breathe. I want - resume- thing pain program now."

Sally picked up the loaf of decrepit bread and ushered Annie and herself out of the bedroom. Shutting the door behind her she said, "Damn, she's determined."

"About what exactly?" Annie snapped.

"Come downstairs with me and I'll explain everything to you," Sally said.

Sally and Annie sat at the kitchen table sipping coffee

as Sally started explaining the circumstances behind Tim's murder. Sally surprised herself at how cathartic it felt to finally talk about it with someone. And she had a choice on how to tell Annie the truth, either she could just drop the bomb or ease Annie into the idea. But as she wasn't sure on how to ease Annie into the idea without sounding condescending she dropped the bomb.

"Tim was involved in some corporate espionage. That's why he was killed. He stole something and then hid it at your house."

Annie's eyes widened, "What?"

"I know. It's kind of," Sally looked around the kitchen, "out there. But now some time has passed I understand why he did it."

"Have you lost your mind? What are you saying?"

Sally immediately realized her mistake. "Okay, I did this wrong. This is my fault; I'm not good at explaining myself sometimes. Let me start again?"

Annie pursed her lips and wrinkled her brow at Sally.

"Let's say there's this big conglomerate who has their hands in a little of everything, human resources, military contracts, toilet paper, you name it. Right?"

Annie nodded.

"And person A works for a small human resource company in silicon valley, and he knows just about everyone. So person A's small human resource company get's bought out by this big conglomerate so now person A is working for this conglomerate with military contracts."

"And person A is Tim," Annie nodded.

"Right, but hang on. Now the National Security Agency and the FBI likes to keep tabs on this conglomerate since they have so many contracts with them for satellites and military materials, etcetera. So the NSA goes to person A, who is in human resources and says 'hey, we need to keep an eye out for who is working on military projects over there in that conglomerate,' and person A says 'sure, I can do that for my country'. Then one day the big conglomerate sends their human resource guy, person A, over to handle the human resources for this small satellite contractor outfit and the FBI, who likes to keep tabs on things too says, 'hold on why is big conglomerate handling the human resources for a small satellite contractor'."

"So Tim was in the middle of all this?"

"Yes. And the FBI reaches out to Tim."

"Why? Why would he do that?"

"He was an informant, for the NSA -"

Annie chuckled and looked up at the ceiling, "Oh Tim, you little idiot. I can see it happening too. You know, I can see him thinking how cool it was then all of a sudden he's surrounded by these sharks - playing spy master like he was ten years old." Annie rubbed her eyes, "Okay, so what happened?"

Sally spread her palms out on the table and sighed with relief. "Well, best I can make out this little satellite agency, called The Hayward, was making a satellite cloaking device for the NSA and perhaps they were blackmailed or just paid, but they made a copy of the device for the big conglomerate as well, which is a no-no. And instead of just telling on them to the NSA Tim stole the copy of the device they made for the big conglomerate and replaced it with a fake." Sally shrugged, "I don't know why, maybe he panicked, or maybe something went wrong.

Annie's face had disbelief all over it. But Sally didn't budge, "I know. Lorna and I thought the same thing. But it's true. The Hayward had contracted out their human resources to Spectorgies. They did that in order to hide and shuffle payments between them. See, The Hayward was developing satellite software for the NSA and Spectorgies wanted to get their hands on it. So from what I gather, Hayward's sale to Spectorgies must have gone through but Tim nabbed the copy and he must have hidden it in your house. I'm very worried that whoever hired the person that killed Tim and shot Lorna is just going to hire another person to retrieve this device."

"Why didn't you tell me any of this before? I mean, why not-"

Sally cut her off, "Because, by the time I was able to piece it all together, I mean, everything just kept happening. You know, and I tried, but I mean, you were kinda in shock after you found Tim. Then Lorna was well, Lorna, and then my parents. And then we thought the police were coming after you for Tim's murder. It was just all happening so fast. And frankly I just felt like I needed to get rid of that immediate threat, *you know,*" Sally eyeballed Annie, "just so I could have a breather and think for a minute." Sally made a quick arm lurch for the key fob and pressed the button. The low hum of the frequency jammer began and she rolled her eyes in disgust that she had forgotten to activate it before.

"So, okay, you did what you had to do or thought you had to do," Annie said accusingly.

Sally looked at her menacingly, "Oh, it would have been better if we left it up to Ohlone Police? The same ones who wanted to arrest you for Tim's murder? They are going to arrest a man with no past, no present, no address, no weapon, no evidence. Sure, they would have been on him like stink on shit. Look, Annie, what happened was," Sally took a calming breath, "horrible, but we may not be sitting here having this conversation had I not acted. Please, I'm having a hard enough time with this, don't make me defend myself to you too."

Annie didn't respond but sat quietly staring at the

table. Sally knew what she was selling Annie was a half-truth here and she stole a glance at the kitchen clock. She needed to set up a meeting between the Nurse and Michael in order to get the ball rolling on his end of their bargain.

Annie nodded in an unspoken agreement with herself, "So Spectorgies killed Tim?"

"All I know is the gunmen was a trained CIA assassin. Who he worked for is up for debate."

"Then why did he shoot Lorna?" Annie was beginning to wrap her mind around the problems.

"Because I think when Tim wouldn't give up the device, he came back. Lorna probably smart mouthed him and he shot her."

To Sally's surprise Annie chuckled at this, "Yeah, she probably did." Annie stopped chuckling and realized something. "Hang on. If he came back to the house, do you think that's where Tim hid the device?"

"Yes."

Annie rapped her knuckles on the table, "I knew it. It all has something to do with the house. Who all knows about this?"

"Just us, and Roberta knows some stuff. But not everything."

"What about your parents?"

"Turns out they were trying to warn me about this. Somehow word had gotten to them and they were trying to protect us."

"What happened to them?"

"I sent them away. I didn't want to risk them getting involved too. This device, it's worth like 30 million dollars, probably more."

Annie shook her head in disbelief, "What about this bread?"

"I don't think it knows."

The humor was lost on Annie. "Do I get a say in this?" Annie snapped.

Sally leaned back, "Of course you do. Absolutely."

"Cause I'm going to be honest, I don't really approve of the last plan you enacted. Not at all, I understand, and maybe I'll grow to appreciate it even, but right now I think it was wrong to do what you did."

"Fair enough."

"That's just not how normal people handle things. That was *abnormal* behavior. Part of your brain has to be sprung to do such a thing."

Sally sat back calmly and listened.

"I think you should see a therapist. I mean, this isn't 1970 East Berlin."

Sally waited as Annie digested everything.

"Of course if you hadn't acted we may not be sitting here debating it." Having had her say Annie looked around again, then tapped the bread.

Sally opened the bread bag pulled out several slices of bread then stuck her hand in and pulled out a small hardcover notebook. She slid the notebook to Annie who opened it. "That night, remember we had dinner and Lorna was cleaning up in the kitchen? She said an Asian man delivered Chinese food to her at the kitchen door. He said that it was from Tim and that he'd be in touch. When she opened a container she found this book wrapped in plastic. But you know, the next day she got shot."

Annie opened the book to reveal Tim's familiar cramped handwriting. She thumbed through the book, but nothing looked remotely familiar to her. It was just gibberish. There was no note to her from Tim. No I love you, no explanation from beyond the grave. Just nonsense. Annie closed the book back. She had tears streaming down her face, "I don't understand. I can't take anymore of this Sally." And collapsed into tears.

Sally stole another glance at the clock. If she was going to make that meeting with the Nurse and make it into the office she was going to have to cut this short or at least find an excuse to get out of here for a while. She berated herself mentally for wanting Annie to snap out of it and buck up. Maybe Annie was right, maybe there is something abnormal about her. Sally got up and poured herself some more coffee and cleared her throat.

"I think I should leave you with all this for a little while. Don't you?" Sally asked.

Annie shrugged her shoulders.

"I think maybe some oatmeal might be nice this morning," Sally tried to sound casual but sincere.

"What are you talking about now?"

"I think oatmeal for Lorna would be a good idea. And I think if you two put your heads together then you'll be able to figure out that code that Tim wrote in."

Annie grabbed the book and opened it again and looked at the pages.

Sally sat back down at the table. "Well of course it's in code. I mean, this is Tim we're talking about."

Annie smiled through the tears and nodded her head.

"I think as far a plan goes, we should just find the damn thing and turn it over to whatever authorities or do it anonymously."

"But I don't want my life destroyed in these shadows. Why don't we just tell everyone? You know, sunlight-" Annie tried to remember the phrase.

"Because it amounts to treason. Despite his best intentions and he was probably, absolutely, trying to do the right thing, the security agencies could just turn it around on him and say he committed treason just to save their incompetent asses. And there ain't enough sunlight in the world to disinfect those assholes."

Annie nodded.

"Look, when Lorna wakes up maybe you two will talk?"

"Yeah," Annie agreed.

"I need to run into the office, just for a bit and then I'll be back before lunch."

Annie nodded.

"Are we okay here?" Sally wanted a verbal confirmation. The last thing she needed was for Annie to loose her mind and do something crazy right now.

"Yes. I'm not going to run off and do something crazy."

Sally squinted at her, "Are you reading my mind?"

To clear the air between them, Annie half smiled and squinted back at her. "Yes. And pick up some more bread on your way home."

Annie pulled out the oatmeal from the cupboard and turned on the flame under the saucepan. Her mind strayed between wondering where Tim would hide something in the house and Sally's explanation.

When the oatmeal finished cooking, she placed everything on a tray for Lorna. As she climbed the stairs, Sally passed by to leave.

"See you later!" Sally called out.

"Okay, we'll be here," Annie assured her.

Sally let herself out the front door and spun the keys around in her hand. Annie wasn't wrong, she thought, her behavior had been abnormal and criminal. But that's not what rang a bad chord in her mind. It was how quickly she was able to slip into that brain space that allowed her to go through with it. How easy it was to revert to the behavior that ruled her parents. Mastering the art of manipulating others. The trafficking of secrets where the only rule was to do unto or be done in. The engine revved up at the turn of her key. Sally decided Annie was right after all and when this was all over she was going to get some therapy.

As she drove off she shook the reverie from her mind. She slipped into a cold, calculating mental space and put her game face on. Convincing the Nurse that Michael was a go between for the Aurora buyer was only half the battle. The other half would be up to Michael.

CHAPTER 5

Lorna lay back on the bed in naked contemplation. I don't feel well this morning, she thought. Say it out loud, her thoughts continued, but surely Sally is tired of her complaining. Don't be a jerk. But there was a break in her string of thoughts, she was trying hard to remember that familiar smell. What is it, something from the microwave maybe? The shower stall in their master bathroom could accommodate two people, that is something true, but only if she sat on the bench. It's these drugs they are giving her, of course, she thought. She needs to say something to Sally. She rolled over to her side and with great effort she inched up a little by pushing her legs down. A wave of nausea passed through her again. No, that's wrong or is it just a new pain? What's that smell? Pea soup? She felt a cramp in her stomach. Come on Lorna, she said to herself, there is something wrong so speak up.

Sally stood at the doorway between the bedroom and bath and watched Lorna squirming in the bed for a moment. Step one, wrapping Lorna in cellophane, was complete. But should she clean herself first then help

Lorna shower or maybe better to shower Lorna, wash her hair and get her out to rest.

"Wow, plastic wrap is hot," Lorna lay back on the pillows of the bed. "Ain't this romantic?"

Sally couldn't keep the laugh inside. Lorna's once shiny blonde hair was dull and streaked with grease; her cheeks sallow, and dark circles shadowed her now dull blue eyes. Her previous fit figure depleted and exhausted by surgery, medicines, and inactivity. Put some garish paint on her face and she'd looked like a refuge from a red light district. "This must be the good times I was promised when we married."

"What? No, dude, like I'm cooking, it's like I'm a pot pie over here."

"You kinda smell like one," Sally said without rancor.

"Really?"

"Yeah," Sally walked over and stood by the bed. "Roll over and slide off, we have to get you up and to the shower bench."

"Turn it on first and let the water get warm at least," Lorna instructed.

Sally went back into the bathroom to turn the shower on and when she returned Lorna had slid off the bed.

"Oh my God," Sally rushed over to where Lorna had landed in a half squat twisted lump next to the bed.

"No I'm okay. I was trying to show you how I could get up myself but I don't have stomach muscles apparently. Whew," Lorna sniffed. "I am ripe. What have you been feeding me?"

"Okay, just-" Sally waffled around trying to figure out how to grab Lorna up without hurting her. "Okay, listen, I'm going to get down here," Sally squatted down on all fours beneath Lorna, "and just flop yourself over me and I'll stand you back up."

"Are you sure?"

"Yeah, just like, lay on my back."

Lorna positioned herself over Sally's back and Sally lifted back up dumping Lorna back onto the bed.

"Okay," Sally overarched her back, "if I can get you in there and wash your hair and sponge you down, can you sit on the toilet and dry yourself while I shower?"

"Of course," Lorna said confidently.

Sally looked at Lorna dubiously but other than hosing Lorna down in the back yard, she couldn't think of how else to accomplish this underappreciated daily task.

~~~

With the shower debacle behind them, Sally set out to dress Lorna. "Roberta will be here any minute to change your dressing," Sally was saying as she pulled Lorna's sweatpants on, "how about just putting on this zipper hoodie and we'll put on a long sleeve shirt afterward."

"Okay. I was thinking maybe it would be a good idea to air me out today too."

"What do you mean?"

"I mean maybe I could go for a ham and cheese?" Lorna was referring to the ham and cheese croissants from the Auld Alliance she had grown to love.

Sally scoffed. "Just because you can make it down the stairs and back doesn't mean you can go for a bike ride."

"I'm not talking about a bike ride. Drive me. Dude, I have another hour, maybe, at most before I go back to la-la land, the pain is a lot better today. Please, I need a ham and cheese croissant, so bad," Lorna lied. She knew she was lying but there was something she needed to say and could not, for anything in the world, get her mind back on the point.

"I thought you told Annie you'd help her decode that book."

"It's called deciphering, and I am, she's over at her house now looking for a book. Please, if I have to eat another rice and vegetable medley concoction of hers I'm going to puke." That's it, she thought, she wants to puke. But Sally continued talking and it took all her concentration to listen.

"What book?"

Lorna paused, there was a thought that was slipping away. "He wrote in several codes. I think one part of it is a book cipher. Another part is in VIC cipher, which is difficult and will take me a while. Although some of it looked a little like a substitution cipher."

Sally finished putting on Lorna's "lucky" socks. An odd pair of tube socks with a red stripe. She rubbed Lorna's feet comfortingly. "How about I go get you a ham and cheese croissant?"

"No. No more cipherin', no more pills, nothing until I get aired out." Lorna said in frustration.

They stopped talking when they heard someone walking up the stairs. Annie gave a quick knock on the door before turning the handle. "Can I come in?"

"Sure," Sally welcomed the distraction.

Annie walked in and smile, "Hey! It smells like soap in here. What's going on?"

"Well, we've had a shower but our diva in distress wants to be aired out now," Sally said truculently.

Annie switched her gaze quickly between them and contemplated. Obviously Lorna's request was demanding, but on the other hand if she goes for a drive she might pass out and sleep more. But then again, she might pull a stitch, and that wouldn't be worth it even if she did pass out. And she shouldn't wish that, she thought, but Lorna's general gracious demeanor has been taking a turn to the sour lately.

"Annie!" The voice seemed to come from the ether.

"What?" Annie jerked back to the present.

"I thought you were taking a day off?" Sally asked.

"I'm sorry, I was up all night taking the house apart and putting it back together. I brought this book for you." She handed Lorna a book.

"*Kim*," Lorna looked at the cover. "Good pick."

"It's for that cipher you showed me. It was Tim's favorite book from childhood. I thought it might have a passage or something to help you."

"Oh right," Lorna seemed to remember, "that is a good idea. But we don't have a page number to match it against, but we can give it a try."

The doorbell rang. "That's Roberta," Sally said and headed out the door for the stairs.

"Did you find anything?" Lorna asked referring to Annie's nighttime activity.

Annie shook her head, no.

"Can you help me up?"

"Where are you going?" Annie asked.

"I want to see if the Auld Alliance is still open."

"Roberta's here," Annie reminded her.

Several thoughts struck Lorna at once. "Not Kim, I'm sick." Lorna looked pointedly at Annie. "I don't feel well!"

Annie shuttered at Lorna's outburst but nodded to appease Lorna. "She needs to change your dressing," Annie explained softly.

Roberta and Sally appeared in the doorway.

"I'll go fix some breakfast," Annie said excusing herself from the room.

Roberta made her way to the dresser and grabbed the plastic box that held the bandages and the necessary medical supplies.

"I'll help you," Sally said to Annie and left the room before Roberta could object.

Downstairs in the kitchen Annie said to Sally, "I thought maybe grits and eggs?"

Sally nodded. "Yeah, something's off though. You see it, don't you?"

Annie busied herself with the breakfast as she spoke, "Maybe she's getting worse? You know maybe those narcotics are backing up in her system or something, in her brain."

"I need some kind of second opinion, she didn't seem paranoid but it's like only one part of her brain is working, like she got cognition but no reasoning. Ya' know?"

Annie nodded, "And no short term memory."

Sally stood at the counter staring at the empty doorway drumming her fingers and chewing her lip.

Annie continued hopefully, "Maybe she'll forget about the ham and cheese croissants."

Sally continued drumming her fingers, only half listening as Annie continued, "I was thinking last night, do you remember when Lorna and I were taking that art class and we got robbed?"

Sally grunted.

"Then, she and Roberta and I had that spat, I wouldn't call it a fight but you remember, we weren't on exactly friendly terms. But Lorna didn't give up, I mean Roberta and I were ready to lay down and play dead and Lorna got mad at us and started yelling about something, I can't even remember what now but she kept referring to herself in the third person calling herself The Lorna." Annie chuckled and mimicked Lorna's voice, "You're gonna turn your back on The Lorna?" She got serious again, "Then Lorna turned around and caught the burglar." Annie snapped her fingers together. "Single handedly, she tied that man up and left him for the police. She gift-wrapped him! And I realized something last night after you told me everything and she and I sat down to decipher Tim's book. I need The Lorna back. So, is she acting crazy? Yes, maybe she's even taking advantage, a little maybe, but not by much. Lorna can be annoying and bellicose and I don't even pretend to know how her brain works but if I'm going to find this thing that Tim stole and we can get on with our lives, we're going to need The Lorna. So." She concluded, "I'm not going to take a day off. The Lorna doesn't get a day off being shot in the chest so The Annie doesn't need a day off neither."

Realizing Annie was done talking, Sally snapped to and saw Annie holding out a tray filled with food in front of her.

"Can you take this upstairs and I'll clean up."

Sally dutifully took the tray and as she left she could hear Annie mumbling something about a grocery list.

"Looks real good." Roberta announced to Sally as she entered the room with the tray.

Sally put the tray down on the bed next to Lorna, who eyeballed the food greedily.

"No," Roberta said to Lorna. "I'll hold it up and you unlatch the table legs." Roberta picked up the tray and hovered it over Lorna's lap as Lorna reached up and pulled down the legs. "Your natural impulse is to use that right arm and you've got to resist the temptation."

Lorna nodded and dug into the grits left handed.

Roberta smiled. "Good appetite."

Sally watched this exchange with confusion. Not fifteen minutes ago Lorna was demanding to be aired out and, really, all morning she had been combative in some way. "That's great." Sally said noncommittally. Then she caught Roberta's eye and gave a quick head toss toward the door.

Roberta raised her eyebrows and nodded. "See you

tomorrow." She said to Lorna.

"Danks!" Lorna called after her with her mouth full.

Roberta shut the bedroom door and followed Sally into the spare bedroom.

Roberta looked toward the stairs, "We got a minute?"

"Yeah, does she seem alright to you? I mean mentally?" Sally asked.

"Quiet, like she's plotting something." Roberta nodded.

Sally shook her head and grunted. "I know this may sound odd, but something is not right with her. Annie and I have both noticed it."

"Like what? How do you mean?"

Sally pursed her lips and looked around. "No short term memory, mood swings, one minute she raring to go and then next sound asleep. I mean dead to the world asleep, and when she wakes up again who knows, nauseas, short of breath, confused, belligerent."

Roberta nodded. "It may be the narcotics. Is she having cramps?"

Sally shrugged.

"Well, have her take notes about it and when you go back to see the doctor make sure you show the notes to him."

"Yeah, but Roberta it's like," Sally paused and her shoulders fell. "Okay, the first couple of days out of the hospital she was one way and now she's another."

Roberta lowered her head and raised her eyebrows at Sally. "Right. I hear you. It's like she's on drugs. She'll come around, this is the hard part, the healing. No, the hard part will be weaning her off the drugs. Getting all that out of her system. Save your energy for that. But look," Roberta lowered her voice, "we need to talk about something else."

Sally nodded.

Roberta paused, "I think we may have found Lorna's shooter."

"What does that mean? You arrested him?"

"No. I mean we found his body, on one of the boats in the marina."

"His body?"

"Crime Scene Unit is going over it now. But he does match Lorna's description."

"So, he's dead."

"Yes." Roberta considered Sally's reaction to the news.

Sally puffed out her cheeks and blew out air, "Good riddance?"

"He was shot twice in the back, one to the head."

Sally had no reaction to this news, she was doing a quick time clock calculation in her head. Once the hit mans murder is revealed they had, at the most, 36 hours before steps were taken by whoever hired him. And they have maybe 24 hours at the most to produce this Aurora. Roberta caught Sally's gaze. "I don't know what to say, I mean it solves a murder for you doesn't it?" Sally added.

"No evidence linking Tim's murder and Lorna's attack," Roberta carefully scrutinized Sally.

"I'll let Lorna know."

"Well, they may want her to identify him as her shooter. That would go a long way in at least telling us who he was," Roberta nudged forward.

Sally let a profound moment pass between them. She knew that Roberta knew what she had done. But what was Roberta going to do about it, if anything?

"Several passports and identifications. This guy wasn't a weekend boater and he wasn't who he claimed to be. Oddly, the place was a mess. Looks like someone had gone through it as well. But none of his very expensive boating equipment was taken, well, as far as we could tell."

"As well? What do you mean someone had gone through it, as well?" But Sally knew at once it must have been The Nurse, hopefully Michael had taken care of any evidence the Nurse had left linking Sally to the murder.

"Ransacked, kind of like Annie's place, after Tim-"

"Huh," Sally nodded.

Roberta paused and looked at Sally knowingly. "Look, you're my friend and I want to help you guys out here, but you're stepping in my yard. I've seen too much, I know too much, and pretty soon this is going to be above my pay grade. He had to be a contractor-"

Sally didn't want Roberta to say too much, "Sorry, Roberta, I've got a deadline now. The clock has started."

Roberta nodded, "I'll see myself out."

But Sally turned to Roberta, blocking the doorway. "No. I mean, thank you for letting me know. I think you are doing everything in your power to help. I know that and I really do appreciate it. Thank you for working with us and you're right, this is as far as you go."

Roberta turned to walk out. "You're welcome." Roberta lowered her voice as she passed by the doorway, "but listen to me now, you gotta get out of this thing. And you better do it soon."

"I'm working on it," Sally nodded.

"Good, I'll see you later."

"Thanks."

Sally heard Roberta letting herself out the door as she poked her head back into the bedroom. Lorna had fallen asleep again midway through finishing the breakfast. Sally lifted the fork from out of her hand and carefully lifted the tray up.

Sally placed the tray on the kitchen counter as Annie ripped off a sheet of paper from the pad.

"You guys are about out of food in here." Annie turned to Sally.

"Okay, there's someone we need to go see."

"Who?"

"I don't know quite yet. But Roberta said," Sally stopped herself before starting again, "Lorna passed out again, I think she must be exhausted from this morning. Let's just go, we won't be gone long."

Annie's eyebrows quivered for a beat. "Then let's go."

~~~

In the car Sally was careful not to be to specific in the lie she told Annie. Roberta, Sally said, had told her about a guy here in town that was some kind of federal agent. Keeling, Roberta's old boss, had worked with him in some capacity a few times so Roberta thought maybe he might have some answers for them.

"That's very kind of Roberta." Annie had said.

Sally held off notifying Annie of the discovery about the assassin. She needed Annie to be on this one track of finding the Aurora. No sense in confusing the issue.

They stood outside the side door at the Lemon Sud bar and looked up at the second floor windows. Annie looked over at Sally who was stealing covert glances at the cars passing by. "No offense," Annie confided, "but I wish Lorna were here. She always knew what to do in these situations."

Sally looked back up at the second floor window. "Knock?"

Annie took a quick shallow breath and jerked on the metal door that swung wide open. "Oh, that was easy."

They slowly made their way up the dingy, creaking stairs. "Well, it's not like anyone can sneak up on him," Sally said approvingly.

Annie knocked on the door. A few moments later the door opened. Michael stood there looking back and forth between the two women on his doorstep.

"Do you speak English?" Sally asked with poignancy.

"Sometimes," Michael said understanding Sally's opening question to actually mean that he must act like a stranger to her.

"Do you know who we are?" Annie asked.

Michael hesitated, "Yes. You'd better come in."

Sally and Annie walked into a dilapidated room with a small kitchen to their right, one of the cabinet doors hung precariously off its hinge. Annie looked around, surprised by the shabby surroundings.

"What is this place?" Annie asked.

"A safe house," Michael answered honestly. He understood at once he was about to shatter any illusions Annie had about her husband.

"Who are you?" She asked.

"I'm Michael Chan. I'm a FBI agent, Tim was my informant." He said softly.

Annie's mouth fell open, she tried to form a question, but the shock was settling in on her. Michael and Sally stole a steadfast look between them. Sally made an almost imperceptible shake of her head to him. "Would you mind clearing up a few things for us?" Sally asked.

"I will try."

"Did you have anything to do with Tim stealing the Aurora?" Sally led the questioning.

"Yes and no. He was helping me monitor the Aurora but he swiped it and replaced it with a fake on his own. But then I helped him hide afterward, here, as a matter of fact. Then he took off and then, well, I'm sure you are aware of what happened next."

Annie joined in the questioning, "But I thought Tim was a NSA informant, why were you involved if you're with the FBI?"

"I work for a special fraud division. We handle corporate espionage and high profile fraud. Tim was an informant for the NSA to keep an eye on Spectorgies and Hayward but I tapped Tim to keep an eye on the Aurora for the FBI as well. Our division feels there have been too many contractors working in the NSA and you can't serve two masters."

"But what is the Aurora?" Annie asked.

"In the simplest terms it's a satellite cloaking device. It makes satellites disappear while in orbit, so it masks the satellites capabilities." Michael looked around. "Would you like to sit down?"

"No," Annie snapped at him. "So you were watching the watchers?"

"Yes."

"Now what?"

"We'd like to have it back, the Aurora."

"Who?"

"The National Intelligence Agencies." Michael looked up at Sally and nodded as he spoke. This was more for Sally's benefit than Annie's. "An alliance has been formed under the Director, and within the next couple of days you are going to be served with warrants and subpoenas. Basically, they are going to dismantle your house and question you, at length. They are building a case, framing Tim as a traitor under the espionage act."

Annie's legs buckled, both Michael and Sally lunged to break her fall but they missed and she landed on her butt. Annie braced herself on the floor, putting her arms down and taking deep slow breathes. "Okay. When is this going to happen?"

"I don't know exactly, but soon." Michael explained slowly as he took a place on the floor next to her. "Tim was not a traitor. He was a good guy, who just panicked.

And I desperately want to help you, please let me help you. We can find this Aurora again and make all of this go away."

"Then why are you not telling them?" Annie asked, scooting away from him.

"Who?" Tim replied and mirrored her movements.

"This Director guy. Tell him not to do this. I'll help them if they'll just let me. I don't want the damn thing," Annie pleaded

"Unfortunately, conciliation is not their strong suit. They've got all these new powers and they like to assert them - test the boundaries."

"Why haven't you come forward to me before?" Annie asked.

Michael rubbed his eyes. "I've tried, so many times. But I'm a one man operation here, there have been a lot of strings I've had to follow and I do have to be very careful that I'm not detected. I had hoped by delivering Tim's codebook, you'd be able to find the device and it would all work out naturally. What I didn't and couldn't have anticipated is the other one, Lorna, getting shot. And now that I've heard about how Homeland Security and the NSA want to proceed with your case -" Michael broke off. "So, actually, you've saved me some time by finding me."

Annie looked at Sally who was observing this whole scene. "I think you're being inappropriately friendly here." Annie scooted away, putting at least two arm lengths between she and Michael. "What do you think?" She directed her uncharacteristically brisk question to Sally.

"I'm sorry," Michael interjected and moved even further away from Annie.

"So. What are you bringing to this? How is it you want to help?" Sally asked.

"I don't want to see these assholes with the NSA, who basically dropped the ball, try to pin this on him. It wasn't Tim who made the second Aurora to be sold to - who knows? An adversary at the least. One of their private contractors did that and now to cover their tracks they want to blame someone else. And Tim, you know, I mean yeah, he outsmarted them, but by doing so he also fell into a trap. We need to start going through your house. I mean really going through it, pulling up the floor, checking the walls. Have you gotten anywhere in this code book he left?"

"No, we'll try again tonight. Do you know cryptology?" Sally asked.

Annie's head snapped back to Sally. "So you trust him?" She said as if Michael wasn't in the room next to them.

Sally raised her eyebrows. "Keeling did."

Michael addressed Sally's question. "Not on that level, all I know is the streaming and blocking we use for digital devices. I mean I know the basics, the early theories and all that. But that book was meant for Annie and I thought Tim would have used a key that only she and he would have known."

Annie looked up, her face wide with a new understanding. "Of course."

"What is it?" Sally asked.

"Nothing, I have to think about it, but I might have an idea. I don't know though." Annie got up slowly from the floor. "Thank you for talking to us."

Michael and Sally looked at Annie searchingly.

"We'll let you know what we come up with," Annie said.

"Hang on, let me give you a phone number to reach me. Let me just find a pencil."

Annie kept moving for the door, "That's okay, we

know where to find you."

"No Annie wait," Sally said. "Just in case."

Annie turned a cold gaze on Sally, "Let's go. He obviously can't help us, or he would have come forward sooner."

"Here you go." Michael handed Sally a slip of paper.

"Whatever." Annie said and left.

As Sally turned to follow Annie, Michael grabbed her wrist and whispered. "Beware, the Nurse."

Sally nodded and quickly caught up to Annie.

After they got back into the car and Sally pulled out into traffic she asked Annie, "So, what's on your mind? Something dawned on you back there."

"It did. But I don't want to talk about it until we get back. I've got to run home for a few minutes anyway."

"Okay," Sally agreed. She didn't exactly like the idea of Annie being in that house alone but didn't want to alert Annie to any danger. "Tell you what, why don't I take Burt and Ernie for a walk, while you do what you need to do and we can reconvene at the house and make lunch. It's about time for Lorna's feeding -oh shit. We have to stop off first, is that okay?"

Annie let out an agitated sigh, "I guess."

"I just want to pick up that ham and cheese for her," Sally said.

"Oh by all means," Annie snapped.

"Hey," Sally admonished her. "What about helping The Lorna?"

"I just found out my house and what's left of my life are about to be raided and you're all, 'Oh, Lorna wants a croissant'. By all means, get her that fucking croissant!"

"Okay. I'm sorry. I'll drop you off first. I just thought we could get more done if we worked as a team. But you're right. You have every reason to feel on edge."

"No. Stop for the croissant. And she likes Gouda cheese. We could just pick up our dinners too. That way we can work without stopping tonight."

~~~

Once they pulled into the driveway, they had a plan worked out for the evening. Sally parked the car. "You know, I was just thinking. If that guy, Michael is right about all this, then we should have an attorney on hand for you. Do you want me to make a few calls?"

"Yes. Thank you," Annie said as she got out of the car.

As they walked down the drive to the front porch Sally looked over to Annie's house. "Did you leave a light on in back there?" She asked indicating Annie's house.

Annie looked up and continued to walk. "I don't know, maybe."

Sally watched Annie cross the street and walk up the front porch steps and into her own house. But then her own front door was ajar and panic shot through her like lightening. She took the stairs two by two and called out Lorna's name but got no answer. She threw open the doors to the empty rooms upstairs and leapt back down the stairs and checked in all the rooms. No Lorna. Sally felt panic crash into her stomach. She threw open the front door and ran across the street to Annie's house.

"Annie!" She yelled as she pushed the front door open.

Annie came around the corner. "She's here," Annie said calmly.

Sally walked into the kitchen where she saw Lorna passed out on the kitchen table. An empty picture frame was on the table near her head and as Sally walked around carefully, looking around the room and back at Lorna, she saw a frothy pool of drool had accumulated from Lorna's mouth to the table.

"She's asleep, but she figured it out, look," Annie said smiling and let out a snot filled cough and pulled the codebook and a piece of paper out from Lorna's hands.

"What is it?" Sally asked.

"Tim and my wedding vows. I had them framed," Annie said. "But Lorna made fun of them so Tim had written funny ones, see?" Annie held out the paper with a shaky hand, "Tim used *that* as the code key."

Sally took a deep breath and looked around. "Okay. Let's get her back home." She stroked Lorna's head, "Lorna. Wake up. We have to go back home."

Lorna didn't budge.

"Lorna! Come on. Back home!" Sally said loudly.

Sally gave Lorna a nudge on the shoulders but Lorna remained unresponsive.

Annie joined in, "Lorna!"

They both gave her a gentle shake and Lorna's arm flopped off the table.

"Call Roberta," Sally directed Annie.

"Smelling salts!" Annie answered. "They're in Tim's emergency pack." She ran to the front closet and pulled out a large green backpack. She turned it upside down and emptied it on the floor. She grabbed a small box, returned to the kitchen and broke open the ampoule and ran it under Lorna's nose. Lorna didn't respond.

"Call Roberta!" Sally demanded and carefully pulled Lorna off the chair and laid her out on the floor.

CHAPTER 6

"Keep her head turned to the side." Roberta directed from the front seat, with a calmness that belied the situation. Sally and Annie both sat in the backseat with Lorna wedged between them. With her patrol car sirens blazing and echoing through the Warner Tunnel, Roberta had the demeanor of a Sunday driver. The two women in the backseat were holding Lorna upright and as still as possible as Roberta careened and jerked through the traffic to the Oakland hospital.

Roberta slammed on her breaks in the emergency receiving bay and medical staff moved in tandem, gliding about in a well-rehearsed crisis ballet. Annie and Sally were pointed to the receiving area and after the initial flurry Roberta moved the car out of the bay.

Shocked silence engulfed them as they sat in the waiting area. Time lurched forward and back again as they sat in that hideous stress pose of impotent waiting. Finally, Roberta broke the silence. "Did you get the bottles from the bathroom too?" She asked Annie, referring to the bag of drugs she had handed to the nurse.

"Yes," Annie said.

Sally shook her head and mumbled, "I'm so glad you remembered that."

Roberta stood up but seemed to change her mind. Sitting back down she spoke in a lowered voice, "Guys, I got to get back on duty. I'm so sorry. Annie, can I run you home real quick and you can bring a car and whatever else you might need. Or maybe I should call Ms. Strangler?"

Annie looked at Sally, who was staring vacantly at the intake desk, before answering, "I'll go with you."

Roberta stood up to leave.

"Just give us a minute here," Annie said and subtly nodded at Sally.

The emergency room doors opened and caught the attention of the three women who watched expectantly. A bespectacled, dark haired, middle-aged man said something to the nurse behind the intake desk and turned to face the women. He had the physique and slouch of an old runner with a bad back.

Sally stood up and immediately introduced herself, "I'm Sally Thompson, Lorna's partner."

Doctor Raether clenched his hands together and abashedly spoke to the floor. "Ms. Thompson, I'm Doctor Raether," he spoke in a clear mumble, "we've been able to stabilize Ms. Tollison. We're running some tests now but," his head jerked up with an inspired idea, "is there anyway Lorna could have gotten into any household poisons?"

Sally and Annie both screwed up their faces. "Poisons?" Sally said. "No. What kind of poisons?"

The doctor bowed his head again, "Well, this is just preliminary, you understand, but it does look like she might have ingested *some* kind of poison. There was some cuticle discoloring - we're going through her other pharmacy med's just to be sure-blood work-" The doctor stopped mid-mumble, looked at all three women and turned to leave.

Sally snapped to attention. She grabbed the doctor's arm, "There were no counter-indicative reactions in her medications. But, I need you to test the actual medications, the pills, for that poison. Whatever it is."

Annie caught on to Sally's idea and said, "But we're the only one's who've been giving those pills to Lorna."

"I know that. That's exactly right," Sally said stiffly to Annie. She turned to the doctor, "I think your initial diagnosis is probably right if not, very close to it. Please check those capsules."

Annie added, "That would explain her strange reaction to those narcotics. Remember, Doctor Stallone said she'd be really out of it but then it would gradually lessen. But she's been like a roller coaster."

Doctor Raether meandered off, "We're going to need to flush her system - I'm going to keep her in ICU and I'll let you know any further developments."

Roberta tapped Annie on the shoulder, "I gotta go."

"Okay, I'm right behind you," Annie nodded.

Sally jammed her hand into her pocket, pulled out the slip of paper with Michael's number on it and handed it to Annie. "This is Michael's number. I need you to call him and ask him to keep an eye on our houses while we are gone. Then I need you to find a quiet spot where you can work on deciphering the codebook."

"What are you going to do?" Annie said as she pulled herself toward the exit doors.

"I'm going to sit here and worry."

"For how long?"

"Until they come back and tell me Lorna's in the clear."

"Who could have poisoned her pills?"

"That's what I'm worried about." Sally said as she gave Annie a little wave.

After what seemed an interminable time Sally approached the intake desk. "Excuse me, I'm Sally Thompson. Lorna Tollison was admitted to ICU a few hours ago, I was trying to get an update." She said to the nurse wearing blue scrubs with colorful balloons printed on them.

"Sure. Are you related to her?"

"Yes, I'm her partner."

"Okay, someone will be out shortly," The nurse reassured Sally.

Sally paced about for another half hour and approached the desk again and addressed a different nurse, this one had puppy faces printed on her yellow scrubs. "I can see you're very busy but I've been asking for an update on my partner in ICU, Lorna Tollison."

"Sure," the nurse said briskly, "let me go get someone for you." Then she disappeared again.

Fifteen minutes later Sally approached the nurse's station again and stared at yet another nurse with dark pink ribbons printed on light pink scrubs. This nurse continued working as if Sally was not standing directly in front of her and staring at her. The nurse found what paperwork she had been searching for and left the station. Sally passed through four hours in this surreal charade repeating her request to this carousel of fashion conscious nurses.

In the intervening moments between the nurses station visits she stared at the fake ferns but watched her questions pass through her minds eye. How did this happen? This poison or drugs that Lorna had taken, when could it possibly have been administered and in what form? When had the house stood empty for someone to enter? She watched the nurses change shifts, fresh emergencies come and go, and she saw the families of patients being escorted through the double doors of the emergency area.

Sally took out her cell phone and looked at it. Strange, she thought, no messages from Annie, nothing from Roberta, not even Mrs. Strangler had called. Something was occurring to her and she squinted as if it was coming from a great distance. It's wrong. This whole set up - she looked around with a clear understanding - they had been separated. That would explain why this day has felt so haphazard. Annie sent home, by her self. Lorna taken ill, but perhaps not life threatening. And she dumped here to wait. She had been too scared to leave and too stupid to realize this was probably a set up. She sat up straight and except for her eyes darting back and forth, she sat still for a moment. Was she being paranoid? Yes, definitely. Divide and conquer, it's an old trick, but effective. Sally stood up with new confidence and walked over to the nurse carousel.

"Hi, I'm Sally Thompson. I brought my partner, Lorna Tollison in about three o'clock," Sally demanded.

"Lorna Tollison? Hang on," The nurse turned to a computer and began typing.

"Thank you."

A moment later the woman looked back up at Sally. "I'm sorry. Ms. Tollison has been moved to a private room and her information is restricted."

"But I'm her partner. Do you need to see our certificate?"

"No, it's not like that. I mean her information is restricted access, even in the computer. See?" The nurse tried to turn the computer screen toward Sally.

"I've asked almost a dozen nurses over the last four hours for information and not one of you even bothered to tell me she was being moved? I'm her next of kin, I brought her in." Sally was reaching rant proportions and heads began turning in their direction, she lowered her voice, "Okay, you know what, this isn't your fault. I get that, but *you* had better get either with a supervisor, or administrator, or Dr. Raether and find my partner. *Now*."

"Let me see what I can do," The nurse said and picked up the phone.

Sally watched as the nurse dialed a number, waited a moment, pushed a couple more buttons and hung up the phone.

The nurse stood up, "I'll just go and see if I can find Dr. Raether."

Sally held up her hand. "Don't bother. Look, I've watched the nurse's here play the nurse shuffle for hours. I come up and ask a question. That nurse disappears and another one returns then someone else asks the new nurse a question and that one also disappears and yet another one returns. If *you* can't provide me with a person who has the authority to override that restriction then I'll be happy to return here with a warrant."

Just then a dark haired Asian woman in a blue suit and skirt appeared behind the nurse, "Melisa?"

The nurse turned around and looked relieved, "This is Lorna Tollison's partner, she brought her in and the computer is saying restricted access and now-"

The woman touched Melisa's shoulder, "I've got it."

Melisa got up from her seat and left the station. The blue suit took a seat at the computer desk and typed in a code. She looked up at Sally. "Ms. Tollison is in a private room, being treated for an overdose. And I'm afraid that's all I can tell you at this time as you are not listed here as her emergency contact."

"What? Of course I am, I'm her partner."

"Says here a Perez Santiago. He authorized the

private room and the restricted access." The blue suit said with finality, "Is there anything else I can help you with?"

Sally's jaw slacked open. She was stunned. They, Quill and Tessa, had changed Lorna's emergency contact in Lorna's hospital record. Her brained wheeled around, of course they probably paid someone off but how could they be so evil as to cut off her contact with her own partner. The hospital administrator watched as Sally's face lost color and take on a pasty film. And in turn, Sally watched the blue suit get up from the desk and walk away.

Sally turned and looked around the ICU waiting area. Pitiful and worried faces reflected back to her. She watched a little boy run in a circle, fall, pick himself up and continue running circle laps. If Lorna is in a private room and perhaps Perez is there with her, then she is safe. But how would they know any of this? Are they a part of this divide and conquer or just the beneficiaries? Actually it doesn't matter, it is very smart she thought, with Lorna safely ensconced in the hospital then she and Annie can look for the Aurora. She left the building and stood where a few cabs waited on the curb. She dialed her cell phone for Annie. When she got no answer she dove into one of the cabs.

"Ohlone Island." She said to the cab driver.

"Through the tunnel?"

"Yes, yes. I'll direct you," Sally said leaning forward.

~~~

Sally could see Annie's house lights burning from within. She looked back at her own place, which was dark and seemed to take on a foreboding air. She walked up Annie's steps and rang the doorbell.

A moment later Annie opened the door, "Hi."

"Can I come in?"

"Of course," Annie said cheerily and stood back. "I'm sorry-"

"I don't care. Did you know that Quill and Tessa had changed Lorna's emergency contact at the hospital? She's under restricted access. They've cut me off from her."

"Is she okay?" Annie asked.

"Yes, I think so. How's it comi-"

Annie cut her off, "Come with me." She took a few more steps into the house.

Sally immediately recognized a familiar hum. "Is that a -"

"Yes, Tim had it installed apparently," Annie said referring to the frequency jammer that was radiating its low frequency hum. She opened the door to the basement.

Sally had a queasy feeling deep inside her gut. "Did you talk to Michael?"

Annie let out a contemptuous chortle. "He said he was laying rat traps."

Sally realized immediately that Annie missed the true meaning of his remark. Michael wasn't laying out traps for mice to fall prey to, as Annie probably thought. He was laying out metaphorical snares to catch people or throw off people away from herself and Annie. "You first." Sally waved her hand toward the stairs.

Sally's eye's adjusted to the dim light, feeling their way around the walls of the half finished basement and landed in the darkest corner where the Nurse sat, perched upon a wooden stool.

"Sally," Annie said, "this is Agent Bernard of the NSA. She's come for the handover of the Aurora." Annie turned away and the Nurse flashed Sally her shoulder holster and gun.

The Nurse smiled and stood up holding out her hand. "So nice to meet you," she said. "When they told me an old CIA operative was working on this I was really relieved."

"I've never been with the CIA," Sally countered, refusing the handshake.

The Nurse, Karen Bernard, shrugged. "At any rate, we're extremely grateful for the recovery effort and I was just telling Ms. Doughall about the reward. She has asked that it be split up between you."

Sally's gaze landed on Annie, who stood with her arms crossed behind her back. Annie looked like a hopeful child, waiting patiently for her prize. "I would love to see it," Sally said innocently.

"So would I," Karen winked audaciously at Annie.

"Okay, but," Annie looked to Sally in a pleading way. "I want a receipt. Something that says I turned over this Aurora to the NSA."

"A five hundred thousand dollar reward kinda speaks for itself," Karen Bernard said.

"No, I mean I want," Annie paused, "an affa-david."

"She means an affidavit." Sally said, eyebrows raised, "And I don't blame her."

"That's fine, but you understand that it has to go in and be tested and everything first. We've been through something like this once before."

Sally took over, "Annie is being threatened with warrants upon her person and her home. I'm certain that she's simply asking for reassurances that these warrants are not issued or acted upon during the time that the Aurora is being tested."

"Absolutely. We'll have it by morning and then we'll make the exchange?"

Annie nodded and looked at Sally for reassurance. Sally nodded back at her.

"Good." The Nurse stood up to leave. She looked at her watch as she made her way up the stairs with Annie and Sally in tow, "Say, 8 o'clock then?"

As they reached the top of the stairs Karen added with all the casualness of a daily routine, "Oh, what I wouldn't give for regular office hours."

Annie shut the front door behind Karen Bernard and paused before she turned to Sally.

"Where's Michael?" Sally said before Annie could speak. "Someone is playing divide and conquer -" A light knock came from Annie's sliding glass door in the kitchen. Sally scurried around to the kitchen and slid open the glass door for Michael.

"What the hell Michael?" Sally demanded.

"I was right here the whole time," Michael said calmly, "down by the little basement window."

"A lot of good that would have done if she shot us," Sally said, incandescent with rage.

"She wasn't going to shoot you. She doesn't have the Aurora," He said defensively.

Annie watched the two of them fight like old friends, she thought. She narrowed her eyes at them and crossed her arms in front of her. "So, how long *have* you two been working together?"

Sally puffed up and turned to Annie, "I am not, nor have I ever been, in the secret services. Now please, will you let it go already?"

Michael chuckled a little. Bringing the ire of both women to his gaze. He continued smiling and shook his head. "I'm sorry, it's just that there's all these men who want in to the services and here you are, a woman, and you're all, I don't want to be -" Michael stopped realizing he just inadvertently made a sexist comment. He blinked at both of their quizzical looks and wiped the smile off his face. "I'm sorry."

"Annie, I'm trying so hard to keep this shit together, now please, what happened?" Sally changed the subject.

"Well I called Michael on the way back." Annie looked at Michael, who nodded agreement and interrupted her by interjecting a finger up at them.

"And just real quick here," Michael rushed his speech, "the moment she told me what happened I realized your two houses were empty and I rushed over in the van. Okay, go ahead." Michael held up both hands to surrender the floor.

Annie nodded at him and continued, "I finished the codebook when I got back here. It only took a little while; Lorna really hit that code wide open for me. I had intended to look for the Aurora but this woman showed up. I didn't know who she was so I thought she was going to serve me with a subpoena or do that warrant thing but she only asked to speak to me."

"And you let her in?" Sally asked astonished at Annie's naivety.

"When someone flashes a badge at you, you tend to do what they ask," Annie explained.

"Where were you?" Sally asked Michael.

"At that point I was watching from the van," Michael said. "But when the Agent went inside I snuck around back to get a better view. Plus, Annie had put up the frequency jammer so I had to get closer."

Sally asked Annie, "When did you do that?"

"Like maybe five minutes before she got here?" The statement came out as a question.

"Okay," Sally paced around in a circle for a moment. Obviously, the Nurse had bought the line Michael was feeding her, that his name was Sunil and he had a buyer for the Aurora and that explains why she would reveal herself to Annie today. Her thoughts moved on to the next problem.

"Annie, was there anything in that book that would implicate anyone in," Sally shook her head from side to side, "I don't know maybe another crime?"

"I don't know what you mean. Like what kind of crime?"

"I'm trying to figure out why someone would poison Lorna? Why go that extra mile or maybe it was simply to get she and I out of the picture entirely."

Michael leaned back on his heals and crossed his arms in front of his chest. "No, you're right. It *was* to get her *and* you out of the way," Michael agreed nodding.

"Well," Annie demurred and moved further into the kitchen, "Lorna has made a lot of enemies in this town." She began making coffee.

This struck Sally for a moment. Annie was an avid tea drinker. Sally didn't even know Annie had a coffee maker. She looked at Michael and said quietly, "So, did you get those rat traps laid out?"

Michael nodded and stole a glance in Annie's direction as they followed Annie into the kitchen and sat down at the table.

"But that doesn't answer your question of who did it, does it?" Annie asked shrewdly.

"No. But for now at least I know she's safe," Sally said.

"Okay," Annie finished making the coffee and clicked the machine on. "Michael, in our bedroom, I mean my bedroom, there is a big doggie bed. I need you to pull up the floorboards underneath it. Sally, you take the basement."

"Anywhere specifically?" Sally asked.

"I don't know, Tim practically redid the whole basement, it could be anywhere down there."

"I just need something to tap on the walls, forget it, I'll figure it out." Sally said getting up to go downstairs.

"I'm just going to need a hammer," Michael said.

"Garage," Annie said and swung her head in the

direction of the garage.

Sally waited at the bottom of the basement stairs listening to the movements from above. She heard Michael leave and come back, then walk up the flight of stairs that led to the upper floor. She heard the kitchen sliding glass door slide open and waited another moment before carefully climbing the basement stairs. She cracked open the basement door and through the slit could see through Annie's dining room and beyond to the outside patio. Which was lit up like the fourth of July, she thought. Annie shifted the dog's house over to the side with great effort. Clearly Annie was oblivious to the fact that she was being watched, and perhaps not just by Sally and Michael.

Sally twisted her wedding band around her finger, if she finds that Aurora right now and someone from NSA or FBI is watching then there is nothing to keep them from storming in right now and destroying whatever chance they have of catching the Nurse. Not that she's had much time to think about it properly or been able to gather any proof but the closer they get to this thing the more dead certain she is that it was the Nurse who hired the man who killed Tim and shot Lorna. Not Spectorgies or the NSA as she originally thought. Sally watched as Annie began touching the stone's beneath the doghouse, then stop and tap one stone in particular again. Sally ducked and skipped down a few steps when Annie turned and walked back inside to the kitchen.

Sally heard loud creaking and light tapping begin upstairs. Once Annie was back outside, Sally resumed her spot to watch the events unfold. Annie went back to the stone she had tapped and began using a kitchen knife to pry it open. The lid popped up and clambered back on to the stones. Annie reached inside and pulled out another box and opened it. She threw a kitchen towel over the shoebox-sized container and looked around. As the seconds ticked by, Sally weighed her options. She could push the door open and alert Annie that she had been watching her or she could cause a diversion. She needed to get the focus off Annie if others were watching as well. She silently crept down a few steps into the basement. "I found it!" Sally yelled loudly and ran back up the steps. "Annie, Michael, I found it!" She pushed open the door to see Annie standing open mouthed in front of the sliding door and Michael, gawking at her.

"What's going on?" Annie wanted to know coming into the kitchen and placing the box on the counter.

Sally pursed her lips as if to shush Annie and put her hand out and lowered it down slowly. Sally did a reverse peace sign and tapped, just below her eyes. Annie nodded perceptively. Michael entered the kitchen nodding perceptively and Sally looked to him. "What's the plan?"

"We need to delay her. I've got some calls to make."

Annie watched them and spoke up, "No, we're turning it over to her as soon as she walks through that door."

Before Sally could open her mouth Michael said, "Annie, she's not a NSA agent. She was, but left them weeks ago. There is in fact a national intelligence alliance working like I told you about but she's not a part of it. The problem now is that someone in that alliance is leaking information to her and possibly others. We need to plug that leak, so we need to let her continue thinking she's getting away with the Aurora."

Sally looked at Michael skeptically. She thought he was about to blow the story line they had fed Annie, and maybe there was some truth to what he had said about plugging a leak in the information. But she doubted it. Michael wants the Aurora for his outfit in the FBI.

"But what about my home? I don't want it torn apart. Why can't I just turn it over to whoever shows up with the warrants?"

"Because it defeats what Tim was trying to do," Michael stated simply. "Tim was smarter at this stuff than me. He foresaw this cyber war, that's why he was helping us. Obviously, we can't destroy it. But at least we can get it in the right hands. And finishing this is how I can help you honor Tim."

Sally looked to Annie. Something emotional has shut down in her, she thought. There were no tears in her wizened eyes.

"Who says I want to honor Tim?" Annie asked. "He does all this without my knowledge, he starts divorce proceedings on me, and then I'm left holding the bag. What's there to honor? Why should I give up my life for something I don't even believe in? I never would have agreed to any of this. I liked my life before and I want it back."

Sally nodded her agreement and added almost absently, "I think Tim liked the idea of being a part of something bigger than just him self. Working in Silicon Valley with all the technology companies, I think he was really trying to protect what he could. I don't think he thought at all about any consequences. He probably thought he was protecting you by divorcing you." Sally set her eyes on Annie. "You've not had any time to mourn or process any of this. When Agent, I mean, Karen Bernard shows up why don't you tell her you have to wait until the bank opens to retrieve the Aurora." Sally turned to Michael, "You've got to give her at least a couple of hours to think this through, without your help."

Michael nodded, "We can do that. Sure. Let's hope she buys it."

Sally added, "And Michael, you're just going to have

to respect Annie's decision."

"Absolutely," Michael assured her.

They worked together to cover up the Aurora's hiding spot from under the doghouse and took the Aurora to the basement. "Lorna always says, 'the best place to hide something is right out in front, in plain view'." Annie said as she set the box on Tim's workbench among the broken radio's and odd electronic paraphernalia.

Michael looked around the space and nodded, "Looks normal."

"Alright," Sally said with finality, "I'm headed back home then. I've got to come up with a plan to deal with Lorna's family after this."

They shut off the basement lights and trudged up the stairs one more time together. "Are you going to be okay?" Sally asked Michael.

"I'll be out in the van. I'll be fine. I better go out the way I came in though, " Michael said.

"Oh hey, Michael, if you need relief out there just come to the side door. I'll probably be awake anyway."

"Thanks," Michael said, turned out the patio lights, and left.

Annie touched Sally's arm for a minute while she made sure Michael was out of earshot.

"Do you not trust him?" Annie asked.

"It's not that, I just think he wants the Aurora for his agency. But we need him, he's our only contact to what's going on with that alliance."

"Right," Annie nodded. "One more thing, do you think Lorna's family poisoned her? You know, to get control somehow? I mean, this thing sounds like something Tessa would be involved in; she's got those government contracts. Or maybe someone trying to get at Tessa?"

Sally inhaled and shook her head, "That's a good point."

"After this is over, tomorrow afternoon, they don't have any reason to keep me away. I'll go over to the hospital and see what I can find out."

Sally raised her eyebrows, "That'd be great, Annie. Thank you."

"They can't keep people apart. It's ridiculous," Annie scoffed at the thought.

"I'll see you at what time in the morning?" Sally asked.

"Eight?"

"No, that's when Karen gets here. Like six-thirty?"

"Oh, okay," Annie agreed.

"Look whatever you decide, it'll be the right answer and we'll just work through it."

~~~

Sally stared at her bedroom ceiling. No matter what decision Annie makes, she's screwed. Turn it over to the Nurse and the government goes after her. Turn it over to the government and the Nurse and whatever Henchman she employs will go after her. I'd take my chances with the government, Sally thought. Really, the Nurse is the most immediate threat to her. If someone poses as an agent then that's not Annie's fault, she could just say that she was acting in good faith since no one from the NSA or any other agency had approached her. Sally sat up in the bed.

"That's it," She said aloud to herself. Sally glanced at the clock. It was only going on two o'clock in the morning. She got out of bed and dressed. She went downstairs to Lorna's office and found a laser pointer from the cat's toy box and went to the front window. Pointing the laser pointer at Michaels van she tapped out an S. O. S. and went into the kitchen to make a pot of coffee and waited.

A few moments later there was a tap at the kitchen door and she let Michael inside.

"What happened?"

"Nothing. I think we should talk. Come on, we can grab our coffee's and watch out the front window."

"Can I use your bathroom first?"

"Sure."

Sally took her coffee into the living room and stared at Annie's house. Michael joined her soon after. "What is she doing over there?" Sally asked Michael as a light from the upstairs turned off.

"I don't know, she's been moving room to room all night. Anyway, I didn't get a chance to tell you last night. But I made a call to my boss when Annie called me."

"And?"

"I told them a second attempt had been made on Lorna's life. That's when they told me about all the group's that are now working on this."

"Who's involved again?"

"CIA, FBI, NSA, and Homeland, believe it or not. That's why the National Intelligence Director is handling it, trying to pull all the strings together."

"Too many chefs in the kitchen. They'll bungle it. I wonder if they even care that there is a leak in their ranks. But I think we should gently encourage Annie to turn the Aurora over to the Nurse. It's not her fault if she turns it over to the wrong person, you know, she acted in good faith. Plus, it'll keep her out of immediate danger."

"Yeah." Michael agreed.

~~~

Annie came up from the basement with two small suitcases in hand. When she reached the top floor of the house she placed them in the bedroom and looked around. She'll put clothes and toiletries in one suitcase and leave one out for valuables and keepsakes. So, this really is what it comes down to, she thought, thirty-four years and just a shitty suitcase full of crap no one else would care about but her self. She looked at the small closet safe filled with documents that provided proof of life to other people; insurance, certificates, and accounts. Why bother?

She moved the closet suitcase over to the side and lifted up the carpeting. She stuck her finger into the hollowed out knot hole in a wood plank and lifted up the cut out of floor planks. Reaching into her pocket she pulled out a small safe key. It was a second key Tim had left her. He had planned out this whole thing. Contingency plans, codebooks, secret keys, had he known this little mission of his would go so wrong for him? Was their life together so bad, so boring that he felt he had to liven it up with a secret life? How could something so abstract like this stupid Aurora be worth throwing your life away?

Annie opened the floor safe. There were two large plastic zip-lock bags filled with neatly stacked cash and a small tape recorder. Annie pulled out the tape recorder and pressed play.

~~~

At four o'clock, Sally looked over at Michael. "Hey," She said quietly. Michael jerked awake.

"I'm sorry."

"It's no problem. Why don't you run to the bathroom and do what you must do. I'll make us some breakfast sandwiches. If anything were going to happen, it would have by now."

"Yeah," Michael rubbed his eyes and yawned.

"I just want to get this over with. As Lorna would

say, *'whatever!'*

"The fuck I would say *whatever*! Why would you leave me in the hospital like that!" Lorna bellowed from behind them. Michael jumped forward and fell to the floor with a roll. Sally jerked her whole body around.

Lorna was wrapped front to back and back to front in hospital gowns and wore a sagging pair of socks. "You super spies left the kitchen door unlocked!" Lorna's volume seemed to be stuck on scream. "I need some money for that cab! It's around the corner!"

CHAPTER 7

"And the next thing I know- this old man is hovering above me." Lorna bellowed. "Who I believe, Michael, is a friend of yours." She looked across the kitchen table at Michael who nodded.

"Where was Perez?" Sally interjected.

"How the hell should I know?" Lorna bawled.

Michael leaned in closer. "His name is Doctor Stritch. He's not really a friend, he was my boss, Pickles', doctor and I know he works with the people from our division. They fought in Vietnam together, Pickle and Stritch." Michael desperately wanted to explain the full story on Dr. Stritch and his little black bag of magical pills and ointments. But it probably wouldn't go down too well that the old man wasn't a human doctor but a veterinarian and that Michael had met him after he was seriously injured in the boat blast. One look at Lorna's dilated pupils confirmed to him that Dr. Stritch had pumped her full of the same kind of drugs he had been put into Michael after the boat blast.

"So," Sally said to Michael obstinately. "Your people

must have come in and taken Perez away? Then this doctor gives Lorna some cocaine or something. Look at her."

Michael looked at Lorna's sallow skin and sunken cheeks, "I don't think he'd give her cocaine."

"I feel great!" Lorna announced and slammed a pill bottle on the table that had been clenched in her hand the whole time. "This shit's better than that other shit I was taking. Look, we need to talk to Annie, I figured it all out on the cab ride over!"

"What else did Doctor Stritch say?" Michael wanted to know. "Was there anyone else with him?"

"Nope!" Lorna answered. "He helped me put my gown and escorted me out to the cab. Which I thought was odd, I mean, there was no one in the nurses station and no one on the elevator, and we just walked past admitting as pretty as you please."

Sally, realizing time was wasting away, stood up. "Okay, Lorna first we need to get you dressed and ready for the day. Michael, why don't you grab a bite to eat while we get ready?"

"Yeah," Michael agreed.

"I'm not hungry!" Lorna announced.

Michael quickly wiped the smile off his face when Sally glared at him. He busied him self in the kitchen as they went up stairs.

"Shit, shower, and shave baby! I'm gonna need a bushwhacker!" Lorna screamed from the staircase.

Sally spent what little amount of patience was left in her reserves on getting Lorna sponged down, dressed, focused on the task at hand. She explained to Lorna how they needed to convince Annie to turn the Aurora device over to the Nurse. The reasoning behind the decision, being that it wouldn't be Annie's fault if she turns over the device to a person impersonating an agent, as well as keeping the Nurse off Annie's back. Once Lorna was calmed down, Sally watched Lorna apply lotion and couldn't help but notice the ease at which Lorna moved now, as if her body was almost healed.

"So, what about the warrants and stuff?" Lorna asked.

"We have to wait on that," Sally answered. "That's why we need that affidavit from the -" Sally faltered a little, "agent, I mean, Karen Bernard."

Lorna caught Sally's stumble and stopped the persistent lotion application. Lorna's eye's narrowed at Sally. Sally braced for another barrage of questioning but Lorna simply nodded at her.

"And in other news," Lorna began rubbing the lotion into her arm again, "what my family tried to do, amounts to kidnapping. It was disrespectful and repugnant. But I'll deal with them later."

Sally was amazed at the Lorna's display of lucidity just now.

"I know it's not your area of legal expertise but I'd like to get them on something, something about the manipulations of my hospital records."

Sally balked at this declaration, "Lorna, I agree what they did was reprehensible, but maybe we can revisit this when this is behind us."

Lorna stopped rubbing her arm, which was in danger of loosing all the hair from the rubbing. "Let cooler heads prevail?"

Sally nodded.

"Fuck that." Lorna said as a matter of fact. "I'll hire my own lawyer. You don't know them like I do. It was an act of revenge, a power ploy, wrapped up like concern. They went too far this time."

Sally was a little taken aback. She had only seen it from her own point of view, not as Lorna was saying, a power ploy over Lorna. "But we need to tread lightly, Lorna, in light of the knowledge they have against me."

Lorna nodded. "Agreed, Counselor. Which is why I'll handle it. What you did was for both of us. Wrong, right, who knows? But it was for us and at least you were honest about it. What they did, was for them, you see what I'm saying?"

Sally looked at her watch. "Do you feel - I mean, how do you feel?" Sally asked Lorna who had resumed the arm rubbing.

"Am I not right? Am I being crazy?"

Sally shook her head with concern.

"I see. Maybe I was given, like, a pain blocker and some kind of speed."

"Do you feel at all tired?" Sally asked.

"I feel like I'm kinda soaring above it. Like at times really focused and then I dip down until a breeze catches me again-"

"Okay," Sally stood up and stopped Lorna's loquacious exaltation. She reached over and gently hugged Lorna and gave her a quick kiss, "I'm just glad you're here."

The gesture gave Lorna something else to focus on and she moved closer to Sally and gave her a long kiss, "Me too."

Sally pulled away, "We've got some stuff to deal with first. Okay?"

Lorna moved into a sultry pose and winked, "Then I will see you soon."

Sally's heart sunk, "No, Honey, you have to come with us. Remember?"

Lorna tsked at her, "Yeah. Just kidding." And added a *pfft* and snort for good measure as she left the bathroom.

Sally and Lorna arrived in the kitchen refreshed and

ready, only to find Michael passed out on the kitchen table.

"Michael," Sally touched his arm.

Michael jerked his head up in alarm, "What!"

"It's okay, you just napped, everything's fine," Sally reassured him.

"I'm good," Michael said with a thick, sleepy tongue.

"Me too," Lorna said. "You know, my arm and chest feel great."

Michael noticed her volume control issue had been corrected, "That's great Lorna."

Sally interjected, "Michael, look, why don't you run up and grab a quick shower, we'll have a bite to eat and then we can get started."

"With what?" Lorna asked.

Sally smiled patiently at her partner, "Remember the plan?"

"Oh right." Lorna said officially, "Michael you will take your shower and we'll eat. Then I'm going with you to the van where we can monitor Sally and Annie's progress. After the exchange at the bank I will leave the van and continue on with Sally and Annie."

Michael stood up, "That sounds fine. Thank you."

~~~

Finally, the night was lifting its curtain on a new dawn and the air was moist with morning when Michael and Lorna left through the side door. Keeping low until they reached the back of the garage Michael stopped before jumping the fence.

"I forgot about your stitches," He said looking up at the fence.

"That's okay," Lorna said casually. She pulled a couple of boards away from the railing. "It's my sneak door. I use it sometimes when the boys won't come to me when I call them inside. I know where they like to hang out, over there by the garden." She pointed to a neighbor's backyard. "They think I'm magic."

"What boys?" Michael asked stepping through the new hole in the wall.

"Patience and Fortitude. My boys." Lorna said placing the boards back.

Michael knew where Lorna was mentally and this could turn out to be a fascinatingly entertaining conversation, but he pulled back from it. He had to try to keep her focused. They walked the long way around the block and quietly cut through another yard before ending back up on Saint Charles Place and quickly hopping into a large white van.

"Wow," She said looking around the inside of the van. The walls of the van were covered with gadgets, electronics, and surveillance equipment. Each side had a small table top that when folded down, revealing small monitors behind it. Two stools were latched to the floor.

"I know. Tim had this built," Michael agreed.

"Really? When?"

"About five months ago. He put together the schematics and used some of his father's old contacts down in San Jose to put it together. Honestly, it's better than what we use in the FBI."

"How?" Lorna asked.

"Well, he was smart and used a lot of analog devices for tracking and listening on this side. But he also actually built the digital devices for storage we use on the left side, here. All of the analog recording is patched back into the digital devices for storage. So there's no beaming anything to and from a home base, it's a contained unit."

"Wow, I have no idea what you just said," Lorna smiled and took a seat.

Michael gave her a pitiful smile. As he began turning

on the devices and getting settled into the van, he weighed his options. He could just let her flounder, wondering why she felt so good or he could fill her in and use her drug induced brilliance to his advantage.

"You seem more focused than you did when you first got home," He mentioned casually as he flipped switches.

"Yeah. I get it. I've been drugged. Again," Lorna agreed. "I need to be careful not to pull my stitches even though I don't feel any pain."

Michael was relieved that either she had figured it out or Sally had already told her she had been *enhanced*. "That's very true. Trust me, you *will* feel that later on. I'm gonna get the recording set up, if you can - just for a few minutes - try to get your mind really focused on our situation. All of your mental abilities have been really, uh, heightened. If you can, kinda harness it, or ride that wave, we can take advantage of the new awareness. Here, take these headphones and listen in. Let me know if anything seems amiss." Michael handed Lorna the headphones and began pushing buttons.

~~~

From the front door, Sally could see lights still burning in the back of Annie's house. She knocked on the front door and waited.

"I'm sorry, I couldn't sleep," She said when Annie opened the front door.

"Neither could I, come in," Annie moved away from the opened door. "Coffee?" She asked moving into the kitchen.

"Please," Sally sat down at the kitchen table and took a deep breath. "Lorna's back."

To Sally's surprise Annie threw her head back and cried out in a maniacal laugh. Coffee went all over the counter, "Of course she is!"

Sally couldn't hold back and joined in the ridiculousness.

Annie sat down with her cup of coffee, "So she's okay?"

"Oh yeah," Sally nodded.

"Well hopefully that's enough for you then," Annie brought her smile to a close and nodded at Sally knowingly.

Sally ignored the insinuation that perhaps she was on some kind of revenge fueled murderous rampage. Maybe Annie thought that this morning's ruse was to lure Agent Bernard into a trap. But Sally simply nodded agreement and changed the subject. "So, have you come to any decisions?" When Lorna and Annie had gone through their crime-fighting phase, Annie had always kept he wits about her. But this time was different and it was important to Sally that Annie stay calm enough to pull this off.

"Yeah. I'm going to turn the Aurora over to Karen."

Sally was greatly relieved. She had prepared herself for cajoling and reasoning with Annie about this decision. "Really? What-" Sally let the question dangle there.

"Something Tim said."

Sally cocked her head to the side, "What'd he say?"

"Just, ya' know," Annie shrugged and let it drop.

Sally didn't press it, but said, "I think it's a good decision. We want to get rid of this woman, I think she's dangerous. And you'll be acting in good faith. You'd have no way of knowing if any agent was lying about who she was. It was smart to ask for the receipt."

"Look," Annie said. "I appreciate all you've done. I just want to make sure I at least say thank you. I would never have gotten through this without you and Lorna."

"You're welcome."

"When this is over, I think I'm going to relocate."

Sally nodded, "Yes. I can imagine that would feel like a great relief for you. Where do you think you'll go?"

Annie looked distant, "Away."

"Like a small island off the coast of Spain *away*, or a small town in Montana *away*?"

"I don't know yet."

Sally nodded, "I totally get that feeling of wanting to vacate this portion of your life. I've been there. Do what you need to, and if you need any help, just ask. Of course you're going to have to tell Lorna."

Annie smiled, "Well, that's no help."

"I have my limits," Sally smiled back.

"Almost there," Annie called to Sally as she placed the Aurora in her large purse and went back upstairs. Karen Bernard showed up five minutes later with her file folder and an empty satchel. Sally perused the affidavit and looked at the judge's signature, an obvious forgery. But whether or not it was real was of no consequence, it was fraud either way. Annie and Sally road to the bank in Annie's car and Karen followed them at a close distance. Sally took a couple of glances out the driver side window across the blocks and caught occasional glimpses of the white plumbers van as they drove.

The South Shore shopping center was like a modern and garish extension built onto an old and stately mansion. The entire shopping area was built upon the dredge material brought up from the canal on the east side that originally linked Ohlone Island to Oakland. The centerpiece of the shopping center was a large grocery mart that was flanked by an electronic box store and a fading bookstore chain. Closest to the road that ran out front was a gas station and a few old original beach front stores, a liquor store, a small diner, and the Ohlone Island Bank and Depository.

~~~

"Just so I'm clear here." Lorna was saying as they pealed off and drove a circuitous route to the bank parking lot. "You sent Sally's parents to Prague and are using them as the buyers for the Aurora. You set the whole thing up?"

"Yes," Michael interjected.

Lorna pondered this out loud, "The Nurse thinks she's selling the Aurora to a Chinese firm. Which, y' know let's face it, is actually the Chinese government. And you did this to flush out the leaks in our Intelligence Agencies." Lorna snorted, "Man, are you going around your elbow to scratch your ass. First of all, I'm not an attorney, but I've pretended to be one on the internet and I'm pretty sure that's entrapment. Second, how do you know who and where she intends to sell it to them? It would seem to me, I mean if I were Karen, the Nurse, Bernard, with twenty years experience in the intelligence agencies, and I knew I was being watched - then I could figure out that you were giving me enough rope to hang myself. Of course I'd go along with your dog and pony show. Prague is a shit load closer to Russian than China. You don't think she could figure out the buyers are Sally's parents? If I were Karen, I'd be all, 'Sure, I'll sell it to these people' to *your face* and then I'd set up my own deal once I got there. 'Cause if you do have a leak, you know, if she's not working alone then they've already set up their own deal and they're using you to get out of the country." Lorna added a, "pfft," and rolled her eyes, "You're just basically financing her deal."

Michael ignored her insult and stared ahead at the road thinking about what she was saying.

Lorna rambled on, "Or, if I was Sally's parent's I'd be all, 'Suuuure, we'll help you out, son. Just give us the Aurora and we'll return it straight back to you'." Lorna added another sarcastic snort and 'pfft' before continuing, "Shit. They could be acting as Karen's unwitting brokers in all this. And you can't do anything about it because you're FBI, you can't operate on foreign soil. What were you thinking? I can't believe someone in your circle didn't stop you. Unless they're in on it too! Using all this to set up the Nurse to take the fall and your operation gets control of the Aurora. That would be the be-all and end-all, wouldn't it? Set up by your own people?"

Michael's face flushed.

"I mean, I don't mean to be rude, but I think you're in the wrong business. But you never know, maybe you're doing Sally a favor here by getting her parents killed. It's not like they've been very good parents, more like absentee landlords in a way. Not that they're bad people. Well, they are, but I mean as far as parents go, they did make sure she was raised in a safe environment and paid for her schooling, maybe they just didn't know how to love a child. I imagine that's complicated. But, Dude, what sucks for you is getting two legendary agents killed in one of your missions."

"Okay!" Michael had enough of Lorna's rambling. "Thank you, I've got enough to think about now." He put the van in park and went in back with Lorna. She sat down on one of the stools and watched Michael click button and flick switches to set up the listening apparatus. He handed her a set of headphones. "Here, the sound will go in and out but keep listening, just in case."

~~~

Annie walked into the bank with Sally, leaving the Nurse to watch from her car. Sally took a seat in the waiting area as Annie walked over to a cashier window and spoke to the cashier who pointed behind Annie to a man sitting inside a cubicle.

Annie walked over to the man and sat down. A few minutes later the man ushered Annie behind a closed door. The small claustrophobic room was lined with grey metallic boxes with just the handles sticking out. They both used keys to pull out a box together and the man set the box on a small table in the center of the room. Annie opened the safety deposit box as he walked out. She clapped her palm to her forehead. It was another Aurora. Or something made to look just like it. Tim had made two dummy Aurora's. Maybe more? She pulled out of her purse the Aurora she had found under the doghouse and set them side-by-side. How could she tell which was which? Tim left no instructions on this. Wait a second, if one Aurora had been built by a corporation then it would have some kind of serial number on it, she thought. She pushed together two metal clips and slid out the main unit from the housing of one.

She stared at the two Aurora's. Okay, she thought to herself. Obviously this was part of his plan. The safest place for the Aurora would be in a bank vault, so the one in the safety deposit box must be the real thing. Which would mean the doghouse Aurora was a plant. Perhaps he had put it there to buy himself some time should someone have come after him, which is exactly what happened. Unless, she shifted her weight, he never got to change them over. What if he was interrupted that night he was killed? She was taking too long with this, she realized. Fuck it, she thought.

"Yeah, you know what? To hell with it." She said aloud sliding the housing back in place. She stuffed both Aurora's in her bag. What does she care which one is which?

Annie walked out of the bank vault and into the waiting area and thanked the bank manager as she and Sally left together.

Outside, Annie and Sally split up. Sally went to her car to wait and Annie spied Karen's car and got in.

"How'd it go?" Karen asked.

"Here," Annie pulled one of the Aurora's out of her bag and handed it over.

Karen immediately pushed the clips together and pulled the housing apart, she looked around the piece and found what she was looking for. "Okay," she said with finality and handed Annie the file folder that held the affidavit. "Thank you -" Karen started to say but Annie opened the car door and got out.

Annie walked across the parking lot and got into Sally's car, "Let's just go."

~~~

Michael and Lorna watched Karen's car pull out and the watched Annie get into Sally's car and they pulled out of the parking lot as well.

"Hey!" Michael said aloud.

"They forgot to get me." Lorna added, "That's not part of the plan."

"Don't worry about it, I'll take you back," Michael said. "Maybe something went wrong." Michael started the van and took off.

"If it was me, and I was you," Lorna started her rambling again, "I'd get ahead of this thing. You gotta get your people, or someone, over there to Prague and intercept this thing. But the first thing you should do is call off Eunice and Wallace, Sally's parents, shut them down. Move them on down the line or something. The two of them are over there with a lifetime worth of contacts. Shit, they've probably already set up an entire outpost or something. All those geriatrics coming out of the woodwork for one last hurrah! You know who you should send? You should send Sally. She probably knows

more than she's saying anyway, or! Or better yet! Send
her grandmother. That old birds sitting in that retirement
village plotting to overthrow the security guards anyway"
Lorna continued rambling on about Sally's grandmother
all the way back to Annie's house. But Michael remained
stuck on something she had said. She was right, of
course, he could not go to Prague, but Sally could.
Michael made a slow turn around the block of Saint
Charles Place before parking the van on the other side of
the main street.

Michael and Lorna found Annie and Sally sitting in
Annie's kitchen table staring at Annie's purse. Lorna
walked through the living room first looking at Sally,
then at Annie, then the purse and back at Michael, who
now stood next to her surveying the scene as well.
"I'll bet you 30 million dollars I can guess what's in
that bag," She said proudly.
Sally and Annie looked up at her. Michael rushed
over and opened the bag to see another Aurora sitting in
it.
"Don't worry kittens, Lorna's got it all figured out,"
Lorna said, referring to herself in third person.
Michael pulled out the Aurora urgently and slid the
casing off. He turned it around in his hands before placing
back into the casing and putting it back into the purse. "I
gotta go," He said.
"Where ya' goin'?" Lorna asked.
"I gotta catch up to her."
Lorna caught him by the arm. "It's all good, Mikey.
Lorna's gotcha covered," Lorna said in a falsetto voice.
Michael maneuvered his arm away from her, "I'm
sorry, why don't you fill them in and I'll catch back up
with you later."
Lorna took a step back and smiled at him confidently,

"Alrighty then, see you later. I'll fill *everyone* in then."

Michael's eyes narrowed as she continued. "Oh yeah, I'm gonna fill *evvveryone innnn*!" Lorna finished with a flourish. "You're thinking," she pointed at Michael, "who's gonna listen to ol' crack pot Lorna with her crazy theories? You know who listens to me? Van Elder." Lorna spread her hands out for emphasis, "Sound familiar?"

Michael scowled and turned to Sally for confirmation. Sally shrugged.

"Don't look to her," Lorna bellowed. "You two think you're the only ones with secrets? You'd better think again." Lorna sat down and patted Annie's hand, "Annie, do you think it would be okay if I had some tea. I think maybe something decaf."

Everything stopped as Annie got up and quietly turned on the electric kettle and sat back down with a tea bag and empty cup.

"I have to pee." Michael pointed at down the hall, "Do you mind?"

"On the right," Sally said.

When the door shut Lorna mouthed the words, *Van Elder*, and put her hands out indicating she had no idea what she had said.

Annie leaned forward and mouthed, *Who's Van Elder?*

Lorna shrugged again.

Sally pointed to herself and mouthed, *I know*. And pointed at Lorna and mouthed, *How did you know?*

Lorna laid her hand out flat, like a book and mouthed, *Read it, in the newspaper*.

They all nodded together. Lorna pointed toward the direction of the bathroom, arched her eyebrows knowingly and mouthed, *He's up to something*.

CHAPTER 8

Sally, Annie, and Michael sat around the kitchen table captivated by Lorna's labyrinthian reasoning. In an unending rapid succession, images and memories raced through her mind and her battle to stay on topic added to their suspense. Every once in a while she would veer off and begin rambling about a technology based economy or how, when she first heard of the band Hall and Oates, she thought they were called Haulin' Oats. Then someone would have to speak up and lure her back to the point. However, her mental struggle was not without merit.

"You were talking about why you think it's important we go after the Nurse," Michael said flatly. He wanted Lorna to continue, as she was his best ally in getting the Aurora back for his bosses.

"There are, like, a thousand reasons," Lorna nodded her head in agreement with herself.

"You were at the planning part," Annie wanted to get this over with.

"So look, Annie, they're coming for you. Right?" Lorna didn't wait for an answer. "You leave out this

Aurora and the paperwork that the Nurse left you. Just leave it out on your kitchen table, and leave the paperwork next to it. If nothing else it will be a trail for them to follow and buy us some time maybe. Let's get packed."

"What?" Sally asked.

"Where are we going?" Annie asked.

"To Prague. We have to save Sally's parents," Lorna answered.

"No, Lorna, it's over. We've done our part. We're sticking with the plan," Sally said with finality.

"I just feel like maybe we should set some rat traps as well," Lorna said, thinking aloud.

Sally's mouth fell open in frustrated disgust.

"Michael, you should do that and, I don't know, plant some confusing evidence as well. Make it look like we were abducted." Lorna continued. "Don't pack heavy, just bring a backpack. You know, like that guy, Stan or Steve what's-his-name with the guidebooks - that one that's always telling people only to pack a toothbrush and under wear and buy everything else. He's always going on about experiencing another culture is what travel is all about. Who does he think he is to define travel for everyone else? Maybe I like my brand of toothpaste."

Sally's rubbed her face, "Oh my God, Sweetheart, what are you talking about?"

Lorna looked confused for a moment and turned to Michael, "Did I not just go over this?"

Michael shook his head, "No. You and I were talking about it in the van."

"Oh, I'm sorry. I think the Nurse is running your parents. They don't know it of course, and they've most likely set up a second sale to another outfit. You know a zebra don't change his stripes. So the Nurse uses Annie to get the device and she's not stupid, she knows she's being watched. She plays along with Michael's yarn while it benefits her. And that get's her a free trip to Prague, playing along with this whole gamut. But instead of selling the Aurora to Sally's parents she has her own buyers or she sells to the people Sally's parents have set up to buy the Aurora, thinking the whole time they are acting as brokers. Because why wouldn't they? They're opportunists, right? This is a perfect opportunity; they don't have to get their hands dirty at all. They probably just made a few calls. They make the sale and disappear into the ether again."

Sally spoke up, "But Lorna, I don't care. Maybe you're right, but that's their business. They've been playing this game a long time. Don't underestimate those old people, they've seen things, they've had experiences. Why should I care if they get themselves mixed up in this?"

Lorna turned to Michael, "Look, I'll bet that your boss, Pirate-"

"Pickles," Michael corrected her.

"Didn't you say earlier that Pickles only brought Sally's parents in to help you cover the cost of your missions while you get on your feet? But then they find out more about what's going on here and they think they can make some dosh and dash."

Sally interrupted again, "Yeah, and the whole time they were here setting up their little Auld Alliance tea shop they were feeding me the line they were retired. They've been like this my whole life Lorna. I'm done. I'm not going off to save them, they wouldn't do the same for me, that's obvious."

Michael looked at the digital wall clock that read: 10:30 A.M. This whole scenario was going to go one of two ways, he thought. Either Lorna was going to convince these other two she's right and he had a chance at the Aurora or Sally would win out and everything would be lost. He looked over at Annie. She no longer cared and who can blame her. He looked again at Sally and Lorna, two women who he believed had absolutely no use for him at this point, so he changed his tactics. "I don't know about the Prague thing. But I think it might be a good idea for Annie to hand over that paperwork as soon as they come knocking on her door."

"Yes, Sherlock, we all know that," Lorna snapped.

Michael ignored Lorna and turned to Annie, "Annie, how do you feel about all of this?"

The question struck Annie. It was one thing for a good friend to ask such a personal question but it was another for this manipulative yahoo to pry into her emotions. "I don't know. What's done is done I guess," She said noncommittally.

"Oh and that's another thing," Lorna boomed. "Did no one here think it was the least bit interesting that the Nurse had worked for the CIA and then that *assassin* was an ex-CIA operative? Didn't you think to pursue who exactly hired him? And who do you think poisoned me?"

"Please Lorna," Sally pleaded.

"I'll tell you who did it, who had knowledge of poisons and how to administer them." Lorna continued. "And if you think I'm gonna let that go you sure as shit don't know me."

Sally's face flushed a deep red as she struggled with her rage. She addressed Michael. "How long before these drugs she's on wear off?"

"Another 36 hours maybe," Michael answered promptly.

Sally stood up, "I'm going to bed. I'm done."

Annie scooted her chair back and was poised to rise when Lorna sat back down and spoke to Michael, "Fine. Michael, we need a plan here. I know you can't leave the country so I'm going to need you to be my point man. We're going to need some type of satellite phones or some kind of secure line to communicate on."

Annie leaned forward, "Lorna."

Lorna had forgotten Annie was there for a moment and she turned to her.

Annie carefully spread her hand out flat on the table. "Think about this for a minute. Okay? Think about why you are doing this."

"Because the bitch tried to kill me. Twice, I think."

"Okay, but she's gone now."

"Yeah, and she's probably going to kill Sally's parents or have them killed."

"So what are you going to do when you find her?" Annie asked reasonably.

Lorna thought about this for a moment and turned to Michael, "Is there any precedent for turning her over to foreign intelligence? Like maybe in a former Soviet block country?"

"No Well, -" Michael stopped and his eyes widened in a realization. "Unless she's caught selling state secrets."

"You mean if she's caught trying to sell a secret satellite device?" Lorna grinned.

Annie interjected, "That's not what I mean. Lorna, you are in no physical shape to do this. This isn't your job, it's Michael's."

"You're right. And I didn't start this so it's not even mine to finish. But I was drug into this thing, so now I'm in it. And I'm going to finish it. Her first mistake was leaving me alive," Lorna stood up. "You don't have to come with me Annie, I'd understand if you didn't."

Annie looked accusingly at Michael, "I'll bet you love this don't you. You've got someone to do your heavy lifting. And look at her! Shame on you."

Michael stood up and gently grabbed Lorna's frail

arm, "She's right. We'll figure something else out."

Lorna looked down at his hand on her forearm, "Did I say you could touch the Lorna?"

Michael recoiled.

"I'm going to find my passport and a backpack. We need to get this show on the road. Do or don't Annie, it's your call. Michael, we need those phones."

Lorna went into her office and grabbed her old backpack. Patience and Fortitude were sitting on the catwalk that lined the wall. She paused, "Mrs. Strangler is going to be feeding you two for a couple of days. Be good boys for her." When she got to the bedroom she found a plaintive Sally sitting on the edge of the bed.

"Please don't go Lorna. This was never our fight to begin with, we have absolutely nothing to gain by chasing this."

"I'm not chasing the Aurora, Sally. I don't give a shit about that. But I'm not spending the rest of my life looking over my shoulder either. Please try to see it from my point of view as well, why does Tim get closure and I don't?"

"Please, I'm begging you, don't ask me to do this again."

It occurred to Lorna that Sally misunderstood Lorna's intent. Lorna sat down gently on the bed next to Sally and placed her arm around Sally's back. "I'm not asking you to *do anything*. We're not - I'm going to do the right thing and turn her over to the proper authorities. The same one's she's been duping and stealing secrets from for years. I can't think of a better and more patriotic gesture than that. Can you?"

Sally sighed, "That's like the third reason you've given me. Which one is it? Revenge, patriotic duty, or saving my parents?"

"With any luck all three and maybe a few I haven't

thought of. But truth be told, it's for me. If I do nothing then I've been just a pawn, beaten up and shifted around the board. That's not me. It's my duty to do what I can to protect myself, I can't just leave it to some random government sanctioned authorities. They don't give a shit about me. And ya' know, if they had any power in any of this they would have acted a long time ago. Instead of letting the killer go and government contractors commit treason. Ya' know?"

Sally shook her head. It was true that there was no way Lorna was going to let this go and turn it over to someone else. And Lorna would not be the only one constantly looking over her shoulder. Sally sighed and looked at her hands when she spoke. "I think this is a huge mistake. There's no plan, no contingency plan, we have no concrete intelligence on the Nurse's whereabouts or intent. I mean really, Lorna, this is all conjecture from your addled brain. And can we talk about what happened with your family?"

"Not yet. They've committed familial treason. Let them stew in it for a while. We can have their trial later, Counselor." Lorna added hopefully, "When we get back?"

Sally rubbed her hands through her hair, "I don't have a backpack."

"You can use your emergency go pack from the front closet."

"I have one caveat," Sally said.

"Okay. What is it?"

"We take one swipe at this. We give ourselves only one chance here. No chasing anyone or anything else, no side moves. If we get there and find out she's already made the deal or she's gone off to another town, whatever, that's it. We go home."

"What about your parents?"

Sally shook her head, "They're on their own. I can't help them. I'm not risking my freedom or my life for them."

"Okay. I understand. Thank you."

~~~

Downstairs Lorna and Sally found Annie and Michael passed out in the seats they had left them in. Before Lorna had a chance to wake them, Sally carefully tugged at her arm, pulling her away from the kitchen and gave a head nod toward Lorna's back office.

Sally closed the office door behind them and spoke softly, "Listen, we need a contingency plan. I'm going to write a letter to Roberta explaining everything so far. By the time she gets it, we'll be gone and if anything goes wrong, at least someone will know what happened."

"I think we should write a note to Mrs. Strangler too, for the boys. But what do you think about Annie?"

Sally shook her head and clucked her tongue, "I don't know where she is, mentally, right now. It's not that I don't think we can rely on her, but I think she needs to work in her own best interest right now. Ya' know?"

"Yeah. Okay. What about Michael?"

"We are his only hope of getting that stupid machine back, I'm not worried about him." Sally said.

"But, that's not our objective."

Sally rolled her eyes. "He doesn't need to know that."

"Oh, sassy, I like that. That's good."

"Okay?" Sally nodded.

"Yup."

Sally opened the door to the hall and they walked into the kitchen where Michael's head had fallen back and his open mouth gave out a choking sound while he breathed.

Lorna gave two short 'sst, sst', half whistle and half

shushing bursts of air. A sound through her teeth she generally reserves for when their cats are being bad. Michael and Annie woke up and looked around.

"What happened?" Michael asked.

"I've changed my mind," Sally announced. "I don't want Lorna going alone and I can't change her mind."

Annie flopped her head down between her legs and let out a long, "shiiiiiiiit." But then lifted her head back up. "Okay."

Lorna shook her head at her, "Annie, you don't have to go. Don't feel like you have too."

"Of course I have to! It was my husband that got us into this shit."

Lorna cocked a hand on her hip and announced in her best authoritative voice. "So, kids our theme for today is: we are not responsible for our relatives actions."

"No shit. It's just, this is just a never-ending stream of, shit. Shit." Annie pounded her first.

"Well put," Lorna said and sat down. We need to at least put together a loose framework here. The first step is getting there."

"Right." Sally sat down and continued. "But then we need to at least find our starting point, who, what, how, or where. We need a point A to go from."

Annie stood up, "I'll be back in a little while. I need to get a backpack-the dogs-I've got stuff. I'll be back in a little bit." Annie sat back down with a pad of paper and a pen. "I need to make a list. It'll be easier."

Michael addressed Lorna, "Just call Air-Berlin or Lufthansa, I think they have direct flights from SFO. Then take the train into Prague. It'll be faster than all those connecting flights." Michael snapped his fingers and stood up. "As a matter of fact I *do* know a couple of people I could call. Wait, don't do anything yet, let me make a call from the van."

Michael started for the front door with Sally calling after him, "Back door. Back door!" Michael changed directions and ran out the kitchen door.

Annie leaned forward and said in a low voice, "Look, Michael doesn't need to know this, but I've got some cash we can use. Tim left it for me."

~~~

That night, Annie, Sally, and Lorna walked down the flight gangway that led to the airplane. Michael had worked furiously to get as much information and documentation he could for them before they left including a diplomatic status for Lorna. And he had slipped Sally a second, empty, dip. pouch. Just in case.

Annie inhaled the last breath of fresh air before entering the plane and clutched at the plastic shopping bag that held a diplomatic pouch Michael had given them. It had been decided, considering Lorna's mental state, that Annie should do the actual carrying of the pouch. The pouch itself was sealed tight with a tamper proof plastic strip. Somehow Michael, or more likely someone Michael worked with, had assigned Lorna as a diplomatic carrier for this pouch. It was to be delivered to the American Embassy in Prague tomorrow afternoon or would that be the day after tomorrow? Annie thought about this for a minute and then let it go. They should just go directly to the embassy when they get to Prague and get rid of this pouch, first and foremost. As they got settled into their center section seats Annie and Lorna sitting in the aisle seats, Annie leaned over to Sally. "How'd we get first class?"

"I don't know, Michael made the arrangements, I'm sure the Dip Bag had a lot to do with it." Sally answered.

"The what?" But it dawned on Annie and she shook her plastic bag that contained the diplomatic pouch. "Oh, got it. The pouch."

A flight attendant spoke to Lorna. "Es ist gut Sie wieder zu sehen, Ms. Tollison."

"Danke." Lorna smiled at the pretty and fit blonde. "Es wird gut, Deutschland wieder zu sehen sein."

Annie's head snapped back and forth between the women. She had no idea Lorna spoke German.

"Annie, would you like a drink?" Lorna asked.

"Scotch," Annie croaked out. How did she not know Lorna spoke another language?

"Rot, Weiss, und eine schottische mit Soda. Bitte."

As the attendant walked to the galley, Annie urgently leaned over to Lorna again. "There is no way. None. Not a single chance you are *even* slightly entertaining the idea of drinking alcohol right now."

Sally seconded Annie's motion with a wide-eyed glare and pursed lips.

"Party poopers," Lorna leaned back in her seat.

Sally quietly asked Annie, "Ask her how she knows this particular flight attendant."

Annie leaned over to Lorna. "Sally wants to know how you know this *particular* flight attendant."

Lorna shrugged, "I guess she recognizes the name, maybe she thinks I'm Tessa."

Annie leaned back over to Sally. But Lorna leaned over as well and stage whispered. "It's happened before."

Annie and Sally leaned in together, "Listen-" Sally started.

"I know," Annie interrupted, finishing Sally's thought. "Do you want the first half or second shift?"

"You take the first one, suddenly I'm not very tired," Sally said contentiously.

~~~

The gleaming steel and glass architecture of the

Bahnhof Zoo (a Berlin central train staion) radiates efficiency. Sally felt her stomach flip and twitch with anxiety as she watched the busy people going home from work. The territory being relatively familiar to her, Lorna had taken charge once they arrived and did the money exchange before they departed on the city train to take them to the Berlin Hauptbahnhof. Both Sally and Annie were duly impressed with Lorna's efficient manor in dealing with the airport shuttle to the city train and now she was taking charge arranging their passage to Prague. Sally glanced at her watch. Michael had said Lorna probably had another 18 hours before she crashed. Lorna had not slept the entire flight. Which now meant Lorna had maybe another 4 hours left before her tank was empty. Sally looked back over at Annie, who looked like she could use a few more hours of sleep as well.

"I'm getting us a sleeping compartment," Lorna said. "It'll still take another five hours to get to Prague. So, we have about an hour and a half before we need to be on the platform." Lorna turned back to the ticket counter and spoke with the cashier.

Annie watched as a hurried woman ran up to the counter and tried to interrupt Lorna's conversation with the cashier in that clipped and, to Annie's ears, harsh sounding tongue. Lorna turned to the hurried woman and spoke severely and was quick to retake her conversation with the cashier.

"Nein," Lorna barked at the cashier who, it seemed, tried to help the hurried woman. Then Lorna continued with her transaction with the now visibly upset cashier.

Annie turned her back on the them and quietly spoke to Sally, who was also watching the scene. "Great, she can piss people off in two languages."

Sally snickered, "You should hear her Spanish. All she knows are the curse words."

"I had no idea, I mean, she's *very* fluent," Annie sounded surprised.

"Well, she did an exchange thing in college. It's not going to be this easy in Prague," Sally confided.

"I don't suppose you know any Slavic languages by chance?" Annie asked her.

"I kinda know some, hello and thank you at least," Sally reassured her.

"Okay," Lorna arrived back to their huddle. "Here are your tickets, put them in your backpacks."

"What now?" Annie looked around.

"Well, the first thing I want to do is burn these clothes," Lorna confided. "This place has a lot of shops in it. I'm going to grab a change of clothes we need to erase some of our obvious Americanisms and get some toiletries."

"Hang on," Sally stopped them. "We're not splitting up and doing some casual shopping in here."

"But, a change of clothes would be nice," Annie said. "All I brought is a pair of underwear and a tooth brush."

Lorna raised her eyebrow at her.

"You said to pack light."

"Okay, how about this, we go get some clothes and toiletries, then we go a grab some food for the trip, and then whatever. I think we might want to find a map of Prague and essential stuff like that."

The three women walked away from the ticket booth and made their way to a casual clothing shop and all picked up a change of clothing and sweaters then made their way to another shop for their toiletries. Once they finally agreed on a soap and shampoo they could all use they found a store that provided them with essentials. There they picked up a couple of maps, a Prague travel guide, flashlights, and batteries. Lorna also bought a Swiss army knife and small first aid kit.

By the time they reached the train platform they were loaded down with shopping bags. "Maybe we went a little overboard with the food," Annie suggested.

"We're only going to have our backpacks once we get to Prague." Lorna assured her, "We'll use most of this on the train anyway."

"I need to brush my teeth in the worst way," Sally complained.

"Shouldn't we call-" Annie started.

"Not yet," Sally said quickly cutting her off. "Not till we're on the train."

At last, they were on the train and shut themselves into the small but efficient looking compartment.

Lorna sat down and smiled at Annie. "Pretty cool, huh?"

"I feel like I'm in a futuristic world," Annie said. "I mean honestly, why can't we have this in America. Or at the very least California."

"Wasn't there some talk of one?" Sally asked.

"Yeah, Governor Schwarzenegger was trying to gin up support for one, but in this financial crisis? I can't see that happening," Sally said and at the same time pulled out the satellite phone Michael had given her. She held it up and gave a 'what do I do?' shrug.

"Wait a bit, I think," Lorna answered. "I think they come around to the rooms and check our tickets first. We'll tip the guy and give him our passports. That way we won't be bothered when we cross over the border. But we should get those maps out and eat something. I think I'm going to have to have a pill soon anyway and I have to eat with those things."

"What are they?" Annie asked.

"That's a good, good question. Anyone have a guess?" Lorna pulled out her pill bottle.

"Oh no," Sally's shoulders drooped.

"It's what that doctor left me. He said I was going to need them."

"Are you in pain?"

"No, but I could eat and I'm starting to feel tired at least."

"Lorna," Sally said. "I think you should have a nap, then you can eat again, and take one of those pills. Because if their going to make you, uh-" Sally wanted to say crazy but thought better of it, "make you feel like you did before then you'll be operating on days without any sleep at all."

"She's right," Annie quickly added.

"And if they knock you out, then at least we can get you into a cab and safely to a hotel."

They spent the next half hour distributing the goods from the bags while the train sat idling. Annie was able to catch only a few words between Lorna and the conductor when he came by to check their tickets and passports. And when they began moving in a slow crawl out of the station they were looking over the maps and eating.

"So, Prague's a small town divided by a river, here," Sally pointed out. "Lots of bridges."

"Holy Crap," Annie said with her mouth full. "This is the best train station food I've ever had."

"I know, it's pretty good," Lorna smiled and took another bite of her pretzel bread sandwich. She wrapped up the rest of it and started rooting through her backpack. "Anyone need to use the bathroom before I go in there?"

"I do," Annie said.

"Me too," Sally said.

Annie got up and went into the small bathroom. "It's like a boat bathroom!" She called out.

"Listen, when I start the shower I think you should make the call," Lorna whispered to Sally.

Sally nodded and took another bite of food.

Annie came back out of the bathroom and Sally went in behind her. "That's going to be an acrobatic stunt for you to shower in there," Annie said and sat back down. "Sally will have to change the dressing."

Lorna nodded but then pointed to herself, then to the bathroom. She held out her thumb and pinky finger up to the side of her face and made like she was talking on the phone. Then she pointed to Annie and the seat that Sally had been sitting in.

Annie nodded understanding of Lorna's silent gestures, when Lorna goes into the shower then she and Sally would finally call Michael. Annie stared at Lorna for another moment. "You look like maybe you're not in tip top form right now. How are you feeling?"

"I'm feeling really tired again," Lorna acknowledged. "I think I'm going to get myself organized here, grab that shower, and maybe crash for a while."

"Okay," Annie agreed, slightly relieved that Lorna's crash was coming now that they'd settled into the train trip.

Sally came out of the shower and toilet room, pulled out the phone again and began pushing buttons as soon as Lorna got into the shower. Annie found a pen and paper in her backpack and waited.

"Michael?" Sally said trying hard not to scream, "Yeah?" She turned to Annie. "Where's that earpiece thing?

Hang on!" She said into the phone as Annie dug out the earpiece and handed it to Sally. Sally connected the earpiece, "Can you hear me?"

"Yes," she said in a normal voice.

Annie leaned over to her and put her head next to Sally's earpiece.

"I've got good news and bad. The bad is the CIA is

now crowding in on this. Fuckin' Lorna was right, it looks like your parents put out feelers to find other buyers. Also, we have an errand for you while you're there."

"Why?" This is exactly what Sally had feared, a side venture that would derail them from their task.

"No, it's no biggy. Someone's going to drop off a package to you at the safe house then when you deliver the Dip bag they'll give you an empty one. Put the package from the safe house in the empty pouch and bring it back with you."

"Michael!" Sally let her disappointment show.

"Look, I had to do some serious wheeling and dealing on this. Word on the Aurora has spread overnight and the players are coming out of the woodwork over here. The safe house is at nine dash one hundred Ramova."

Sally watched Annie write down the address. "Okay. Got it. So what about the Nurse, any word?"

"She's operating under the name Barbara Rutledge. She took a flight to Moscow and boarded a train for Prague but the trail goes cold from there. And, I don't mean to be stupid about it, but, I don't think you're going to have a hard time finding an African-American woman in that part of the world."

"She's probably holed up somewhere and having people work for her. We'll have to draw her out," Sally agreed.

Annie had been looking at a map and pointed to a spot on it.

"Hang on," Sally said to Michael.

Annie quickly pointed out that the safe house on Ramova was in the Old City but the embassy was across the river from there, "That's a long way."

"Michael, the safe house is all the way across the river from the embassy."

"Okay."

"I'm saying I think," Sally watched Annie silently mouth, 'do-it-last'. "I think we should do the Dip Bags last."

"No. Look, you have to do it first. It's how I got you into the safe house, they were pretty insistent on that point. Okay, there are a couple of other things. There's a violinmaker there in the city. I don't have a name but he has a small shop. He's a friendly, you know?"

"Yeah, I got it," Sally understood his use of the words, "a friendly" to mean he works with the American intelligence services.

"Worst case scenario, find his shop. Also, what do you know about The Cheese Maker?"

Sally's blood went cold, the name The Cheese Maker stunned her for a moment. Annie pulled her head away from listening and furrowed her brow at Sally.

"Nothing," Sally spit out.

"They call him The Cheese Maker 'cause he makes money for Russian Mafia's. We're talking about a lot of money changing hands in all this so that's going to draw him in like a fly to shit. And he's your worst case scenario."

Sally was not feeling good about this phone call, "Michael, do you have any good news?"

"Yeah, listen, I've got some back up for you. Two women. They'll be staying in the Old City."

"Yeah, and?"

"They belong to our division, so they'll find you."

"What? What kind of help is that?"

"When you need them, they'll be there." Michael reassured her.

Annie leaned away again and shook her head at Sally in an 'I can't believe this' way.

Sally rolled her eyes. "Anything else?"

"Just keep this phone on so we can keep in contact.

I'm going to keep trying to track the Nurse."

"Bye."

"Good Luck."

A moment later, a very soggy Lorna threw open the bathroom door. "Nothin's easy," She said and collapsed on her bunk.

CHAPTER 9

"I've seen only two violin shops listed in here," Annie said softly, showing Sally the guidebook.

Sally looked at the guidebook and back at the town map. "Heaven forbid they be in the same part of town," she grumbled.

Lorna let out a soft whimper as she rolled onto her back. The train made a smooth rocking movement and an almost rhythmic sloshing sound that was comforting.

"If things go bad here," Anne continued quietly, "shouldn't we find a safe place for us to all meet up or something?"

"Yeah, I was thinking about that. I'm just torn between finding a spot where lots of people would be or somewhere secluded."

"A big hotel, I thought."

"There's one here," Sally pointed out a spot on the map for Annie to study.

Annie nodded.

"Then if we need a secluded one, there's this synagogue near it, just here."

"That's good. It's weird how you can go over the maps but then you still have to kinda get your bearings straight once you're in the city."

"Well, it looks to me like while you're in Prague, if you always know where the river is, you're in good shape."

Annie yawned and put the guidebook down. "Okay well, I'm going to wash up and have a nap."

"Right," Sally said absently and picked up her backpack.

While Annie showered, Sally reorganized both her own and Lorna's backpacks. And once Annie crawled into the bunk above Lorna, Sally took her turn in the shower. Afterward she settled into her bunk across from Lorna, ate the rest of her sandwich and watched Lorna sleep fitfully. What she really wanted to do is curl up next to Lorna, but instead she thought about what Michael had said about the Cheese Maker. Even just a whisper of this Cheese Maker being involved raised the hairs on the back of Sally's neck. Everyone who was in the wrong kind of business knew horror stories of him.

She had heard rumors and innuendoes about this infamous man from her time in Bosnia. The more dramatic stories said he was a shadow of a man but other's say it was a gang of thugs. Whether or not he was a myth or a man was almost irrelevant in the light of the atrocities for which he was accredited.

Her thoughts floated back to that time in Bosnia. The atrocities she had seen there, supposedly as a peacekeeper, were simply unspeakable. Life, for all its precious quality had been diminished into a trembling lump of dread for those people. Children set on fire. Women raped and beaten until their bodies were mangled and disfigured. The loss of human life, the men decapitated, the memories came flooding back to her.

And the rest of the world did nothing to stop the horror for those people. She wanted nothing to do with anything involving governments, wars, intelligence services, or so called peacekeeping missions ever again. But here she is, sitting on a train, hurdling irrevocably towards the same part of the world and brought by the same forces that brought her here the first time. Only this time they're calling it a cyber war. New technology, how do you arm yourself in a cyber world? Sally sighed. Nuclear energy was a new technology once too she thought sardonically. She rolled Lorna's pill bottle in her hand. The sticker on the bottle had a hand scrawl across it: 2 x 12hr.

"Save some for me," Lorna said from her bunk.

Sally looked up at her partner. "Here," she opened the bottle and slid a couple of pills out.

Lorna popped one into her mouth and washed them down with what was left in her soda bottle. "I need to brush my teeth and get my shoes on," Lorna said and tried to lift herself from the bunk, "oh, shit."

"What's wrong?"

"I'm just, everything's kind of heavy."

Sally scooted into the bunk next to Lorna, "Good, I need a cuddle."

"Just stop right there," Annie said from the top bunk, "we all know what that leads to."

Lorna laughed, "Oh come on Annie, I'd cuddle you."

"No. You. Wouldn't." Annie said. Her voice partly muffled by the pillow.

The final half hour on the train was spent preparing for their campaign. In the only way three women nearing middle age, in a foreign country, with no discernable tools or weapons at their ready, and absolutely no tactical or reconnaissance training can prepare; they finished eating and having their coffee. And by the time the train was slowing down it was clear that the mystery pills Lorna had swallowed were taking effect.

"I'm not saying the intelligence services drum up business to justify their existence but I had this theory, right?" Once again her train of thought had derailed and her voice was louder than a conversational tone. "So I was doing research and came across Van Elders name on some online newsletter thing-"

Sally made a counterclockwise circular gesture with her thumb and index finger, as if she were turning down a volume knob.

"Sorry," She said with less volume. "But Michael fell for it."

When no one responded it dawned on Lorna that Sally and Annie were waiting for her to get back on point. "I'm just saying I don't think Michael's that clever. Basically, he is having us act as couriers for the embassy."

"Kinda, yeah," Sally agreed.

"And who works for our embassies in foreign countries?"

Annie furrowed her brow, "State Department."

Lorna lifted her head up and spanned her arms out. "And who works secretly for the state department in foreign countries?"

Annie rubbed her forehead, "the CIA?"

"So he has us doing a CIA courier job to the state department. This, Lorna does not like." Lorna said cupping her hands in her lap again.

Oh, here we go, Annie thought, its Third Person Lorna again. But on second thought, maybe that's not a bad thing in this case. Annie cut her eyes to Sally.

"So what do you think that means?" Sally asked The Lorna.

"Michael said that the CIA was horning in here.

Either they are going to try to double cross us, something to do with the courier bags. You know, play a shell game with these things. Or they're setting us up. I do think it's strange he didn't mention anything about the NSA. Which means, despite whatever this *team* national defense game they're playing, the NSA is running their own mission here. If we run these Dip bags then we're really opening ourselves up here. What's the consequence if we don't deliver them as instructed?"

Sally shrugged. "He didn't say."

"I know we said we wouldn't split up, but that's exactly what I think we should do. Look, I'm the weakest link here, and the courier bags are under my name, let me go to the safe house and you two take off for-," Lorna paused waiting to hear from one of them. "What's after the Dip bags?"

"We should find my parents," Sally offered.

"Good, where would Wallace and Eunice go?"

"I think I should start with that violin maker, he's supposed to be worst case scenario but if he's been a player in the past he might be a good starting point at least."

"Fine. You head there and I'll go to the safe house. We'll set a time and meet at a hotel. Which hotel? Where's that travel guide?" Lorna asked hastily.

Sally pulled out the travel guide from her backpack and Lorna snatched it from her hands.

"Let's see, I want a good five star," Lorna caught Annie and Sally stealing a weary glance. "Where do you think two rich old spies from the cold war era are going to stay? The Come On Inn or The Posh Suites?" She flipped the pages until she found what she was looking for. "Here, this one. Annie, get us checked into The Continental."

"Hold on. Lorna, I want Annie to go with you. Please.

You two handle the Dip bags, hopefully there won't be too many violinmakers in town. Let's say we meet back at the hotel in three hours? We'll call Michael and see what else he's found out and see where to go from there."

"Good, then it's a plan," Lorna agreed.

~~~

Any train or bus depot looks eerie and desolate at five o'clock in the morning. But to Annie and Lorna's western eyes, the Prague Nádraží Holešovice (Holesovice train station) was a uniquely sketchy looking affair. Dark shadows loomed across the aged tiled walls. Stark lighting shone on filthy alcoves filled with sleeping residents. Men in black leather jackets stood outside on the curb next to unmarked cars hoping to be mistaken for proper taxi services. Sally put Annie and Lorna in what looked to be a legitimate A-1 taxi service and made sure he knew the address and that he'd accept Euro's as payment.

Sally stayed behind and changed some of her Euros into Koruna's at a machine and then headed over to the tourist information booth. The information booth was closed but Sally perused the pamphlets and flyers on a carousel outside the door. Sally grabbed anything that had music or music type events on them and used the carousel to conceal her appraisal of the men on the curb next to their cars. With an affected confidence to her gate, she headed back out to where the taxis were stationed.

"Dobry den." Sally greeted a young swarthy looking fellow leaning on his taxi.

He flipped his head up in acknowledgment.

Sally smiled and said hopefully, "Anglicky?"

"Sure," he said. "You need ride?"

"I'm gonna need a long ride, I have several stops to make. I'm looking for a violin maker and I understand you have several in town."

"Ano," he said in agreement, "but it's not open now, too early."

"Yes, that's not the point though, I just need to know where they are. I need to see them."

The young man pulled out a cigarette and lit it absent-mindedly and thought for a minute. He blew out a puff of smoke. "Ano. I know a couple of places." He looked at his watch and pulled out a cell phone. "Hold here." He said and went into his car. Sally watched him through the windshield as he pulled out a piece of paper and a pen from his glove compartment and spoke on the phone. A moment later he came back to the sidewalk next to Sally.

"Okay," he said. "I've got the list, there are six places. We like violin here. This is not going to be a cheap ride." He eyed Sally suspiciously.

"I understand. How much?"

"50 Euro. Including tip."

Sally almost jumped into his car but thought he might enjoy haggling. "You mean 50 Euro plus the tip?"

"Yes, I say that. They are very far apart. Two trips across bridges."

"50 Euro total." Sally said and cut her hand across the air in front of her.

"Good." He nodded and scrambled back into the driver's seat.

"Good." She said and opened the back door to his subcompact car.

~~~

Annie couldn't help but feel a little awestruck by the architectural grandeur of the city. In the distance she could make out the iconic Prague Castle lit up with stage lighting. It was stunning and felt magical in the dark morning hours as they traveled across the cobblestones.

The pleasing symmetry of the high-topped windows across the width of a street imposed order among the creamy baroque facades that syncopated with gothic, neo-classical, and renaissance edifices.

Lorna broke the silence, "I can't wait to meet our tour guide in the morning."

Annie looked at her questioningly before realizing Lorna was not saying this for her benefit. Annie nodded, her eyes floating to the front seat before she joined the charade, "By the time we unpack and have breakfast it'll be time to meet up with her."

They paid the taxi and as they got out they took a moment and looked around, the cool, moist fresh air felt good on their faces. Annie looked up at the neo-classical building in front of them. "This is it," she said and stretched a hand out for the door handle.

"I'm guessing there won't be an elevator here," Lorna said and followed Annie inside.

They took the four flights of dilapidated stairs up to the fifth floor and paused in the stairway. The paint was peeling in some places but in other's the wall had been completely ripped up to show the stones beneath. Centuries of remodeling had not diminished the quality of the construction, only the plaster.

"What a shit hole!" Lorna exclaimed upon letting Annie and herself into the safe house apartment and placing the key back on top of the doorframe. Annie instinctively scanned her surroundings. The tall ceiling had beautifully carved wood beams and ornate window moldings. Her eyes adjusted to the darkness and focused on a bare light bulb hanging precariously from the ceiling. She followed the black electrical wire across the ceiling and down the wall on her right to a small black button framed by black painted wood. She pushed hard on the button and the light bulb popped on. Lorna whirled around and lunged to push the button back off. "No, Annie. Flashlights. We don't need the whole neighborhood knowing we're here."

Annie dug around her backpack for the flashlight and then closed the door to the hallway shutting them in darkness. Using their flashlights, they both quickly inspected the small apartment and met back in the large main room.

"Back here," Lorna said and moved back to the bedroom, which was the furthest room from the front door and faced a courtyard in back. Annie followed her back and stood in front of a window that had a cardboard piece covering where the glass had been. "If you look down you'll see a zig-zag fire escape."

Annie stood on her tiptoes and looked over the cardboard. "Wow, modern," Annie said humorlessly.

"So," Lorna said. "This is the safe house Michael set up for us."

"Classy. I think someone mistranslated crack house," Annie replied.

"Once upon a time I imagine it was beautiful in here," Lorna said as they moved back to the front room.

"I have a really, really bad feeling about this," Annie whispered, her flashlight catching a dark corner and showing several used hypodermic needles and other drug paraphernalia.

Lorna's flashlight beam rested on a wall, "Are those bullet holes?"

Annie focused her flashlight beam on the wall, "You think we should just leave? And maybe watch from the street?"

Lorna walked over to the oversized windows and looked down several floors to the street. "Well, if they've been watching then they'd know we're both here. I guess one of us could go out that back window. We'd have to separate, one of us down there in the street and one back there in the courtyard. That's risky, don't you think?" Lorna asked.

"Well, let's go in the back and wait by that fire escape. At least we'll be out of direct sight," Annie added.

"We've got, around, three or four hours still before the sun-" Lorna stopped and clicked off her flashlight at the same time she heard several rapid door knocks.

A man's voice said something in another language. The two women froze for a moment. At the same time that Lorna jerked into motion and reached to open the door she heard sounds that were all too familiar: whiz thud, whiz thud, whiz thud. The door pitched open, splintering the door jam. Lorna was in retreat before the large figure sprawled across the floor. The package he had been carrying slid across the floor to Annie's feet. Annie didn't miss a beat in sweeping the package up and scrambling to the bedroom behind Lorna.

Lorna dove head first through the bedroom window knocking out the cardboard. The rusted metal of the fire escape gave way under her weight and she crashed to the landing below. Annie leapt through behind her without looking but landed on her feet straddling Lorna's body. Lorna popped back up, thus body checking Annie pushing her flailing backward down to the third floor landing. Annie bounced off the railing like a rag doll, down the stairs to the next landing where she glimpsed sight of Lorna sailing mid-air toward her. At the last landing Annie began carefully crawling over the railing but Lorna picked her up by her backpack, pushed her over to the ground then came flying down on top of her. She picked Annie up by her coat lapels screaming, "Run!" They ran through the courtyard to the farthest end where a doorway led into a little stone walled tunnel and out to the street.

Lorna kept Annie in front of her chanting, "go, go, go" as they turned onto the street. Annie realized she was still carrying the package the man had dropped and she threw it down. Lorna reached down and swooped it up again. Five blocks later and out of breathe, Annie ducked into a doorway and doubled over, hands on her knees. Lorna slammed herself against the wall next to her and slid to the ground, tucking the package under her as a seat. For a few moments they didn't speak, their bodies heaving in great gulps of air.

"What the fuck was that?" Lorna gasped out.

Annie slid down next to Lorna. "I think I broke something," Annie sucked in more air.

"What?" Lorna turned to her.

"I don't know, something." Annie said, then looking around she pulled out a map. "What street is this?"

Lorna cautiously moved her head forward to find a street sign, leaned back in again, and tried to sound out the word. "Mysleevesarecoldah. My-slee-kova."

"Where's the river?"

Lorna gave her a quizzical look and shook her head.

"I need to know where the river is, Lorna," Annie admonished her.

Lorna stuck her head out of the doorway again and looked around. "I think it's that way, down the street," Lorna pointed the downhill direction of the sloping street.

"Okay, we go right and then one, two, four, okay whatever, just go straight until we get to here and then right again. That'll put us at the hotel."

"I think we should find a hiding place for this," Lorna patted the brick she was sitting on, "in a church or something."

Annie looked down and spoke sharply, "Lorna, get rid of that, it's drugs."

"Really?" Lorna pulled out the package from

underneath her and turned it over in her hands, feeling its heft, "I want to keep it."

"Why?"

"I don't know, because, who knows, we might need it," Lorna said and stuffed it into her backpack.

Annie looked at Lorna and said with deadpan seriousness, "Right, when in a foreign country, one never knows when a couple of pounds of drugs might help one out."

Lorna was taken aback by her sarcasm, "I said we could hide them in a church!"

"Did you see who was chasing us?" Annie asked, her fear bubbling to frustration.

"No. And I told you this would be a set up, didn't I? The Lorna knows, man."

Annie let it go and stood up, "Come on, we have to get to that hotel."

~~~

The time conscious taxi driver was careful to take the shortest routes between violin stores. As they drove off the modern paved thoroughfare and onto medieval cobbled stone alleys, the affable taxi driver spoke incessantly to Sally. He spoke of his day job working in a hotel, his two children with another on the way, his dream about working on the Internet, and his hatred of Russians. Every once in a while his eyes would veer into the rearview mirror at Sally who was staring out of the car window trying to get a sense of direction. Then he would go into a monologue about the history of the area they were driving through. The first two stops they made were uninspiring. Sally would get out of the car, look both ways down the streets, look around the front window of the music store and walk back to the car.

By their third stop the taxi driver couldn't take the

suspense any longer and he turned around in his seat to face Sally. "You know what I think?"

Sally took a beat and said as kindly as she could, "I'm sure you will enlighten me."

"I think you are spy. You are looking for someone. I think you must be Polish, everyone knows the Poles are just American puppy."

"Congratulations you figured me out. Now just drive, please." Sally was curt in her response but she gave him a quick reassuring smile.

As he turned back around and restarted the car, Sally leaned forward and continued, "It's interesting you should think I'm a spy. It must mean you hear a lot of talk about things like that."

The taxi driver nodded, "It's the Russians. They think they're bragging about things they think they know. But they don't know. The more they talk, the less they know. Me? I know nothing. I don't want to know anything so I won't have to talk to them."

Sally nodded agreement to his reflection in the rear view mirror. Then, off the top of her head she added, "I'm not Polish. The man I am looking for was a friend of my father's. We have some personal things to speak about. But we won't be trading state secrets."

Sally watched his head nod in agreement. "Okay. Then it is personal visit."

Sally nodded, "Yes."

"Your father, Czech?"

"No. At least I don't think so."

"Oh, I see." The taxi driver assured himself he had rooted out the reason for Sally's visit.

They came upon their fourth stop and Sally got out of the car. There was something very familiar about the small storefront. The bay window displayed various violas, and violins. She looked around the immediate area. Gift shops and restaurants lined the town square behind her. There was a large circular fountain in the center of the square. Nothing else seemed familiar to her. Staring at the storefront before her, her brain spun around searching for the memory until it stopped on the image of a postcard.

Throughout Sally's life her parents had mailed her hundreds of postcards from all over the world. Most often they were from the capitals of the countries where they worked. Between her parents they spoke eleven languages and she had always been told they either worked as translators or administrative assistance at the embassies. Of course that cover story had been completely blown up when Sally came back from Bosnia to confront her grandmother. And now, looking at the storefront of this Czech music store Sally had a pang of regret for that innocent time and burning all those postcards. But her unsentimental grandma had been so insistent on it. So Sally resigned herself to staring at each postcard, burning the image into her memory.

Sally had taken a few steps toward the music store and stopped. She turned around and retrieved her backpack from the back of the car. "This is it," She told the taxi driver through his window.

"But it's not open, why don't I take you to hotel now, you come back in daylight." The taxi driver offered genially.

"That's okay. I've got it from here," Sally offered. She didn't feel like haggling.

"This is not a safe area for you," the driver pleaded.

Sally turned around and said firmly, "Thank you so much for getting me here safely. I know where I'm going now." She handed him the money and added ten extra Koruna's.

"Okay," he said lifting his hands off the steering

wheel momentarily. And then rolled his window up before putting the car in gear and taking off again.

Sally watched the taxi until it turned the corner and then she took a stroll around the block first. She walked up to the storefront door and looked inside. There was an inner door in the back that had cracks of light shining out from its edges. She knocked lightly and then saw a doorbell. She rang it once and saw the light cut out from the door. Someone has been waiting, she thought hopefully.

Sally took a step away from the door and looked down the winding empty street arched to her right.

"You are the same age I was when we first met. How did you get so old?"

Sally turned around to the left and smiled into the twinkling eyes and wizened face of her old friend, "Luck." Her smile faded as she took in his whole figure and the arm that was stuck in his jacket pocket had the unmistakable outline of a gun pointed at her.

CHAPTER 10

Basing their misguided opinion that Prague was a complete "shithole" on their experiences at the train depot and safe house, Lorna and Annie stood in dismay at the opulent surroundings in the Continental Hotel.

Annie pulled self-consciously at her casual clothing and backpack while Lorna perused the place very *un*self-consciously, assessing all that met her eye. The erudite European booking them into the suite gave them a warm welcome in the foyer next to his writing desk that presumably was all he needed to complete the transaction so efficiently.

Upon entering the room the bellboy handed over their room key. "Tea service will be up momentarily." He declined the tip Annie handed out to him with a wave. "No thank you, madam. I hope you will enjoy your stay with us. Call down for me if I can be of service." He backed out of the room giving them a congenial bow as he shut the door.

Lorna watched this with bemused fascination. "So that's why the peasants riot," she said dropping her bag and looking around.

"For what I paid, they should predigest our food for us," Annie countered. Her eyes caught the frescoed vaulted ceiling then and added a, "ooooh."

For a few moments they absorbed the adornments of the suite. Lorna walked to the large windows with ornately carved rosewood frames and looked through the sweeping gauze curtains down into the street. Annie let herself through the double glass doors that led to a bedroom filled with a canopied four-poster bed and oak armoire. The bathroom held a vintage clawed foot bathtub for two. The skylight above it was a baroque stained glass that shone decorative shadows onto the glistening surfaces below.

Lorna's voice was solemn when she asked, "Do you think David Bowie was the leader of their Velvet Revolution?"

The question rocked Annie out of her dream like state. "No, Lorna, but I could see where you'd get the two confused." Annie turned and led Lorna back to the sitting area. "The Velvet Revolution, if I remember correctly, was the overthrow of the communist party by the citizens. I think it happened here in Prague. And I don't know who the leader was. David Bowie had nothing to do with it. But you are confused because Bowie was all into the androgyny thing with his Ziggy Stardust phase. Which led you to Glam Rock, which led you to think the velvet revolution was a gay thing here in the Czech Republic. It wasn't." Annie sat on the neo-classic sofa and took a deep breath. She leaned back and stared at the ceiling fresco. "Now what? Are you feeling okay? Any pain in your chest or anything?"

"No. I'm good, honestly. We should go," Lorna said pulling on her backpack over her shoulders.

"No, we're supposed to wait here for Sally."

"Well, she's not going to find us *in here*, is she?"

Lorna countered.

Annie looked around disappointedly, "That's true." A knock at the door sent Annie to her feet.

"The tea," Lorna said and moved toward the door.

Annie looked around frantically for another exit as a large swamp of a man in an ill fitting uniform wheeled in the tea service. Lorna looked at his shoes. The bellboy had classic paten leather tie-ups whereas the Ogre before her wore dingy black service shoes.

He shut the door behind him. Lorna reopened the door. He smiled at her and shut it again. He gently touched his chest and bowed his head. "I am -"

Lorna grabbed the door handle but he slammed his heel down barring her from opening it again.

"I am Count Von Wallenstein. Please. I cannot chase you anymore. You must go, but first, you meet me in the catacombs at the castle. Bring that package."

Annie and Lorna exchanged a confused look. "What package?" Lorna asked.

The Count lowered his head and peered up at her, "The one in your rucksack. Do not give it to others. You understand?"

Annie nodded.

He removed his foot and swung the door open. Lorna shut the door again. "I read this article once about these people in Africa who shirked international law and opened a Diplomatic bag and it caused an international incident. It didn't say the people who were transmitting the bag were arrested. You hear what I'm saying?"

The Count looked confused and turned to Annie. Every crackpot in the city must be after them, Annie thought, grabbing her backpack. She moved around the tea service tray to the door. "Excuse me," she said and opened the door for herself.

Lorna followed Annie down the gilded hallway. The

elevator bank held two sets of elevators with floor to ceiling mirrors. Annie looked up at the ceiling mirror down at herself and said disparagingly, "I don't know what just happened, but I look like a Romanian refugee."

Lorna looked up at the same ceiling mirror at herself. "I look fantastic," she said with relish.

The elevator bell sounded and the doors yawned open and they jumped inside. As they stood watching the doors close Lorna caught a reflection of two uniformed Prague Policie getting off another elevator.

"Did you see that?" She asked Annie.

"No."

Lorna's brain went into overdrive. Either the front desk called the police or possibly they were spotted and followed here. There could be an A.P.B. out for them and the guy who checked them in could have been alerted. Lorna reached out and hit the "2" button.

"What are you doing?" Annie said in surprise.

"We're taking the stairs."

The elevator bell sounded and Lorna stepped into another mirrored elevator bank. She grabbed Annie's elbow and headed for the exit sign at the end of the gilded hallway. "We need to find another way out of here."

"The restaurant is back here I think," Annie said and turned left and saw the double doors leading to the restaurant.

"Just go through the kitchen, don't stop," Lorna said throwing open the double doors.

Much to the shock of the breakfast wait staff, the two women wound their way around the tables at break neck speed and headed for the kitchen doors.

"Pardon." Someone called to them. "Pardon!"

Lorna swung around the side of the banquet table that was being set up. When her feet left the carpeting and hit the tiles she slid across the length of the floor and popped through the kitchen doors. Steam was rising from all sorts of stainless steel ovens and stovetop burners. Careful not to reach out and grab anything she half slid and half skated her way across the kitchen floor. She caught the open back door by its doorknob trying to regain her balance. Annie came sliding up behind her and pounded her through the open door. Lorna did a face plant onto the wet and greasy cobblestones and caught sight of Annie's shoes stepping over her. The tugging on Lorna's backpack helped set her upright and she followed Annie's lead, once again taking flight.

After an exhaustive sprint across several blocks, they ducked into another alcove. Heaving and gulping air they looked around the street in front of them.

"We have two choices at this point," Annie said.

"Sally or the embassy," Lorna agreed. "How much time do we have before Sally gets back?"

Annie looked at her watch, "Less than an hour."

"We can't let her walk into an ambush, but we can't exactly stake out the joint."

Lorna stood up and took her jacket off.

"What are you doing?"

"Does the inside of your jacket have a lining?" Lorna began unzipping the lining of her jacket.

Annie rubbed the exterior of her puffy jacket. "No, it's one piece."

"Okay, look, put my jacket shell over your jacket."

"Oh, I get it."

The two women changed their appearance by trading jackets. Lorna put her hair into a bun and put on Annie's beret.

Lorna looked Annie over critically. "Look, can you find an inconspicuous place back near the hotel and keep a look out for Sally? I'm going to head over to the American embassy."

Annie grabbed Lorna's arm. "No. We can't separate."

"Annie, we can't let Sally walk into a trap."

"What if your walking into the embassy is a trap? You think that this morning was a mistake? That they won't be waiting for you there?"

Lorna put her hand over her mouth. "Fuck. I think you're right."

"Right?"

"Yeah."

"Now, think," Annie said soberly. "Is there any way you can signal Sally? Any kind of personal joke or did you two have a secret signal that you'd use at parties?"

"You mean the I-want-to-leave signal? No, not really."

"You guys don't have a code sentence. Like, *oh my look at the time*."

"No."

"Okay how about, remember in college when a sock on the door meant don't come in?"

"Annie, I swear to you I've never put socks on the door and Sally and I never had secret party co-" A thought struck Lorna, "Oh wait, my lucky socks. I wear them everyday."

"Ew."

"I have more than one pair," Lorna explained as she swung off her backpack. "If we can like drop a pair near the entrance of that hotel and she sees them, she'll know they're mine. If nothing else it will alert her to something."

Annie looked at the tube socks. "Is that the best you got?"

"That's all I got." Lorna handed the pair of socks to Annie.

Annie swung her backpack off and handed it to Lorna. "You stay here. Seriously, stay. And if I'm not back in 15 minutes, you'll have to find Sally on your own."

"Here, take the beret." Lorna handed Annie the hat.

"Okay, whatever happens, don't go to that embassy. Just dump the drugs and get on the next train to Berlin."

"You'll be fine. Just act casual. Like you're headed to a job."

"Okay. Stay." Annie pointed her index finger down at Lorna.

~~~

Sally followed the old man into the back door of the music store. They stopped in a large workroom that had stringed instruments in various stages of repair and construction lying about. She watched the old man take off his jacket and place it on a hook on the back of the door. An act he had performed thousand of times, and she relaxed a little. Janis, the man who had gotten her out of Bosnia safely, had aged gracefully it seemed. He had a full head of gleaming white hair and a well-trimmed beard to match. The bluish circles under his dark brown eyes spoke of his lack of sleep. And his small paunch of a belly disclosed a well-fed retirement.

"I was shocked to find out you had gotten involved in all this stuff again. You didn't learn your lesson the first time?" His voice rode the music scale in a staccato fashion.

"Janis, I didn't get involved with it, it got involved with me," Sally corrected him.

His tone softened, "Ohhh, I see. Yes, that sometimes happens." The old man suddenly turned on Sally brandishing his gun. "Just when I thought that I was out, they pull me back in," he smiled and plopped the gun down on the desk, "Al Pacino. His movies are good. You like my beard?"

Sally relaxed again. "Yes, it's gotten snowy." She noticed he had cataracts on his eyes.

"Well, I'm disguised as an old man now. Where are you staying?"

"There's a safe house on Dhoula?"

"Dhoula? Dhoula," Janis thought for a moment, "Oh, Dlouha. Down the road just a bit, in the residential section."

Sally didn't know she was so close to the safe house and felt relieved to be near Annie and Lorna. "Janis, is it safe to talk here?"

Sally watched his body for mixed signals as he answered. "Yes, of course it is. I am just an old musician here."

"The Cheese Maker. I've heard stories, ya' know, but I have to ask you," Sally's voice dropped down, "is he my father?"

Janis' peal of laughter turned into a wheezing cough. "Well. Yes and no. The legend of the Cheese Maker is your father's gift to the world. Who the hell makes up a name like the Cheese Maker?" Janis laughed and pounded the table with his fist. "He is genius, your father."

"But, are the stories true?"

Janis stopped laughing, "Well," he shrugged. "Some of them are. He is wealthy man, and you got top education in America." Janis pointed an accusing finger at Sally as the color drained from her face. "Look, in this business you do what you have to, and there are - casualties. He did his best, your father, not to kill." Janis' voice began its musical scale again and rose in pitch. "He never carried a weapon. He was everywhere at once. And I can say with all certainty, that he saved more lives than he took." Janis slammed a hand on the workbench. "Many, many more lives. All of those torture stories, the war stories, they are not true, that is just legend he made."

Sally inhaled deeply, "Thank you. Um, look, I know you are, well, I didn't know you were even here but then my handler said 'The Violin Maker' and I had to come by, he gave me your name as a last resort, in case I had trouble."

"Ah, but I knew you were coming!" He said with gaiety. "The Cheese Maker, he is here, with his cow."

"My mom."

"Yes."

Sally felt a sudden urge to slap him, but thought better of it.

Janis continued, "I couldn't believe they'd come back here but there they were. He does have many enemies around here with the Roma's, they will kill him indeed."

Sally took this in for a beat and opened her mouth to speak, but Janis continued, "you must have eluded Josef. That wouldn't be hard. He was to wait for you at the train station."

"Who's Josef?"

"My wife's sister's boy. He is imbecile, all those inbreeding, but a good heart."

"What?"

"He read *The Scarlet Pimpernel* and now he thinks, ahh, I don't know what he thinks." Janis shook his head with regret.

"He knows? About us? What does he know?"

"Only to keep an eye on you. But you eluded him, it doesn't matter."

"What does he look like?"

"Oh, you can't miss him. Big man." Janis rounded his arms out in front of his chest and tapped his brow. "Wandering eye."

Sally scanned her memory of the figures at the train depot but had no memory of anyone with that description. "Okay, so, my parents, are they at the safe house?"

"No, they have their own place in Bilkova, the Jewish quarter. Their own private safe house, have you been there?"

"Not yet, I need to get to Dhoula first."

"No, you shouldn't go there. I think it closed many years ago. It's a," Janis held his arm out and mimed pushing a syringe into his arm. "pfft. pfft."

"A shooting gallery?"

"Yes. A drug den. Very bad. Why would your handler send you there? It is not safe."

Janis watched the color drain from Sally's face again. "Because," she said, "it was a set up." Sally looked for the gun on the table that was no longer there and sighed, "was this a set up too?"

"No," Janis looked at the empty table and realized Sally's meaning. "But I don't just leave guns lying around. Sally, dítě, your father is many things, but he is not a traitor and he does not kill children, especially his own, dítě. Find the cheese shop on Michalska."

"Janis, I'm not alone, I have civilians with me. *They* are at the safe house." Sally grabbed her backpack to leave.

But Janis grabbed her arm. "Wait. Do not go to that place Sally. Here take this," Janis pulled the gun from his pocket to handed it to Sally, "I tell you those places, no good."

With any luck, Sally thought, Lorna and Annie will have made it back to the hotel by now. "No, keep that," Sally indicated the gun, "but, I must go. Thank you Janis."

~~~

Annie slammed herself against the wall in the alcove and sunk down next to Lorna. "Well, what now?"

"We're running out of options here, we need to keep

moving. This was a total set up. But by who? Do you think Michael was working with the Nurse from the beginning?"

"No. I don't. I think he's stupid. Not evil, but he clearly has no idea what he's doing." Annie said.

"I think whoever he reached out to in the CIA is setting us up then. They did that whole crack house thing to get us out of the way. And, if that doesn't work then whatever the embassy was going to have us shuttle back to the states would have gotten us. Ya' know, 'cause they were so insistent we take care of the Dip bags first."

"Okay that's fine, but what do we do about it? Damn. This shouldn't be this hard."

Lorna cut her eyes. "We keep our eye on the prize."

"What does that mean?"

"We can't stay here. We have to intercept Sally. We hang back a couple of blocks from the hotel, and we're going to have to split up again. But, you take this end and I'll go down further on the other side. And keep circling around those blocks don't stand still, ya' know, just keep moving. We don't have too much time left-"

Annie interrupted Lorna. "And walking in circles isn't going to help."

A shadowy figure breezed across the alcove where the two women sat.

"Sally!" Lorna said whispered urgently.

Annie jumped up and went after Sally. A few moments later the two women returned to the alcove. "I was just around the corner, off that big square down the block," Sally was saying. "How'd it go?" Sally turned a concerned eye on Lorna who was still crouched down in the corner of the alcove.

"I have drugs," Lorna said.

"I know," Sally said in a placating tone while trying to read Lorna's face and body language.

"No," Annie explained. "She means she's got *drugs*, a bag of it."

"I got shit."

"Meth?" Sally was shocked.

Lorna looked unsure but nodded, "Yeah."

"You could be carrying around a bag of baking soda and you wouldn't know the difference," Sally said accusingly.

"Not this bag," Annie said confidently. "A man was shot in front of us and we ran. He had dropped the bag and I guess I picked it up, although honestly I don't remember it. We fell down a fire escape. Then when we were running I realized I had it with me and threw it down. Lorna was behind me and picked it up."

"This was at the safe house?" Sally asked.

"Yes." Lorna answered and continued with the story, "Then we went to the hotel and checked in and the police came, so we ran again and here we are all runned out. And we met a Count."

Sally looked to Annie for clarity. Annie shrugged and nodded. "He said he was a Count and to go to the catacombs below the castle."

Sally cut her eyes but looked back at Annie, "Was he a fat guy?"

"Yes," Annie said. "Wonky eye."

"And damp. He was dampish," Lorna added.

"Okay I think I know what happened. I think he's harmless. The nephew. What did he say?" Sally asked.

"Shouldn't we be moving?" Lorna asked looking at the sunlight creeping down the side of the opposite building.

"Hang on," Sally said. "What did he say?"

"Just that." Annie said, "Meet him in the catacombs. Then we left, we saw the police on the way out. How did your excursion go? Any sign of the Nurse? We think

Michael may be working with her."

"Why?" Sally asked.

Lorna butted in from her crouching position, "Because that *safe house* was a set up. Meant to get us out of the way. And Michael set it up."

"Look, I don't think Michael's working with the Nurse. He's just being used. But I did find out where my parents are staying. That'll lead us to the Nurse," Sally said and then turned to look down at Lorna. "Are you stuck there?"

"No," Lorna said truculently.

"What about the safe house and the drugs?" Annie asked.

Sally shook her head. "I don't know. Look, even if Michael is working with the Nurse he's so far out of the picture now-" Sally stopped mid-thought remembering what Michael had said about the two women, "Michael had said he had some back up for us, two women."

"We could use some back up," Annie agreed. "Can we trust them?"

"But if Michael can't operate out of the states, how could he have sent two people, he said were in his division?" Lorna questioned.

Sally pulled her backpack down off her shoulder and pulled out the satellite phone. She held out the phone, pressed a couple of buttons and waited.

"Hey," Michael's voice rang through like he was standing right next to them.

"What the fuck, Michael?" Lorna screamed.

Sally pushed her hand out to stop Lorna as Michael said, "Okay, what happened?"

"Are you tracking this call Michael? Have you pinpointed our location?" Sally asked calmly.

"Give it a minute, what do you need?"

"I'm guessing in about an hour you are going to be

arrested for treason. And they're going to send your scrawny little ass to a black sight. Do you understand? We figured it out," Sally continued.

"Sally, what the hell are you talking about? Are you guys okay?"

"No thanks to you!" Lorna yelled at the phone.

"Sh! Lorna. Voice," Annie admonished her.

"Sorry."

Michael cut in. "Sally, look, things are changing quickly here. Don't go to the embassy. Your contacts are on Michalska Street."

Annie rolled her eyes at Lorna, who shook her head in agreement.

"Please, for God's sake Sally. I don't even care what," Michael stuttered for a minute, "what treason theory you've stumbled on over there. What the hell can I do about that right now? And don't go to that safe house either. I think we should just abort this. Head over to Michalska so we can get you out of there. We think, I mean, I think I've found another leak on our end, and he was in direct communication with the Nurse. So she's known their plan this whole time. So, she's one step ahead of us at least."

"But she couldn't know about *our* plans," Annie said.

"Annie," Michael said. "There are two many chefs in the kitchen over there, and a few butchers. We can just let them handle it from here. She won't get far."

Lorna said softly, "but the Aurora might." Lorna watched a realization dawn in Annie's ever widening eyes and stood up.

Annie grabbed the cell phone from Sally's grip. "Michael, we're not going to Michalska. We're heading for the embassy then back to the hotel. We'll call you from the train to Berlin tomorrow." Annie blurted into the phone. She pushed the off button and leaned up to whisper to Sally, "If he can track us, so can others." Annie dropped the phone in the corner where Lorna had been sitting and pulled out her map.

"Where are we going?" Lorna asked.

"To the cheese shop," Sally answered.

CHAPTER 11

The Michalska road is a long and winding stretch that runs from the tourist infused Old Town Square with its infamous astrological clock, bohemian garnet jewelry stores and garish souvenir markets all the way down though a large residential section of Prague. Gothic and Renaissance apartment homes stretch and tower over the passersby on their way to the local cobbler, cafe, or hardware store in the residential section, or Staré Město. Plaster cherubs and gargoyles watch over the ancient cobblestone alleys from partly concealed doorways. Flooding that occurred in the thirteenth century prompted the cities elite to raise the streets to a higher level. So now only certain modern doorways can now lead to underground networks of medieval tunnels and passageways below the city. The underground network remains as a testament to the Resistance fighters who used them to shuttle about the city undetected during the Nazi occupation in World War II.

Sally, Lorna, and Annie walked anonymously past these portals in front of sgraffitoed walls occasionally dodging the Czech Policie cars by ducking into covered entryways. As the daylight was fast settling in and finally, in a sudden outbreak of good sense, Sally stopped walking. "I know it's circuitous but I think you two should walk down the side cross streets and look down each Michalska block for a cheese shop. So look, the Czech word for cheese looks like an S, Y, and R. Some variation of that, S, Y, and R."

Annie and Lorna nodded.

"Annie, you take the south sides of the street and look down there," Sally pointed out the direction. "Lorna will walk on the north side. When you walk up the parallel streets don't acknowledge one another. I'm going straight up Michalska. I'll wait till I see you two coming before moving on, but if you don't see me, you'll know I've found the place so double back. Got it?"

Lorna looked at Sally with a vague expression.

Sally explained further, "You'll do figure eights around Michalska and work your way up the street."

Annie stuck her left index finger in the air and made curly cues around it with her right index finger. "Like this," she said. "And work our way up."

Lorna looked annoyed with them. "I get what your saying, but this isn't a New York City grid we're working on. You'll have to wait for us, that's a long walk we'll be making."

"It's fine," Sally reassured her and took on a casual air. "I'm just out for my morning stroll. It's you two who'll have to watch your back. As a matter of fact, let's switch out our jackets again. Annie you take my outer shell and give me Lorna's. Here Lorna, put on my inner shell."

Lorna took off the black colored lining of her jacket and put on Sally's grey colored lining. "Do you still have that scarf?" She asked Sally.

"Oh, yes," Sally pulled out the scarf and stopped.

"Here, just trade me backpacks."

"You know what I'm packing," Lorna said significantly.

"Yes, Lorna. I'm taking your baking soda," Sally said with some frustration.

Lorna stopped abruptly and cut her eyes at Sally.

"I'm sorry," Sally said begrudgingly.

"No. I'm not letting that one go, we're gonna talk about that shit later."

"Okay," Sally agreed.

Annie stood by watching with some fascination but snapped out of it and asked Sally, "Do we have a plan for when we get there?"

"I think we're going to have to just take it head on," Sally said.

"Okay then, let's do this," Annie said with bravado.

A half an hour later, Annie saw Sally standing on a street corner casually looking at her watch. Sally waited as Annie approached closer and nodded at her before moving on. This was not in the playbook, Annie thought as she followed Sally down a side street. When Sally led her under a stone archway into a mini tunnel where Lorna was waiting against a wall. Annie looked behind Lorna beyond the iron-gate into a grassy garden courtyard.

"Do you have any water left?" Lorna asked Annie.

"Yeah," Annie pulled off her backpack and handed Lorna a bottle of water. "Take the rest of it, if you need it."

"Thanks," Lorna pawed out a couple more pills from her medicine bottle and swallowed the pills with the rest of Annie's water.

"I thought you were supposed to eat with those things."

"It's okay, I had a cheese pretzel left over from the train."

"Honestly, I could use one of those right now," Annie said indicating the pill bottle.

"Yeah," Lorna agreed. "You should have one. Or like a half, since you're smaller than me."

Sally had been looking out at the garden but returned. "She's right, we should half one," Sally said to Annie's astonishment.

"Really?"

Sally had a deadpan look in her eyes. "Yeah, I'm totally serious," she turned to Lorna, "gimme one."

"Sure," Lorna pulled another pill from the bottle that Sally snapped in half.

Sally offered a half to Annie.

"No. No I don't think that will help me. I don't want to take drugs."

Sally popped half the pill in her mouth, "Suit yourself."

They stopped talking when they heard footsteps echoing across the walls of the tunnel. Sally plastered herself against the wall and didn't move as two large men with slicked back hair, blue jeans, and black leather jackets passed by.

Annie didn't skip a beat and stuck her hand out, "Gimme one of those."

Sally said with in a soft voice, "Those were Russians. I passed by, like, six of them up and down Michalska."

Lorna looked out of the passage and into the street. "What do you think they want?" She whispered.

Annie leaned over to Sally and Lorna, "I imagine, *Lorna*, they want their *drugs* back."

"I didn't see their name on it," Lorna hissed.

"Please. Both of you," Sally stopped them. "The building on the corner over there is a building of flats. So there's going to be a door to the right of the shop you saw out front on the bottom floor with a backdoor that leads out here to the garden area. But the fire escape is over on this side here in front of us, on this corner street. Now, my father is going to have taken the flat on the third floor of this corner building."

"How do you know?" Annie asked.

"Because that gives him views of three sides of the building and the third floor because that gives a better chance of escape. Down the fire escape or he could still have time to go across the roof tops."

"Are you sure about that?" Lorna asked.

"Positive. He also has a direct view of the streets below. Now listen," Sally added pulling the small travel soap and shampoos out of her backpack. "Put this all over those hinges of this gate so it won't squeak."

"What is it?"

"The left over shampoo and soap from the train. Just slather it on as best you can. Here Annie, I have some more in this bottle," Sally handed Annie another bottle.

Sally and Annie worked quickly on the hinges while Sally seemed to be fiddling around with the giant lock on the gate. Finally, Lorna heard a pop and the gate swung a bit before Sally stopped it.

The gate door opened with barely a squeak and they slipped through the garden area but the building door Sally wanted to enter through had no outer door handle and could only be opened from the inside.

Annie and Lorna looked to Sally questioningly. Sally silently assured them it would be okay. She took off one of her leather shoelaces and made a little lasso on the end and slipped that under the door on the other side and rolled the lace between her fingers until the lasso part seemed to catch on something then she repeated the procedure for the top part of the door. "Annie," Sally ordered, holding out the top leather lace to show her what to do on the bottom door corner.

Annie bent down and grabbed the lace.

Sally continued, "Gently, and slowly we're going to open the door, just a little, and hold it there."

The two women tugged on the laces and millimeter-by-millimeter until the door came out toward them.

"Now Lorna," Sally said softly. "Take out a credit card and slip it between the door jam at the lock. You might here a click, and then if you can get your fingers into the door jam, pull on it gently. Annie if you can get your little fingers under the door that would help too."

Lorna quickly took out a credit card and fumbled around near the door lock. Feeling the resistance, she jammed it in until she was able to get her fingertips into the crack and she gently pulled the door open.

Sally grabbed up her shoelaces as Annie and Lorna looked at each other in astonishment. Sally smiled and flicked at the credit card Lorna was holding. "Now put that away."

Lorna grabbed her arm. "Did you learn that in spy school?"

Sally grimaced. "Law school. But it only works if you have two accomplices."

Inside the long hallway, three large trashcans sat against the right wall under the stairs and the door that led to the cheese shop was on the opposite wall. Rustling noises and footfalls could be heard coming from inside the cheese shop. Sally took a few steps further inside and looked up the stairwell. She turned to the other two, held up a finger to her lips and then pointed up the stairs.

They followed in Sally's footsteps up to the third floor landing where they gathered outside the apartment door. Sally silently pointed Lorna to stand over to the side of the landing that led up another flight and pointed Annie to go back down a couple of steps. Sally stood against the wall to one side of the door and knocked.

Annie turned a little, facing back down the stairs and held her breathe for a moment, half expecting gunshots to ring out. The three women poked their heads around the stair banister to make eye contact with one another. They waited another moment and Lorna nodded her head at Sally and Annie.

Sally moved over to the other side of the door and knocked gently again when she saw a painted over door buzzer. She pressed the buzzer once and stood back again. Sally rolled her eyes and dropped her shoulders in exasperation. She looked carefully around the landing and walked over to the wooden staircase by Lorna. At the handrail, she rubbed her hand along the edges giving it a squeeze in certain areas. To Lorna's surprise the wood gave way and rolled open popping out a key at Sally that she caught when it hit her on the stomach. Sally walked over and unlocked the door. She ushered Lorna and Annie in with a swoop of her hand before replacing the key and shutting the door behind her.

Lorna took a few steps in and rolled her eyes in slack jawed amazement. "What the fuck did I just see?" She whispered to Annie.

"What happened? Where'd she get the key?" Annie asked.

Sally gave the sparse but expertly appointed apartment a quick once over. But shushed the other two as she passed by the entry-hall where they stood whispering.

"We good?" Annie asked when Sally returned to the room.

"Don't go near the windows and don't turn on any lights." Sally ordered them again.

"Are we just waiting?" Lorna asked.

"Do you have a better idea?" Sally snapped.

"We should at least keep an eye out on the streets,

Sally," Annie argued.

"Stay close to the wall, don't let the curtains flutter. Lorna, you take the back. Annie you take the side. I'll stay here."

Before taking her perch, Annie went into the kitchen and refilled her water bottle. She gulped it down, then refilled it again and tucked it back into her backpack.

Lorna walked into the bedroom. It struck her that everything was oblong. The room itself, but also the windows, the bed, the armoire, the dresser, the pillows, the rugs, and the picture frames. Everything was oblong. On one of the nightstands she saw a framed law school graduation announcement with a blank where Sally's name should have been. How horrible, she thought. It was the first sign of parental pride or love or even acknowledgement she had seen either of Sally's parents display. In the few months she had known them while they ran the Auld Alliance Cafe they never really gave off that familial air of pride about their daughter. So now, Lorna thought, her own father and sister, the only real family Sally's known has turned their backs on her. Lorna scowled at the thought. "Shame on them." She said softly to herself. Looking around she saw no other significant pictures or personal items. She carefully looked over the dresser and the other nightstand; nothing here indicated a past or a personal history. Maybe this framed announcement was a sign or code thing meant for Sally.

Lorna walked back into the living room but stood next to the bedroom door and watched Sally for a moment. Sally was standing with her back against a wall, next to a window, looking intently into a handheld mirror that was facing the street below. That's weird, Lorna thought. Sally's becoming a super spy. And that's when it dawned on her.

"Sally," Lorna said quietly, "I need to talk to you."

"You *need* to get back there and keep a look out," Sally said without looking at her.

"No. You know how these drugs," Lorna paused, "make me talk loud and I don't feel any pain in my chest and arm?"

"What?" Sally dropped her hand down and looked pointedly at Lorna.

"You took a half a pill, not fifteen minutes ago, and you're acting weird. You're all focused and mean and shit."

"No, my actions and reactions are appropriate to the given situation I find myself in," Sally said aggressively.

"Actually," Annie said from another corner of the room, "you're kinda being bitchy."

"Are you kidding me? We've got the Russian mob, Czech police, probably the CIA, and who all else after us, and you're gonna boo-hoo about my tone of voice?" Sally pulled a face.

"Yes. I think your judgment is clouded," Lorna said neutrally. "You need to realize that you are acting weird. It helps to control the drugs affects on you. Look, we need to be thinking two steps ahead here. But I found something in the bedroom I think you should look at."

"What is it?" Annie asked.

"Sally needs to see it. Maybe a message," Lorna beckoned from the doorway.

Sally crouched down and crawled away from the windows and followed Lorna into the bedroom. Annie took Sally's place at the window.

Lorna pointed to the framed college announcement. "What do you make of that?"

Sally's parents had not attended her law school graduation. She hadn't even sent out announcements. However, despite the name blanked out in the middle of the card, it looked like the genuine article. Sally hadn't even known where they were stationed during this time of her life. Sally picked up the frame and looked carefully at the script on the card. It was correct in everyway, the spacing, the typeface, the words and the date.

"What are they trying to tell you?" Lorna asked finally.

"Hang on," Sally pulled the frame apart and slipped out the announcement card. She held it up to the light and flipped it over a couple of times, eyeballing the edges. Using her fingernail, she flicked the corner of the card a couple of times until the paper separated. She peeled back a corner and then took the whole back off the card. She handed Lorna the front half of the card. "Put that back," She said and walked out of the room with the paper.

Lorna followed her out of the bedroom. "Ya' gonna keep that to yourself are ya?" She asked Sally truculently.

"What is it?" Annie asked from the window.

"It's a note from Wallace and Eunice," Lorna answered her.

"What's it say?"

"Ask Captain Deadly over there," Lorna snapped.

Sally whirled on Lorna.

"See?" Lorna pointed and took a step toward her. "See? What you're feeling right now, how you're acting aggressive, that's not normal. Sally. Listen to me. Personally, I want to run a marathon across glass in my bare feet while solving a rubics cube and singing the national anthem at the top of my lungs. You have to focus all that energy. It's like adrenaline or something. Annie, how do you feel?"

Annie answered quickly, "Clairvoyant."

"Right." Lorna gave a quizzical twist of her head. "I don't know what that means, do you feel like you can read my mind?"

"Yes. You have a plan," Annie confided.

"I do! Oh my God, that's amazing."

"Shut up you two," Sally demanded.

Lorna ignored the demand, "What did the note say?"

"Nothing," Sally handed her the paper.

"But shouldn't you put lemon juice on it or look at it over an open flame?"

"No," Sally said plainly.

"But that doesn't make any sense. Why would they go to all that trouble and then nothing?" Lorna asked.

"Maybe it's not supposed to make sense," Annie offered graciously. "Maybe that's the point."

"Stop it," Sally said. "Just get back to your look outs. I'm giving this another fifteen minutes and we're done. I think it's just another ruse."

Lorna went back into the bedroom but she could hear Sally talking to Annie.

"That's what spying is," Sally was saying. "Trafficking in secrets and manipulating others to your own ends, like getting people to steal for you. They're just like a bunch of old gossips. You know who gossips? Stupid people, because they have nothing better to do than to feed off of others hard work. Like those sucky fish on whales."

A stony silence followed Sally's angry diatribe just in time to hear a knock at the door. Lorna came bounding back into the living room and froze. The same rhythmic tapping came again.

Sally moved Lorna to the side and flagged Annie to move into the bedroom. With Lorna and Annie out of sight, she opened the door.

"What's the matter with you?" Wallace wanted to know. "You don't ask who's knocking? I could have been a burglar or worse, the policie."

"Hello, sweetheart. You look awful," Eunice said

grabbing Sally's arm.

Wallace moved past Sally as Eunice closed the door. Wallace was looking his usual balding self, he still looked natty but he'd put on a few pounds, Sally thought. But her mother was looking radiant. Her hair recently dyed pitch black and coiffed in defiance of her facial wrinkles. And her long fingernails, which were red and pointy, looked to Sally as if they had been recently sharpened.

"How'd you guys get in here?" Sally asked.

"With a key, unlike yourself," Wallace said accusingly.

Eunice busied herself looking around and pointed to Annie and Lorna's backpacks. "Where's the other two?"

Sally called out, "Guys! It's clear."

Lorna and Annie walked into the living room.

"You gotta get outta here," Wallace said. "We have a date."

"I'm sure you do. But we're not leaving without the Aurora," Sally said.

"Ha, ha! Did you hear that Ivy? One day on the job and she's demanding a piece of the action! What's your price sweetheart?"

Sally seethed.

"Lek, stop teasing her," Eunice/Ivy said.

Annie muttered to Lorna. "Who's Lek?"

Lorna, mouth agape, continued watching but muttered back. "I think maybe it's Wallace's real name. And she's Ivy, today."

"Who's teasing? I'm *proud* of her." Lek/Wallace pleaded with his hands out. "Come on Sally, let's get you and your friends out of here before the fireworks start. But you did good. I'm proud of you."

A quick glance at Sally and Lorna knew the fireworks were going to start earlier than he thought if she didn't step in right now. "Sally didn't want to come here," Lorna stepped forward into their conversation. "It was us," she turned to Annie for backup.

Annie nodded, "We felt like we needed to warn you."

"About what?" Eunice/Ivy asked.

"Well, a couple of things. We think the Nurse is running you guys as brokers so she could get out of the country even though she knows she was being followed and she's set up a separate sale. There was a leak in the CIA, so she's known this whole time. But we also think Michael was working with the Nurse."

Ivy and Lek exchanged a meaningful look.

"Michael? Where did you get this information, Dear?" Ivy asked.

"I figured it out. It's the easiest line between the two points. Point A, being where the Nurse gets a hold of the Aurora and point B, where she escapes with the money. She was very zen about it and just let everyone do the work for her. I don't even think Michael knew she was getting information from him."

Ivy eyed Lorna with a mixture of pride and suspicion. "That's very good."

Lek stood up again. "Almost, but not quite. Now then ladies, I don't mean to be rude but you really must be going."

"Did you sell it to the Cheese Maker?" Sally bated him.

Lek smiled at his daughter but said truthfully. "He is just a legend, there's no proof such a man ever existed. He's a boogey man. Someday I will tell you the whole story."

"Save it for your memoirs," Sally said.

"I will," Lek said truculently.

Lorna watched this exchange in amazement, for the first time she saw the strong resemblance between Sally and her father. The cut of their jaw was identical. So much for Sally's adoption theory, Lorna thought.

The knock at the door froze everyone for a moment. Everyone looked at each other for a beat. Lorna and Annie instinctively grabbed their backpacks. Ivy put a boney finger to her mouth to hush everyone and waved the three girls into the bedroom and shut the door.

There was no closet in the bedroom and the bed was a good two feet off the floor, there was nowhere to hide. Annie pointed to the window and gave a questioning shrug at Sally and Lorna. Sally shook her head no and put her ear to the door. Sally pointed to the far side of the bed and pushed her hand down showing them how to take cover behind the bed. Carefully the two women hunched down behind the bed watching Sally listen at the door.

Suddenly, Sally deftly leapt to the far side of the large ornate wardrobe. Ivy's hand came in and plopped a gym bag down just inside the door and shut it back.

All three women poked their heads around and looked at the gym bag. Lorna scampered over to the bag and hovered above it. As she moved to open it, Sally slapped her hands away and waggled a finger in her face.

Lorna flicked her hand backwards under her chin at Sally in a piss off gesture and continued.

Sally slapped Lorna's hands away again and mimed an exploding bomb gesture.

Lorna shook her head at Sally and rubbed her fingers together in a money gesture.

Annie watched this pantomime in numbed absorption when a thought slowly came into focus. She jumped up from her crouched position bringing Lorna's backpack over to them.

Sally and Lorna stopped and looked at Annie. Annie opened Lorna's backpack and extracted the drugs from it. She held up the drug package and pointed to the gym bag. Lorna's mouth fell open and she nodded her head vigorously. Sally nodded but put a finger up to them while she inspected the zipper on the bag. She looked up at them and shook her head, but then nodded agreement and gently tugged at the zipper. When nothing happened she opened the bag fully and exposed the neatly stacked piles of Russian 5000 Ruble notes. Annie smiled scurried back behind the bed with her. Sally nodded at Lorna and stood up to listen again at the door. Lorna lifted up several of the note stacks and pushed the drug package down into the bag and replaced the notes.

As Lorna ever so slowly and silently zipped the bag back up, there was a slight creaking behind them. All three women startled and turned around but saw nothing. They heard the creak again and looked under the bed. Slowly the floor under the bed began to shift and was lifted up.

Sally looked around in vein for a weapon. Lorna slid herself under the bed feet first and waited to strike with the heel of her foot. A hand popped up with a small white napkin that was waved at them. Then to Sally's complete and utter shock, Katie, the administrative assistant from her office at Housing and Urban Development in San Francisco, popped her head up from the floor. Katie smiled broadly at Sally and waved her over.

Despite her shock at seeing Katie, Sally shook her head no. Sally didn't even have time to figure out how Katie, the world's most efficient and loyal administrative assistant, could possibly have gotten messed up in this business before Katie frowned accusingly at Sally. Katie cut her finger across her throat at her and then pointed at Sally. Sally's mouth fell open in horror. But Annie, watching this exchange, grabbed her backpack and got down on her belly to slide under the bed and follow Katie down the ladder.

Lorna slid under the bed headfirst and looked down

the hole in the floor to see Katie and Annie waving her down. Lorna dropped her backpack and swung around to face Sally. She mouthed the word, *please*, to Sally. Sally nodded and followed Lorna down the floor hole.

CHAPTER 12

The ladder to the floor below was positioned between two single beds with a nightstand at the head of the beds. Sally climbed down and looked around the economically appointed room. "What the fuck?" She demanded of Katie.

"I know, " Katie said glowingly. "I moonlight for Christy."

Sally tossed her head to the side nonchalantly, "Oh! Of course." And then got serious, "Who the fuck is Christy?"

"I am."

Sally whirled around to see a small meaty woman, in her mid-thirties, with clunky round black-framed glasses and black hair worn like a swim cap. She looked like a French clothing designer from the 1930's. She took a small step forward and smiled at Sally. "Forgive my attire I was doing krav maga." She patted her waist. "Baby fat."

Sally blinked at her.

Annie was delighted, "What did you have? No wait, you had a girl."

"A girl," Christy nodded happily.

"I can't believe *I'm* saying this but can we stay on track here?" Lorna said.

"Quickly. Katie, could you?" Christy tapped the ladder and looked up at the ceiling.

"Sure," Katie said and busied herself with packing the ladder back into the ceiling crawl space.

Christy led them into the living room and sat down. "I'm Michael's boss. But I don't want to talk about Michael's performance on this mission. Needless to say, the fact that I'm doing the fieldwork here tells you everything you need to know."

Sally shook her head and stood back up again. "Unless you set Michael up too. It's very easy to make Michael look stupid. He barely knows his ass from a hole in the ground. And that's your fault because you didn't train him properly."

Christy nodded her head. "Agreed. But I don't have time to prove to you my sincerity. We really don't." Christy shook her head. "We're in the worst case scenario here and it behooves me to be truthful with you."

Sally smiled sardonically. "So that's where you are. Your last ditch effort is to be honest."

Christy looked around as Katie came back into the room. "Yep. Right now the CIA thinks they are getting the Aurora, thanks to your parents," she looked at Sally and then to Lorna, "and the Russians think they are getting it, thanks to Nurse."

"So Lorna was right?" Annie looked surprised.

Christy paused, waiting for Annie to continue speaking but then moved on. "It is vital that you do *not* approach Nurse. She'll kill you in your tracks. The Nurse was trying to disguise herself as a Muslim woman when she came into the city." Christy rolled her eyes. "Like she needs to attract any more attention to herself here. So, Katie has been monitoring the CIA's movements and she thinks they're going to nab Nurse when she comes here in about two hours."

Lorna interrupted, "I'm sorry, then who is that upstairs now?"

"He's the drop off man for the Russians. We've been trying to figure out if Nurse is going to do the Aurora drop off in person or use a carrier."

"Do Sally's parents know that's why the Russian is in their living room?" Lorna asked.

"Yes, and that's also why the CIA is going to grab her before she arrives. They are clearly aware of your parents," Christy paused, "abilities. Anyway, I say she's going to use a carrier and Katie thinks she going to create a diversion and do it in person." Christy shrugged. "The point is though *we* need to grab her before she's noticed."

"How?" Annie asked.

"It's not exactly like we're a tactical strike force," Lorna said.

"Well, we don't need her exactly, we need the package she'll be carrying. I'm thinking a smash and grab. It's sloppy, but who the hell cares at this point. Thankfully though, we got a sighting of her checking into a pension on the other side of the river on Nosticova. Street. Sally, Katie, and Lorna can go out for her. And since you'll be on that side of the river you can drop off the package to the embassy. Annie, you stay back with me to monitor the Russian upstairs."

"Whoa. No." Sally blurted out. "How can you, in all consciousness, send civilians in for a thing like this? Do you know how dangerous she is?"

"*I* sure as hell do." It was Lorna who answered.

Sally continued, "And Lorna's wanted all over town by the police for that drug debacle. Thanks to you, I might add. No. You go and we'll stay here and monitor."

"I can't. It's actually a much better plan. She, and

whoever she's recruited to work with her are expecting some kind of tactical maneuvers. What they aren't expecting is three women walking up the street as big as day. But if I get caught the whole mission is blown to shit, not to mention our department. If Lorna gets caught, I can get the state department to step in under diplomatic status. You remember those papers Michael had you sign for the dip bags?" Christy asked Lorna.

Lorna nodded.

"That puts you under official diplomatic status. You'll be fine. By the way, it was an I.T. guy in the CIA who set the diplomatic status up for Lorna. And now we know for sure he had to be the leak. In his effort to get you arrested over here in Prague, he also gave you an immunity status when he assigned you the diplomatic bag. Those things have to be signed off on. How someone from I.T. could get the assignment past a supervisor-"

"Hang on. How do you-" Lorna began to ask.

Katie answered her quickly, "Michael told Christy about the safe house before you got there. You know those bullet holes you discovered? I stuck a teeny tiny little camera in one of them just before you guys got there."

"I saw the whole thing. Scared the shit out of me too," Christy added.

Lorna frowned at Sally.

"But you didn't see fit to help them," Sally stated knowingly.

"At that point there was still a chance that it was legitimate diplomatic exchange," Christy explained. "I'm sorry that it wasn't. But you guys handled it well."

"Who was the guy who got shot?" Lorna asked.

"And who shot him?" Annie added.

Christy shrugged. "We couldn't see. It's very possible that it was just a drug deal."

"But, we stole the drugs. And no one ran after us?"

Katie and Christy both shook their heads no. Christy went on. "Whoever shot him stayed out of the apartment, perhaps they ran the other way, back down the stairs."

"The Count?" Annie asked Lorna.

"Well, he didn't say anything at the hotel." Lorna answered.

"Who?" Christy asked.

Sally stepped in. "No one." Sally cut off the conversation and looked over to Lorna who nodded her consent to Christie's plan. Sally shook her head no, but then said, "Okay."

"Great. Katie can fill you in on the rest of the plan on the way over." Christy said.

Lorna grabbed her backpack to go. "Hang on, let me get some water in my bottle," she said squatting down and opened her backpack. Looking into her backpack as the others muttered and gathered their things. "Oh," Lorna said softly. "Oh, no." Everyone stopped and looked at her.

Lorna looked up at them and let out a long groan.

Sally rushed to her side, "Are you okay?"

Lorna swallowed and pulled out a Dip bag, "I switched the wrong bags."

"What?" Christy asked.

"I switched the wrong bags," Lorna repeated. "I stuffed the embassy bag in the money bag upstairs. This," she pulled out another bag, "is the drugs bag."

Annie covered her open mouth and gasped a little.

Everyone stood stalk still for a moment exchanging glances. Christy pulled off her great round glasses and smiled. "Genius," she said.

Sally stood up. "What?"

Christy took a step forward. "What's better than a gym bag filled with money and drugs?" Christy put her glasses back on. "A gym bag filled with money and a diplomatic pouch!" Christy rubbed her hands together, turned around, and paced back and forth for a moment. She assessed Annie from head to toe, nodding to herself.

Sally had enough, "Okay. Lorna, let's-"

"Wait," Christy put a hand out to stop her. "I got it. Okay. This is perfect." She looked at Sally. "You want this Nurse out of your life forever and ever? I can make sure of it." Christy lowered her head, "Katie, put the beeper on. Sally and Lorna, you are going to the embassy, but not with a dip bag. Instead," Christy scrambled back into the living room desk, "you'll be taking this note. You don't have to wait for a response. Just hand it to the doorman."

Katie walked over to the desk and pulled out a black key fob. She attached it to the zipper of her jacket.

Christy was quiet for a moment as the other women watched her writing on a single sheet of paper. When she was finished, she handed the paper to Katie. Katie, in what Sally recognized as Katie's natural milieu, handled the administrative tasks for that piece of paper efficiently. Then Katie handed the finished envelope to Lorna.

Christy nodded approvingly at Katie. "Okay. Same plan, different details," Christy announced. "The three of you." She indicated Katie, Sally, and Lorna. "Go across the bridge together. Katie you take up a post at the Nurse's pension. Beep me when she leaves. If you see someone enter, stay a bit, then leave. Beep me. You know the deal."

Katie nodded.

Christy continued, "Lorna and Sally, I need you to take that letter to the American Embassy and leave it with the doorman. This is less dangerous and will tie this thing up in a nice, neat, little bow."

"What does it say?" Sally asked.

"It says to get the Director of Intelligence on the line, immediately."

"What's that going to do?" Sally challenged her.

"It's going to put the State Department up the Directors ass for one," Christy answered knowingly. "Thus clearing our path to finish this job and get the hell out of here."

Graphic, Lorna thought while placing the envelope in her backpack, I like this little Christy dynamo.

~~~

Katie, Lorna, and Sally walked down the front stairs of the building and let themselves out the back door into the garden courtyard. From the garden they walked out of the gate on the far side and onto a side street.

Lorna looked over to Katie, "You know where we're going from here?"

"Yeah, I got it," Katie assured her.

"Katie, how long have you worked in this division?" Sally asked before Katie could give detailed street-by-street instructions.

"Oh gosh, I was an informant for them almost from the moment I got my job at HUD. I worked for Michael's predecessor, but then after he got blown up, Christy came to see me and asked me to take a more active role until things calmed down. Michael doesn't know about me though. But let me tell you, this has been kicking my ass."

"What do you do?" Lorna asked.

"I'm Sally's, and well, several other of the counsel staff's, administrative assistant. But really for the last few weeks I've been shuffling Sally's workload to Christy, who then has it completed and then I just put it in Sally's out basket, then I dispense with it. Scott has no idea."

"Who's Scott?" Lorna asked.

"Our manager," Katie answered.

"But I've exchanged emails with Scott," Sally countered.

"No, you've exchanged emails with Christy. She's good," Katie smiled.

"I could get disbarred for this," Sally said, more frightened than angry.

"Only if anyone finds out, and they're not going to. I read some of the work, it sounds like you."

"Listen Katie, when we get back, I want to see every piece of paper with my name on it. Every file, everything."

"Sure. But it'll be a waste of time for you."

Sally groaned inwardly.

Katie had never hung out with Sally outside of work. And although Katie liked her at the HUD offices, she was beginning not to like her. Sally seemed so gruff and antagonist. Not at all how she is in the office.

"What did you do for Michael's predecessor?" Lorna asked Katie.

"Oh, anytime I thought there was a fraud case coming into the office, I gave him the heads up so he could use his cover story and turn it in to the FBI fraud division."

"What's his - I don't understand what *his cover* means."

"You know his cover story is the Special Fraud Division. The *special* just means it's in a higher classification. The *special* is our division's designation. So anytime I see a case that could fall under fraud I'd give him the heads up. So he could get some credit for it under the regular fraud division."

"That's confusing."

"That's the FBI."

Sally felt like her eyeballs were boiling, she stopped walking. Lorna and Katie turned to see a fractious Sally, her hands balled up into tight fists, eyes staring at the

2

sidewalk, her chest heaving. Katie had had enough; she stepped back over to Sally.

"Look," Katie said. "For what it's worth, if it wasn't for what Christy and I have been doing, you would have been out of a job."

Lorna stood in front of Sally and turned to Katie, "She's on drugs, you know."

"Really?" Katie was astonished. "Imbalanced?" Palms down, Katie waggled her hands back and forth.

"No," Lorna watched her. "Just today. She took one of the pills that doctor gave me and she hasn't learned to harness its properties."

"If it wasn't for Christy, I wouldn't be in this position in the first place!" Sally spat out.

Katie backed down and continued strolling. "Well, I don't know about that Sally. This whole thing has been brewing for years, and it looks to me like it originated with Tim. Not for nothing, but Christy held this whole thing together despite the odds. She's very good at what she does. Very good. If I found myself in your position, I'd want to have her on my side. And honestly, of all those people in that swamp of pestilent incompetence we work in, I'm so glad it's you that I'm helping out. So, please try to look past the blaming and your anger for a little while longer."

"Boy," Lorna butted in, "you hate your day job don't you?"

Katie flashed Lorna her effervescent smile, "We gotta keep moving. We just need to cross that bridge ahead, the Mane-suv most."

"Mánesûv most," Sally pronounced it correctly and added in a dry tone, "you need to work on your dialect skills."

Lorna took a nonchalant glance around as they made their way to the bridge. "How do you know if you're being followed?"

"What is it?" Sally kept moving.

"There are three guys in jeans and black leather jackets. They stopped when we stopped and now they seem to be gaining on us. I'm afraid to turn around again."

"Just keep moving," Sally said.

Lorna couldn't help herself, she turned around again and the three men ran toward them, "Run!"

All three women broke into a sprint and headed for the bridge. They rounded the corner onto Karprova and saw the bridge splayed before them. The impressive stone bridge expanse could handle two car lanes and a pedestrian walks on either side.

Lorna slowed until Sally caught up with her. "Keep running!" Lorna called to her.

"What?" Sally could see Lorna was purposely falling back, "No. Damn it. Go Lorna!"

"Keep running! I've got diversionary tactics!"

Katie had been lagging behind them and now passed them at the base of the bridge.

Lorna let Sally keep pace ahead of her but as they crossed center of the bridge Lorna held back until she slowed to a stop. She turned around and made sure the three guys saw her and she flipped up her middle finger at them. Then she climbed on top of the thick ornate bridge guardrail and jumped into the icy Vltava river water. Sally heard a splash and stopped when she got to the far end of the bridge and looked back. Lorna was gone and the three men were staring down into the river. One guy made eye contact with Sally and gave chase. Sally instinctively started to run again.

~~~

For the first time in a long while Annie felt at peace. It did not occur to her that to have this feeling, right now and in this space was at all odd. She looked down into the courtyard below. How many generations of families picnicked down there? She watched an elderly woman pulling a cart filled with groceries walk out of the tunnel and into the courtyard. The distance from the window down to the courtyard gave Annie a new perspective. "Our lives are so small," she said to herself.

Christy had only taken a few minutes to change clothes and come back into the living room. "Okay, you and I have a job to do as well," Christy said to Annie. "I hope you work well under pressure."

"Me too," Annie agreed complacently.

"First, we are going to divert the CIA," Christy said almost cheerfully.

Annie smiled, "By floating them some disinformation by way of a bogus message from Nurse, or by setting up some unsuspecting tourist, or both? You've got to outflank them somehow."

"How did you know that?"

"I know things," Annie said furtively.

Christy's eyes narrowed. "Yes. Well," she began pulling her laptop closer to her, "let's give Michael a call and get him to call on his leaky friend."

The two women huddled down together at the desk and began to execute their phase of the plan.

~~~

Katie finally caught up to Sally who was sitting outside a corner cafe on Nosticova Street staring bleakly at a wall.

"What the hell are you doing?" Katie asked her.

"Lorna jumped into the river. I turned around and she was gone. Why would she do that?" Sally asked, tears welling up in her eyes.

Katie stuck out her chin, "Because, she knew she

would survive."

Sally shook her head remembering the drugs Lorna had been taking.

"Now, come on Sally. We have to go over to that pension."

"Fuck it. I'm really done this time. I'm going back for Lorna, hopefully someone fished her out and she's in the hospital."

Katie stood in front of Sally and stopped. "You're right. I'm so sorry, *of course* we need to help Lorna." Sally avoided Katie and kept moving. Katie continued walking with her, "What do you think her plan was? Is she a strong swimmer?"

"Not in ice water she's not. I need a phone. I should call the hospitals," Sally looked around.

"Okay. Sally please stop and let me help you."

Sally kept moving forward.

Katie continued, "I'll call the hospitals."

Sally finally stopped and faced Katie, "No. I don't want your help. Go, do your thing you came here to do."

"But we can't go back to the river because those Russians are probably staking it out. Then if they get you, what help will you be to Lorna? Sally, think first."

Sally shook her head in disgust, "Piss off."

"Fine, but you're making a mistake here. Know that," Katie said definitively.

"Yup, one I should have made a long time ago," Sally said and turned the corner.

Katie watched Sally turn the corner and remembered what Lorna had said about the drugs. She took off around the corner, but it was too late. Sally had disappeared into one of the alleys. Lorna had that letter to the embassy, so I can't go there, Katie thought. But then again, I can't go to the Nurse pension and leave Sally.

Katie grabbed a hold of her key fob. The code she

and Christy had made was a single push of the button to indicate when the Nurse was leaving the pension. And two beeps for when the Nurse was close to their apartment. Katie kept walking and ducking into alleys while pressing the fob three times, waiting a beat and pressing it again three times. She repeated the three beeps once more. It wasn't exactly Morse code, but close enough. Katie doubled back and took another alley before repeating her three-beep code.

~~~

Annie sat back down on the couch, "That was actually *fun*. Will they go for it?"

Christy sat down at the computer desk next to the couch.

"Of course they will. They fall for that shit all the time. The trick with the CIA is they always want a second source, so you have to not only create the disinformation but also a believable second source. It's just a step away from saying, "Annie, you shouldn't smoke pot *every* Friday night.""

"I don't smoke pot every Friday night."

"Well, you really shouldn't smoke it at all, it's illegal."

"But, I don't smoke pot."

"Yes. But if someone were listening to that conversation all they'd have to do is say there was a question of marijuana use. Then the record of drug questions would be in your file."

"So the next time any kind of drug question would come up, that would be their second source material." Annie finished.

"Exactly."

"Wow. That's almost evil."

"Almost. It's what we do best. This whole Aurora

mission is out of our purview, but then we also have to consider our mandate and we would be flying blind in the cyber world without it. It was right of Tim and Michael to pursue it. There is no consolation I can give to you for losing Tim. I won't even try. But if it helps at all to comfort you, I think Tim really believed in our division and I think he did his best to help us."

"Really?" Annie began impassively, "'Cause I think he was having a mid-life crisis, and it spiraled out of control. I think he got lost in the fantasy of it all. I just don't believe for one moment that he ever thought it would get him killed."

Christy leaned forward in concern.

Annie continued, "I'm serious. Tim's reality was really dull and he was prone to things like fantasy football and spy novels. He hated working for a large corporation like Spectorgies. But then he's given a chance to inform on them in some kind of covert corporate espionage involving the FBI and the icing on that is you paid him for it. Why I am chapped at you people is because I don't think you fully explained the dangers to him."

"And I don't know that either, it's something we'll have to question Michael about in the debriefing. I'm glad you brought that up. What I *can* tell you is that in general we don't do violence of any kind. If we can't operate inconspicuously we don't operate, so that's an important point going forward. This whole thing has been sideways from the beginning. It's *really* not how we operate."

Annie looked around the room. Christy seemed to be telling her the truth, but who knows with these people. They seem to say whatever anyone wants to hear. Annie wondered for a moment if Christy felt better for saying that crap to her. She looked back at Christy whose attention was drawn to a small red light from the key fob in the palm of her hand.

"Oh shit," Christy said looking down at the palm of her hand.

"What?" Annie asked.

"I don't know yet," Christy furrowed her brow and placed the fob, just like the one Katie had, on the desk. "Do you know Morse code?"

"No," Annie said and wandered around the room. Remembering what Sally had said about staying away from windows, she stepped away, but not before looking down into the garden courtyard. Annie caught her breathe at the sight below. The Count was carrying a lifeless Lorna in his arms through the center of the courtyard bellowing something unintelligible. Something had gone terribly wrong.

CHAPTER 13

Annie ran down the stairs to the back door that led to the courtyard and waved the Count over to her. If Lorna were dead then he wouldn't be carrying her, she thought. And she didn't see any blood. The Count's face was red from exertion but he lumbered over cradling Lorna in his arms. "There's a flight of stair," Annie said as he carefully turned sideways and shuffled through the back door.

The Count nodded as he maneuvered through the stairwell. Annie turned back and watched him climb the stairs leaving a trail of water. She threw open the apartment door to find an expectant Christy standing in the hallway. "What happened?" Christy asked.

"I don't know. It's the Count we told you about."

The Count swayed around the banister and doorways skillfully, considering his size. "Voda," he said, "voda in tub."

Christy turned and said, "In here." She ran into the bathroom and turned on the water in the tub.

The Count followed her inside and placed Lorna in the tub. Annie watched from the doorway as the Count and Christy took off the unconscious Lorna's backpack, shoes, and socks. The Count started fumbling with Lorna's pants zipper and Christy shooed him away. "I've got it," Christy said. The Count looked hurt and helpless for a moment and turned to Annie.

Annie sprung into action. "Come with me," she said grabbing Lorna's backpack. "Are you hurt?" She asked him.

"No. The Count is okay. Maybe some voda," he said.

"Of course." Annie jumped up and poured him a glass of water and brought it back in and handed the glass over to him, "What happened, Count?"

"The Count, he is standing outside watching. He sees people come and go. Then he sees the three women. But one he knows."

Annie nods, "Lorna."

The Count finished the water and handed the glass to Annie. "More?" She asked trying to look him both eyes.

The Count nodded. Annie looked for a bigger glass in the kitchen and opened a cabinet door to see a full row of bottled water. She grabbed two of them and returned to the living room. "Then what happened?" She asked.

"The Count sees men following the women. So the Count follows the men. Then, *zoom phssshew*!" The Count made a buzzing sound and slapped one hand out in front of the other. "So the Count watches. Everybody running. Then she jumps and everyone stops running. But the Count now runs down the river-"

Annie put her hand on his forearm. "She jumped into the river?"

"Yes. Is cold."

Annie blinked.

"So, the Count runs down river and he sees her," he made a bouncing movement with his hand and said, "blub, blub, blub."

"She was bobbing up and down? Swimming?" Annie

tried to help him.

"Stucklin. Like this." The Count flailed his arms around.

"Struggling. I understand." Annie said.

"Yes so I wave to her. Here! Here! I say. But she is not well. So I take down street sign and I grab her, by the rucksack."

"And you carried her all the way back here?"

"Yes."

Christy came out of the bathroom. "I need my medical kit." She glowered at the Count, "Who are you?"

Annie stood up and stepped forward in his defense, "This is the Count."

The Count stood up, put his foot forward and bowed, "Count Von Wallenstein."

"Count Von Wallenstein, and he's saved us *twice*."

Christy looked at Annie. "Go in there, make sure she doesn't drown," Christy ordered Annie.

Annie stood firm, "he's saved us *twice*." She repeated.

"I got it." Christy said and turned toward the bathroom. "Please."

Annie turned to the Count and put her hand on her heart. "Thank you."

The Count lowered his head as she left the room.

Annie rushed into the bathroom door to see Lorna sprawled out in the tub. Annie noticed she had a blue tinge to her skin. Christy had propped Lorna's head on a washcloth on the side of the tub, "Lorna?"

Lorna didn't moved.

Annie bent down and touched Lorna's wet hair, "Lorna?"

Christy came into the bathroom. "Look out," she said.

Annie turned around and watched Christy break open an ampoule and run it under Lorna's nose. When nothing happened, Christy pulled out a metal probe and touched it to Lorna's cheek. Lorna jolted awake and splashed down in the tub. Christy grabbed her arms and pulled her back up. Lorna's eyes fluttered. "I got you," Christy said then continued louder and slower, "you have to stay awake or I'll do that again!" Christy turned to Annie, "this woman's got nine lives. I take it they didn't make it to the embassy."

Annie shook her head.

"Okay, keep her awake," Christy said putting Lorna's arms down and left the bathroom.

Annie returned to the side of the tub and pulled up her sleeves. "Lorna." Annie grabbed one of Lorna's hands and rubbed. "Lorna." Annie grabbed the ampoule and held it under Lorna's nose. Lorna's head moved to the side. "Lorna. Come on." Finally, Annie grabbed the probe and tried to touch it to Lorna's cheek. Lorna jolted again and an arm came out of the tub striking the side of Annie's head. "Okay Dokay." Annie said touching her face to her sleeve, "I see how that works."

"What are you doing?" Lorna mumbled, her eyes struggling to focus.

"You jumped in the river. The Count fished you out. You are in Christy's apartment," Annie summarized.

Lorna adjusted herself in the tub, "Where's Sally?"

"We don't know," Annie answered.

"Did she get away?" Lorna's head flopped down to her chest.

"We don't know, Lorna. Stay with me."

Lorna took a gasping breath and shivered. Annie remembered that shivering was good, it meant that the body was trying to produce heat. Her body is fighting, Annie thought hopefully. She grabbed the hot water handle and turned, pouring more hot water into the tub. "Come on." She grabbed Lorna's chin. "Come on." She patted Lorna's cheeks repeatedly for several minutes.

Finally, Lorna burst from the water and grabbed Annie's shirt, pulling Annie down. "Do it again. Smack me again," she said threateningly.

"That's it!" Annie smiled up at an awkward angle. "Fight me. Come on you-" Annie struggled for some fighting words for Lorna, "ditzy blonde. Fight me, fat ass."

Lorna's eye's blinked open, "Annie, why are you calling me a fat ass?"

Annie leaned her head back and blinked back tears.

"I'm so cold," Lorna said looking at her naked body. "How-"

Christy walked into the bathroom and looked down at Lorna. "Good. So, you avoided a snatch squad by jumping in the river." She tossed her head around, "not my first choice. Now I've had to send Count Crazy to the embassy with *your* letter."

Annie couldn't believe Christy's callousness.

Lorna leaned up, "Count Crazy?"

Annie interrupted, "Count Von Wallenstein pulled you from the river and carried you all the way here."

"Yeah, I'm surprised he could find it. One eye look'n forward and one eye look'n back." Christy added.

Lorna struggled up from the tub again, "Hey. Four Eyes, watch your mouth."

Christy smiled at Annie. "Just gotta give her something to fight against. I heard you from the hall, very clever. I've got some broth warming in the kitchen for her," she said leaving the bathroom.

Annie turned to Lorna, whose teeth were now chattering. "Hot water?" Lorna said.

Annie reached over and turned on the hot water and let it run for a moment. "I just noticed something," she said, trying to keep Lorna awake. "You're in your birthday suit."

Lorna laughed, "I haven't heard that in forever."

Christy returned with a steaming mug. "Just let this cool a little bit," she said setting it on the back of the toilet.

"Is it brandy?" Annie asked.

Christy chortled. "Not with what she's got running through her veins. No, vegetable broth."

"What's a snatch squad?" Annie asked.

Christy ran her hands through her hair and frowned. "CIA" Christy crossed her arms in front of her chest. "It's not good. But," she leaned forward, "until we hear otherwise, we can't worry about them right now."

Lorna leaned up from the tub again, ready to dispute Christy's choice. "I thought you guys were all on the same side now. That's why they have the Homeland branch, to help coordinate you all together."

Christy spat out a guffaw. "Yeah, that'll be the day." Then she put her hand out at Lorna. "Hang on. I know what you're going to say but this thing upstairs can go down at any moment. And it's very likely that if Sally and Katie are out there, they are checking hospitals or Katie is still waiting outside the Nurse's pension, or they are hiding. You see, there are too many variables there. We can't disburse when we know this thing upstairs," Christy made an upward jabbing motion towards the ceiling, "is definitely going down today. Just one thing at a time."

Lorna shook her head, no. Her limbs were heavy and stiff; she tried to rise from the tub but was barely able to sit up straight.

Christy didn't back down. "So we just abandon the entire thing, after we've gotten this close, to what? Wander around the streets of Prague? We've got to trust that Sally and Katie can fin for themselves a little."

Christy had too much to do and left the room abruptly. She couldn't worry about what she couldn't control right now. She sat back down at her desk and put a headphone up to her ear and listened.

~~~

Katie followed Sally to the Nemocnice Milosrdných Sester (Sisters of Charity Hospital) and watched the street after Sally went inside. About ten minutes later Sally came back out to see an antsy Katie waiting on the street corner. "They still behind us?" Sally asked Katie as they strolled up the street.

Katie casually pulled out her street map. "Yup." They stopped and spoke over the map in front of them. "The problem is, the next two hospitals are further afield and I don't think we want to go that far away."

Sally shook her head, "I was hoping she'd have turned up at one of these hospitals."

"I don't get it. Why are they just following us?"

"I think Lorna must have been their target. What better way of finding her again than to follow us?"

Katie nodded.

"Okay, let's just walk around here," Sally sighed as they began to walk around a corner onto a cobblestoned alley that reached a small road that ran parallel to the river.

"If we're going to go to the other hospitals, it would save time if we got a cab," Katie offered.

"What was she thinking?" Sally said abruptly, "How could she possibly think it would help to jump into a freezing cold river?"

"It worked didn't it? I mean, we got away, and she probably did to."

"I'm tired of leading these morons around. We need some help." Sally caught sight of a door sign and stopped suddenly.

Katie also looked at the sign on the building where

Sally was staring. The sign read, Konzervatoř pro zrakově postiľené. It also had several rows of protruding dots. To Katie's surprise, Sally started laughing. "What is it?" She asked.

"It's a school for the blind, I think," Sally looked around and pointed to the sign. "Look at the dots. That *just happens* to be on the bank of the river. Come on. I think we found Lorna," Sally said happily.

The two women walked up the path to the building and rang the doorbell. The woman who answered it was wearing glasses and looking just past her callers and to the right.

Katie followed the woman's gaze and looked behind them.

Sally stood very still but smiled, "Dobry den. Pardon, Anglicky?"

"Yes. Some." The woman answered.

"My name is Sally Souchek. I am looking for my partner, Lorna Tollison. She's Tessa Tollison's sister and I thought she may have visited you today."

The woman didn't answer but moved her head around, somewhat like a bird, Katie thought.

"This is also Tessa's friend, Katie." Sally offered.

The woman shook her head no, "No, no one is here by that name."

"You know Tollison Tech? The computer programs for the blind? That is Tessa Tollison. Her sister is Lorna." Sally said, desperation creeping into her voice.

"I'm sorry, no." The woman said and quickly shut the door.

Sally's shoulders dropped in defeat. She turned to Katie, "she was hiding something."

"No." Katie said. "She's not here Sally." Katie turned and glanced a small walkway to their right and got an idea. "Follow me." Katie stepped away from the door and went into the alley.

"What are you doing?" Sally asked following Katie into the crevasse between the two buildings. "This is private property, Katie."

Katie shushed her. "I know that. But they can't exactly see us, can they?" Katie jabbed her thumb behind them indicating the men who had been following them, "and they sure as hell don't know that. They don't know what she said to us, they think she told us to go around back. Now hopefully there's a back yard and we can just jump some fences and double back before they know we're gone. I'll bet we can get a ten minute jump on them and get back to the apartment."

Sally looked back at the street again before following Katie over the fence.

~~~

Annie stood on one of the single beds with one hand grasping a rung on the ladder that dropped down from the ceiling in between the beds. She was watching Lorna, who sat in the doorway wrapped in a large white robe, her feet in a pan of warm water. Lorna was watching Christy who sat at her desk with a headphone held up to one ear. Christy had one arm extended with her palm out, in a hold gesture.

The only thing Annie could hear was the blood rushing through her ears. Her heart was racing and a she could feel a thin layer of cool sweat accumulating on her upper lip. What was the hold up? At least 5 minutes had past since Christy heard someone come into Lek and Ivy's apartment upstairs.

Christy waved excitedly and stage whispered, "Go."

Lorna looked up at Annie and nodded, "remember, you're playing quiet mouse."

Annie stood up on the ladder, climbed a couple rungs,

unlatched the ceiling tile and dropped it down to the bed. Her hands already shaking, she unhinged the floor above and lifted it gently. She peaked around the flooring before lifting the floor cut out up and carefully, silently, sliding it to the side. She climbed a few more steps up the ladder and belly crawled onto the floor.

Christy jumped up and tiptoe ran over to Lorna. "Go over to the headset. Say something quiet if you hear trouble. Say *trouble* loud enough for me to hear it. I'm going to stand on the ladder."

Annie heard something and looked back down in the hole. Christy appeared and waved the package of drugs at her. Annie shook her head. Christy pursed her lips together and made a big mime crossing her arms over one another.

Annie shook her head again and Christy again waved her arms making a big x and pulled them apart again. Annie understood and nodded. She pretended to pull out an Aurora and replace it with the drug package. Christy nodded and handed the package up.

Annie slid out from under the bed, stuffed the drug package in her belt, and looked around the room. There was no duffel bag and no sign of the Aurora or any other bag it could be stored in.

Annie squatted back down and looked under the bed. Christies head was sticking out of the floor. Annie shrugged at her. Christy shook her head in disappointment and waved her back down. But Annie held out a finger to her indicating to Christy to give Annie just another minute. Annie remembered the layout of the apartment and there may be a small chance she could still look around. The bedroom and bathroom were around the corner to the living room so no one would be able to see if she opened the bedroom door a little. The kitchen was a walkthrough with a service bar that came out near the front door.

Annie carefully opened the bedroom door just a crack and listened to the people talking, some of it was in a foreign language, some in American. The conversation sounded agitated, but not to an argument level. She realized someone was acting as the translator. Annie opened the door further and poked her head out. She got down on all fours and crawled out. She could hear Christy call to her with a quick low "sst". But she didn't turn back. As she crawled across the floor she could see the foyer on the other side of the kitchen where a blue backpack sat. Hugging as close as she could to the side of the cabinets Annie made her way over to the other side of the kitchen.

When she got to the other side, she waited. She needed to reach over to the other side of the foyer and get that backpack. She remembered Sally using the mirror to look out the window earlier and cursed herself for not bringing a mirror. But then she also remembered that backpack was not there before and must be the bag that held the Aurora.

Annie could feel bile rising up in her throat and she swallowed hard. She leaned back on her knees and was gripped in second thoughts when a pair of skinny, black stocking legs under a black skirt stopped in front of her. Annie looked up to see Ivy Soucek not looking back down at her. Ivy took a few steps away toward the door and purposely tripped over the backpack, before picking it up and taking it back into the living area while speaking to someone, maybe in Russian or Czech. Annie could hear only a verbal to and fro taking place. Someone guffawed and tsked several times. Ivy chortled and said something back, in French? Were they speaking French?

Annie looked back from where she had come through the kitchen. She needed to get back downstairs; she shouldn't have even attempted this *little* caper. Annie got back on all fours and began crawling back through the kitchen when Ivy came back into the kitchen without looking down at her and plopped the blue backpack down on the floor. Ivy was still talking and Annie realized Ivy was making a big show of playing hostess to someone at the service bar. This was it. Ivy was giving Annie a chance to change out the Aurora. Annie was hugging the drug package to her chest so tightly she'd forgotten to breath and heard herself taking in an audible gasp of air. She realized she was shaking and couldn't steady her breath. She was missing it, she was missing her chance, the last chance they'd have of recovering the Aurora.

Letting the drug package slide down to her knees and setting it carefully to the side, Annie took a breath. She reached across and gently unbuckled the top flap of the backpack, flipped it open, and took a breath. Sweat burned her eyes. She pulled open the drawstrings of the bag and opened it up, and took another breath. She reached in and felt the metal of the Aurora, grabbed a hold of it, and pulled up. She set the Aurora down on her left and placed the drug package from her right hand side in its place. Then she closed the drawstrings back and fastened the top closed.

She looked up at Ivy who was placing a tray of drinks on the service bar. Ivy crossed back in front of Annie and grabbed the bag again and casually moved it back over to the far foyer wall, never once did she look down at Annie.

Using only one arm to crawl with, Annie made it back to the other side of the kitchen and back through to the bedroom, carefully closing the door behind her. She looked under the bed and saw the crack of the floor widen. Christy's head popped up as she shifted the floor cut out over.

Annie crawled all the way over and slid under the

bed. She handed the Aurora down to Christy first before dropping her legs over the ladder and letting Christy steer her feet to the rungs below.

They didn't speak until Annie had gotten down safely to the floor and they had disengaged the ladder from the ceiling and replaced the tiles.

Christy wrapped her arms around Annie as Annie melted into tears.

"Shh," Christy comforted her. "It's just the stress. Let it out."

Annie seized up and then released the stress in convulsions. She looked over to Lorna who held her arms out to her.

Annie went over and hugged Lorna. "You did it," Lorna said. "You finished it."

Annie nodded, the tears streaming down. Lorna watched Christy grab the Aurora and leave the room as she comforted Annie.

Christy came back momentarily, "Okay guys, that was the easy part. Let's hope the Crown Prince of Prague made it to the embassy."

"Count Von Wallenstein," Annie said defiantly.

Christy smiled, "I know! But I'm serious, if he made it to that embassy, I am going to lobby to make him the Crown Prince."

"Are you forgetting something?" Lorna asked.

"No," Christy said back to her. "But before I head out of here, I need you to help me pack this place up. We're a ticking time bomb at this point. Annie, can you pack up as much of my crap over here," Christy pointed to the living room. "Just stuff it all into that suitcase that's open. Lorna, your clothes are in the dryer. Do you think you could get dressed?"

Lorna nodded, "The violin maker. If things went tits up she was to go to the violin guy."

"Where?" Christy asked.

"Here," Annie pulled out a map from her backpack and pointed to the street off the big square. "Around here, it had to be located around here because the hotel we were to check into was here."

Christy stared at the map again and arched her neck around. "Okay, got it. I'll be back in a short while. Oh," Christy stopped. She went over to her suitcase and pulled out a small phone and flipped it open. She pressed a number and waited. "Dinner reservation for a gold star member. Let's say three hours. There will be five for dinner. Thank you," she said authoritatively and closed the phone again. "That's hoping I'll be back."

They watched Christy hustle out the door. Lorna shrugged, "Worst vacation ever."

Annie nodded and began cleaning off the desk that held Christy's electronic gear. Lorna didn't move and Annie looked up and scowled, "What's wrong?"

"I'm just gathering strength," Lorna said.

~~~

Katie stood in the deli shop across the street from the apartment building idly fondling the various olive samples and staring out the front door. She watched Christy burst through the apartment door and hustle her way across the street. Katie dropped an olive and made her way out of the store. She finally caught up with Christy as she turned the corner on the next block.

"Hey," Katie said loudly.

Christy whirled around and they met on the sidewalk. "Where've you been?"

"Waiting. What's going on?" Katie asked.

"I've got Lorna, now where's Sally?"

"How?" Katie was shocked.

"Later," Christy swiped her hand in the air. "Where's

Sally?"

"She said for me to stay here, she had to go see a man about a violin."

"Alright that's where I'm going. Please, just go upstairs and make sure Lek and Ivy don't go near the refrigerator. As a matter of fact don't let anyone near it. Understand? Make sure everything is packed up and swab the place. No fingerprints. We've got to be out of there a.s.a.p."

"Sure."

Christ took a few steps away and tossed over her shoulder, "I'll be back as soon as I can."

As Katie turned around her eyes glanced an unwelcomed vision. Katie did a skip step shuffle and hurled herself into an alcove. When she poked her head out again she saw the three men turn around in unison and begin to follow Christy.

Katie looked back at the apartment building and licked her lips in thought. If she goes inside these goons might get Christy or worse yet they might get both of her bosses. If that's the case she, Annie, and Lorna will be screwed for sure. But if she doesn't go inside they may not make it out of here at all. Shit. Katie shook her head. No, she should go after Christy. But, then again, if they go after Christy maybe the three of them could make it to a train and head to Berlin.

Katie whirled around again and popped back out in the street. Running parallel with the street Christy was walking on, Katie tried to keep a few streets ahead. Sally had said the big square, Katie thought trying to remember the map of the city. She had to detour Christy somehow. Katie ran up the side street and waited. She poked her head out to see Christy heading toward her at a quick clip. When she poked her head out again and Christy was on the same block. Katie counted to three, popped out from behind the building in front of Christy, did the three-step Thriller zombie claw moves and popped back around the building and ran away. Christy's mouth fell open but she instinctively looked around and saw the three goons behind her and closing in.

CHAPTER 14

Lorna shucked the robe off her shivering body as Annie tossed the clothes from the dryer onto the couch.

"You could have dressed in the bathroom." Annie slung over her shoulder and bent down to open Christy's suitcase.

"And rob you of my art?"

Annie chuckled but shook her head disapprovingly.

With her pants pulled up, Lorna flopped back down on the couch next to the clothes and began struggling with the bra. Her arms felt heavy and stiff, and she took a break to stare at the shirt. Thank God it was a pull over, she thought. She looked up to realize Annie was watching her.

"Need some help?" Annie asked consolingly.

"I think it's all catching up with me," Lorna admitted.

Annie got up and helped Lorna put on her bra, shirt, and socks. She gathered Lorna's backpack, shoes, and coat and set them on the couch next to her.

"Here," Annie handed her the mug of broth, "you should finish this."

The staccato knocks on the door came suddenly and without the prelude of echoing footsteps from the hallway. They both froze midway through Annie handing Lorna the broth.

"Lek and Ivy?" Lorna said quietly.

Annie furrowed her brow. "Yeah, right? It has to be." She went to the front door, disappointed there was no peephole, and opened it.

Lek and Ivy smiled warmly at Annie and let themselves into the apartment.

~~~

Christy ran straight through the big square, past the circular fountain and tried to get lost in the throng of people gathered to watch the antique clock chime and do its show. She didn't dare look behind her. On her left, on the side street she saw people milling around the street tchotchke market filled with what looked more like Russian than Czech memorabilia. There must be at least six streets leading off the big square and she was going to have to look down each one to find the violin shop. She looked both ways down a side alley as she made her way down the street and turned the corner.

She pulled her jacket off and tied it around her waist; the cool air on her skin was a welcomed relief. Across the street she scanned the faces lined up for something outside a building. In front of her people milled around a street vendor hawking his wares. People were simply going about their business all around her. She turned the corner and saw a red flag. Below the red flag were a group of Japanese tourists. The leader, who held the red flag was speaking in low tones into a microphone and the followers all had earphones in their ears. They stopped in front of a shop where two stuccoed fiddles were jauntily positioned above the door. Christy waited patiently and perused the florist shop window behind her, keeping an eye on the reflection in the window. When the tourist group strolled past, Christy turned around and paused a moment before approaching the storefront.

Looking into the window, she could see a light emanating from the door in back. Which means they have a back door, she thought. Christy rang the bell next to the door and waited. An elderly man with a neatly trimmed beard opened the inner door and looked out past Christy. He closed the door again not acknowledging Christy. The inner door opened again and a lanky, well-tailored man with dark hair emerged. Christy watched a policie close the inner door behind him. The man opened the front door for Christy and gave her the once over before saying, "Ano?"

Christy smiled, "I'm here visiting and I was shopping for a bohemian violin, maybe an antique?

The man smiled down at Christy, "Ah, eh. Yes."

His dialect was thick as he searched for the words. But his tailored suit said, unmistakably, high-ranking government official.

He continued, "Later? We have uh, student."

Christy pointed in the shop, "Student now, come back later?"

"Yes. Later, you come back."

Christy nodded, "Thank you. I will come back later then."

She heard the door shut behind her as she walked away, pulling her jacket back on. She turned the corner and walked the length of the block and turned again looking for the doorway that led to the alley between the buildings. The violin shop was two stores down from the end of the block, so once she got to the alley she turned again and found the second backdoor, hoping it led to the violin shop. As she stood looking at the door, configuring a diversion to get Sally out of there, she felt a mass of heat across her back.

The voice was low and deep. "It is I, the Count."

Christy whirled around but he covered her mouth with a meaty paw.

"How did you get here?" Christy blurted through his sausage fingers.

The Count nodded at the door, "He is my uncle."

To Christy's annoyance she couldn't follow Count Von Wallenstein's floating eye and she chose instead to rest her eyes on his long thick uni-brow when she spoke. "Do you have a key?"

"No, he doesn't trust me."

"That's too bad," she said. "Did you-"

"Yes, I handed the letter to the doorman." The Count cut her off.

"That's really good, Count. Is there any other way in here? Maybe a side door?"

"No, he lives above the shop. The stairs are inside."

Christy looked at her watch. "Count," she said rigidly, "I'm getting desperate. If I start a fire out here, do you think you could get the people in these buildings out in time?"

"No. No. You are so destructive."

As they spoke the knob on the door began to turn. The Count jerked Christy to the side and positioned himself to charge the door. He moved with such agility Christy barely got her footing again before he was taking the door with the brut force of a rhinoceros. The door splintered off it's hinges - the Count and the door falling inward, flattening whatever, and whoever was behind it.

~~~

Katie made a mad dash around the corner and plastered herself against the wall. She waited a few moments before breathing a sigh of relief. She had to get back to the apartment and deal with that business. She looked around the street in front of her before continuing at a regular pace.

~~~

Lorna adjusted herself on the couch as she watched Lek and Ivy walk into the apartment. Ivy stopped Annie in the hallway and spoke quietly to her as Lek walked over to Lorna and stood in front of her.

"What happened to you?" He asked.

"I fell in the drink," Lorna said staring at the blue surgical gloves on his hands.

Lek was eyeballing her and Lorna steeled herself as his giant hand reached down and touched her forehead. Honestly, Lorna thought, the more I look at him the more I see Sally.

"Ivy. Get in here Love," Lek called out.

Ivy teetered over in her heels and stood next to Lek and they stared down at Lorna. Lek pointed to Lorna, "this ones got hypothermia. Feel her."

Ivy put down the plastic bag and a package of handy wipes and sat down next to Lorna. She pulled Lorna's cheek next to her own and felt Lorna's hand's. Then she reached a thin, vein-mapped hand behind Lorna's neck and held it there for a moment. Lorna didn't move but kept an eye on Ivy's pointy fingernails.

Ivy stood back up. "She's dehydrated and is suffering from a physical shock I think."

"That's what I thought," Lek said and looked at Lorna. "It's your pallor. You need electrolytes and some blankets." He looked around the room and spotted Christy's black medical bag while Ivy disappeared into the bedroom.

"Annie!" Lorna tried to keep the alarm out of her

voice.

Annie came into the room wearing the blue surgical gloves and carrying handy wipes. "I'm busy."

Lek dug around the medical bag and looked up at Annie, "Get me a couple of glasses of luke warm water, will ya'?"

Annie wanted to protest but did as she was asked.

Ivy also wore the blue surgical gloves when she came back into the room carrying a quilt and draped it around Lorna. "You need to keep that heart pumping into your extremities, so do this." Ivy demonstrated squeezing her hands back and forth into fists. "And squeeze your toes together." Ivy turned quickly and returned to the bedroom.

Annie came back with the water and handed it to Lek, then disappeared into the bathroom. He broke a capsule into the water and watched it fizz before handing it to Lorna. "Drink that slowly."

"What is it?"

"Potassium, sodium, bicarbonate. Tastes like pond dregs but it's what you need so drink it," Lek ordered. "Then drink some regular water. Keep drinking till you start peeing every five minutes."

"Okay," Lorna took a sip and choked up a bit. She made a face and held out the glass shaking her head.

"It's either this or we warm you up the old fashioned way," Lek said straight-faced.

"What's that?"

"We all get naked and make a Lorna sandwich."

"Where's Sally?" Ivy asked noncommittally as she strode briskly into the kitchen.

"She's out," Annie fielded the question following Ivy into the kitchen.

"And the other two, who live here?" Ivy came into the room and snatched the glasses off the table Lorna had drunk from and returned to the kitchen with them.

Annie returned and handed Lorna a bottle of water with a meaningful look but Lorna answered truthfully. "I don't know. I think one is looking for Sally and the other is MIA."

Lek handed Lorna a pair of surgical gloves, "Put these on and don't take them off for anything."

Annie did not like how Lorna was taking Ivy and Lek into her confidence and wondered how much damage these two could possibly do at this point. She sat stiffly on the edge of the couch and watched the clock on the wall. They hadn't pulled a gun and demanded the Aurora back yet, so just maybe they actually were trying to help them. Annie perished the thought almost as fast as it occurred to her. This sitting still was annoying her. They needed to keep moving, she thought.

"I think maybe they were Russian and I jumped in the river and that's when Sally and Katie ran on."

Lek laughed and Lorna shot him a dirty look. "Sorry." Lek smiled. "They were probably Poles, for the CIA of course. Tall, beefy guys, short black hair?"

"Yeah."

"Poles. Hired by the CIA," Lek said knowingly, "but you're sure Sally got away?"

"I don't know."

Lek disappeared into his thoughts for a moment.

"There's one more thing," Lorna said. "Before we left, I dropped a bag of dope into the duffel bag you put in the bedroom."

"Dope?" Ivy asked.

"I don't know it may have been cocaine or heroin."

"How much?" He asked.

"A couple of pounds," Lorna said.

"Where did you get it?" He asked.

"It's kind of a long story."

"Did you get it here?" Ivy asked concerned and looking around the room.

"No, at the old safe house. It's a crack house."

Lek and Ivy once again exchanged knowing looks.

"Lek, be a dear," Ivy said.

"I'm going," Lek said begrudgingly and stood up.

"Where are you going?" Annie asked.

To Annie's great relief, Lek said, "I need to inform the police that I witnessed a drug deal and give them a description of that Nurse woman. The Prague police do not like it when foreigners bring drugs onto their streets."

Ivy laughed, "No, they don't."

"But there's more," Annie confessed.

Lek furrowed his brow at her.

"I replaced the diplomatic bag with the Aurora, when I was upstairs."

Both Lek and Ivy's eyebrows shot up.

"You did what?" Lek asked.

Ivy threw her head back in a wheezing jolt of laughter. "She caused an international incident!"

Lek shook his head but chuckled, "From the mouths of babes. I'll be back." He took a few bouncing steps toward the front door and paused, listening, before opening it.

"Where's he going?" Annie asked.

Ivy smiled at her, "He's going to the embassy, I'm sure. They put tracers now in these pouches. They'll be able to retrieve it soon."

Annie heard a noise in the hallway and jerked to her feet. But Ivy continued talking, "Lorna, have you ever been down under?"

"Australia? No." Lorna said.

"Then you must come visit us on your next holiday," Ivy offered. "You too Annie. We'd love to have you.

With or without Lorna and Sally, you're always welcome." She lowered her voice and nodded to Annie, "You have a particular kind of promise."

Annie turned to Ivy. Ivy recognized the confusion and hurt cross over Annie's eyes.

"There will be a tomorrow," Ivy said softly.

The door swung open again and Katie barged in to see the three women sitting comfortably in the living room. "What the hell are you doing?" Katie said with bated breath.

"Waiting for you," Lorna answered.

Katie shook her head, "We gotta go."

"But Christy made dinner reservations," Lorna whined.

"No. She was ordering a plane for us," Katie's tone grew indignant and she rolled her eyes.

Lorna's eyebrows shot up at this Katie's indignant jab.

Annie jumped in, "Katie, the plane isn't for another couple of hours. I think we should wait for Christy and Sally."

Katie shook her head.,"No, you don't get it. There's a group of men out for us."

"Oh!" Ivy chuckled. "To be young again."

Katie rolled her eyes and shook her head, "Do what you want, I'll be on the plane."

Annie stood up, "Katie, no. Please. Let's not separate again. Christy's got enough on her plate."

"Lek is taking care of the men that are after you. He's upstairs now making the phone call."

But Katie was insistent, "I don't think it's a good idea to wait here. I mean, we should at least change our position."

Annie and Lorna exchanged a glance. Annie looked to Ivy, "What do you think?"

"It's your mission, girls," Ivy responded.

Lorna's shoulder's fell, "That doesn't help."

"Well, your Russian's are going to get picked up for the Diplomatic pouch, and that woman will be picked up for the drugs. I don't see any reason to panic. It seems to me the longer you wait here, the more distance you will have and the more likely your path would be clear by the time you leave here."

Annie and Lorna nodded.

Katie sat down but added, "You didn't see what I saw."

"Sure I did!" Lorna gave Katie a disapproving cluck.

"What happened, dear?" Ivy asked Katie.

"I was outside waiting, over at that deli across the street. When I saw Christy come out. But then I saw some guys from somewhere, I don't know, I guess they may have been in a car or something, cause I didn't see them before, but they were following Christy."

"How many?" Ivy interrupted.

"Three. Anyway, I ducked around the block and ran ahead so I could get Christy's attention from the other direction. I didn't want them seeing me, but I didn't want her to lead them straight to Sally. So I ran up ahead and waited to see her coming and popped out from behind the corner and I *know* she saw me. Then I just turned back and ran. But then I got lost. I don't know how that's even possible. But I got turned around and had to find my way back here. So I waited again and made sure I didn't see any vans or guys sitting in cars before I came back up here."

Ivy nodded approvingly and then thought of a follow up question, "Could you recall what they looked like?"

"One had a blue jacket. Let's see, jeans. Then another guy had like cargo pants and a dark blue, maybe black jacket, like a windbreaker. And the other guy, I don't know, it was so fast. Jeans and brown jacket maybe."

Ivy cut her eyes to Lorna, "Same?"

Lorna shook her head, "No. Our guys were wearing leather."

Again, the front door swung open and Christy came rushing in. She didn't acknowledge anyone in the room before rushing into the kitchen. Behind her The Count lumbered into the doorway at the same time they heard a thud against the doorjamb.

"Ow Fucker! Put me down," Sally cursed.

"I'm so sorry," The Count said.

Ivy teetered to her feet as Annie rushed over to help.

"I got it," She said to him. "Thank you."

Blood covered the front of Sally's neck, shirt, and coat. Lorna hobbled over as Christy came in with a wet kitchen towel.

"What happened?" Lorna asked.

"I saved them," The Count offered.

"At the violin shop, he broke in the back door. I was standing behind it."

"Are you okay?" Lorna asked.

Sally nodded.

"The police were there," Christy said handing Sally the towel.

"They were there to arrest me. The guy that was shot at the crack house? He was undercover drug enforcement."

The Count gasped and bit his lower lip, "He was policie? Nooo."

Annie and Lorna looked at him. Annie cut her eyes at him. "How do you know about this?"

"Because, I shot him. I thought he was a bad man. He had a gun. I saw it. My uncle, he told me to protect you." The Count chewed his fingers in horror.

Annie watched as Ivy, waifish and elderly, comfort his shaking bulk.

"I will be prison," The Count muttered as Ivy steered him to the couch.

Christy reappeared, "We gotta go. That wasn't the police after us." Her eyes widened when she saw Ivy, "Hi. You're Ivy Soucek."

Ivy smiled broadly and nodded.

Christy stuck out her hand, "It's such an honor. I can't tell you-" Christy fumbled. "I've read all about you. I mean, just in Virginia and Pickles of course."

Ivy nodded.

Annie and Lorna rolled their eyes.

Lek filled the doorframe, "Holy shit, are you guys in trouble now!" He exclaimed shutting the door behind him.

Katie jumped up, "I told you guys! See! I said 'leave'. But noooooo-"

"Katie!" Christy stopped her.

Lek stage whispered, "You shot a cop?"

"No. We didn't," Annie said.

"Well, they are saying you did. Said they had eye witnesses too."

"But we didn't," Lorna said.

Ivy came over with her hands in the air to shush everyone. She spoke to Lek. "Darling, they are using the incident to get to the girls. If they take them in to custody then they will have a bargaining chip with this Aurora. It's just a ploy to get them to the table. You know that. Now girls, Katie, Annie, get your maps out and go to the couch. Lek, Christy get in touch with whomever you need to so you can throw dust on our trail."

"Yes, ma'am," Christy muttered and turned to Lek.

"Lorna and Sally, go to the bathroom and get Sally cleaned up. Count, where is your uncle?"

The Count, who was weeping softly on the couch, shrugged.

"Well, don't you think it would be a good idea to find him, and make sure he's okay?"

The Count shook his head no.

"Then maybe you should go to your castle and wait to hear from him?"

Lorna turned and went back to the living room. She sat next to The Count and put her arm around him. "Thank you for saving my life. I will *never* forget what you did for me. When all this is cleared up and some time has past, will you come see me?"

He lifted his head up and touched her cheek. His chest lifted and he inhaled deeply, "I will come for you."

"Okay," Lorna said and moved quickly off the couch.

Ivy showed him to the door and rejoined Annie and Katie on the couch. She smiled at them calmly. "Have you ever seen the Keystone Cops?" She asked.

~~~

Lorna was the second downstairs behind Sally and soon after Christy joined them. Christy's suitcase had been stashed in the small ceiling crawlspace between her apartment and Lek and Ivy's apartment. The suitcase was to be retrieved and mailed to her office by a courier Lek had set up for her. Sally helped Lorna put on her backpack. Katie and Annie joined them at the bottom of the stairs nodding and the two groups separated. Katie, Lorna, and Sally stood at the front door. Christy and Annie walked to the back door and waited. Lek and Ivy walked down the stairs. Lek carrying his European man satchel and Ivy toting her paten leather purse looked as though they could simply be going out for dinner, Christy thought. When Lek and Ivy reached the interior door to the cheese shop she paused and made eye contact with each of the girls who were waiting patiently for her signal. She nodded her head and three doors flew open.

Christy led the way out the back door and into the courtyard garden. Annie looked out from behind Christy for a quick scan of the various doors that let into the buildings and darkened alley tunnels which led to the streets. Each portal, with it's various centuries old adornments, looked less charming and more ominous than the one before it. She popped out the door and closed it behind her with a firm shove.

Christy made a right and walked around the courtyard. But Annie made a beeline across the courtyard. As Annie entered the opening to the tunnel she was to exit through, she desperately wanted to turn around to see if Christy had made it to the other exit. It was the closest exit from the building and had that great rod iron fence that they had oiled with travel shampoo earlier, so she wouldn't hear it squeak. She fought off the urge to look back and chanted to her self, 'make a right, red hatchback', 'make a right, red hatchback'. As she took her first steps out of the tunnel and onto the sidewalk she could hear a distant bird screeching. Walking with purpose, but not hurrying so much that she'd draw attention to herself, Annie scanned the car rooftops parked on the side of the street until she saw a red one. Hopefully, she thought.

"Ruuuuuuun!"

Annie stole a quick glance behind her to see the bespectacled Christy approaching at a high rate of speed.

~~~

Sally, Lorna, and Katie filed out of the front door like school children on a field day, jackets zipped up and backpacks securely in place. Sally led the group down the slight incline of the sidewalk. Remaining single file allowed them to maneuver around the other pedestrians quicker. Each woman, in turn, took surreptitious glances at their surroundings as they strolled. And each one had noted the two men, both wearing khaki cargo pants and fleece pullover's walking parallel to them on the other side of the street. American's, Sally thought and made a sharp right onto the side street.

Sally pulled out a set of keys, swerved her body around a parked car and looked behind her as she opened the driver's side door. Lorna stood next to the passenger door and peered quizzically at the odd look on Sally's face.

Before Lorna could turn around she felt a gun placed firmly in her ribs and a large hand grip the back of her neck. She watched Sally step away from the small grey sedan, and purposefully kept her hands in sight. Ivy came tottering around the front of the car in her heels and jumped behind the wheel. Lek pushed Lorna down into the backseat and followed her into the car.

As the little sedan spun off Sally ran over to Katie who was hunched down against a wall and the two of them watched the khaki pant's race down the street and jump into a car. Sally smiled at Katie. "You alright?"

"Dude, your mom is tiny but damn," Katie said rubbing the back of her head.

Sally helped Katie up and the two women strolled casually down the street.

~~~

Annie held onto the door-strap like her life depended on it. And it very well might. The cobblestone alley they had turned onto was so narrow and wound around the buildings in such precarious ways that the fastest a sane person would drive it would be five miles an hour. Christy was lurching along at fifteen miles and hour and had a hard time keeping the wheels of the car from scraping the raised curb.

"Look," Annie was able to proclaim before a wheel of the car hit upon a stone that made her jaw slam shut. "Look, I don't see anyone behind us. I think we can take it slow for a bit, just till we get off this street."

Christy jabbed her eyes at the rearview mirror and back out the front window and let off the gas, "Okay."

"That was awesome driving by the way."

Christy groaned, "Don't thank me yet."

Annie looked down at her map, "Two more streets."

Christy looked back at the rearview mirror, "I don't know, those guys, they didn't try very hard, you know? Did that feel right to you?"

"How should I know? I'm not Ivy Soucek."

Christy eyes widened and she nodded positively, "Oh, she's wonderful."

Annie furrowed her brow at Christy.

"Here we go," said Annie, "they're raising the door for us. Right here."

A large loading bay door was rolled up as Christy maneuvered the car next to a small delivery van inside the surprisingly cavernous loading dock. The loading dock door rolled back down automatically with a clang but no one appeared. The two women looked around for a moment.

"Uh," Annie choked out, staring at the ominous looking loading dock.

"Oh shit," Christy agreed.

"Make a run for it?" Annie asked.

"No. They may be waiting for us to make a move," Christy said looking around the bay from the inside of the car.

"I don't know. Maybe we should, like, ram the door with the car or something. I mean, put up a fight at least."

"No, no, no," Christy put up a halting hand. "They may want to make sure we are who we're supposed to be, and may not be allowed to show us who they are. Just get out of the car slowly and put your back pack where they can see it - away from you."

Around the side of the bay a small cement staircase with a modern metal banister led to a steel door. The steel door opened and an elderly woman walked into the loading bay. She stood there, a bright red and blue striped scarf wrapped around her curlers, in her mismatched polyester skirt set with a mangy fur wrap around her shoulders. With her fists on her hips she watched the two women get out of the car.

It was definitely Slavic, whatever the old woman had said, Annie thought.

"Dobry den?" Annie tried to greet the woman.

"Oh!" The woman threw back her head and said mockingly, "Do-bry Din."

Annie looked to Christy for help. Christy said nothing and took a step away from the car. Annie wanted to run out of there so bad she felt like she would hyperventilate. A door on the back wall opened and a man, in his mid-50's walked out fumbling with a set of keys. He shook his head and smiled as he walked around the back and down the stairs to the floor of the bay. "I'm sorry, I dropped my keys and had to retrace my steps."

His dialect was surprisingly without the sharp slavic accents, Annie thought. He opened the back of the van. "Okay, a half hour and you'll be home free."

Christy threw her backpack in first. "Thanks," she handed him a wad of bank notes.

But he held up a hand refusing the money. "No, for Ivy."

Christy insisted shaking the notes at him. "Please, for me. Take it. For your mother." She said indicating the door behind her.

"My grandmother," he said smiling.

Annie mentally recalculated his age and got in the back of the delivery truck.

~~~

"What took you so long?" Lek asked Sally through the driver's side window.

Sally grimaced at him but said nothing. Ahead she could see Lorna and her mother sitting in the car together. Katie got out of the passenger side and walked over to the other car holding Lorna and Ivy and got inside.

"Well?" He said holding out his arms. "Not bad for your old man."

Sally smiled and got out of the car.

"And not a shot fired I might add. A good spy never carries a gun Sally," He said lecturing.

Sally looked over the flat field in front of them. Maybe he was a great spy, she thought, but at the cost of being a father. Not a great father nor a good father but just a plain old dad. In the distance she could see the lights of Prague beginning their nightly glow. And for the first time she saw her father, as a human, with all the human flaws attached come into her view. Living under the legacy of his own father, he was just a person trying to make a way in a very messed up world of shadows and lies.

They spoke and stopped at the same time. Sally smiled. "Dad. Thank you for your help in this-" she shook her head and let the sentence drop.

"Hey, it was your first mission, I had to be here. I missed your dance recital."

"What?"

"The one your grandma took you to. Ms. Charlotte's School of Tap." He said.

He's trying to make up for lost time? She thought. But smiled, "Oh right, well, you didn't miss much. A bunch of little kids tripping over each other looking dazed and confused."

He laughed out loud. "Yeah. I would have given my right arm to see that." He lifted his right forearm and rubbed it.

Sally looked at his craggy face in the dying light. "This was the only mission, Dad. I need to make my own life. Just a basic, boring, run of the mill life; with dinner's at home, weekend grocery trips, and gardening."

"You like gardening?"

"Sure."

"Oh, you should see New Zealand then. Gorgeous."

A small white delivery truck came bouncing across the roadway and into the field. It came to a sliding halt a few feet from the little grey sedan.

The driver got out and shook Lek's hand.

Sally's mouth dropped open and she shrugged empty handed at the guy.

"Oh, sorry," He said and opened the back of the van.

Two very nauseas, disheveled, and angry women spilled out of the back of the truck. Sally moved to help them out as Christy straightened her glasses on her face and tried to right herself. Christy yanked her arm away from Sally and adjusted her shirt. The driver made the mistake of chuckling at her. And Christy, without saying a word to him, hobbled over and kneed him in the groin.

Annie crawled to the truck doors and handed Sally her backpack. Sally helped Annie out of the truck and practically had to carry her over to the car holding the other women. Christy and Sally leaned against the back bumper of the car.

"How'd we do?" Sally asked.

Christy checked her watch. "Well, we made it. For better or worse."

"What's next?" Sally asked.

"Well, this, Christy patted a backpack, goes to the Director, also for better or worse. And then we have to let the justice system do its work."

"Fraud?" Sally chortled. "It'll never see the light of day."

Christy nodded. "I hope not."

EPILOGUE

Lorna returned to a hospital in San Francisco and was unceremoniously escorted into a private room. There was some internal repair done in her chest, among other tweaks, a drip was added to her chest cavity. After a couple of weeks in the hospital Annie stopped showing up and answering her phone. It was Sally who finally told Lorna that Annie had left town, whereabouts unknown.

Lorna returned to Saint Charles Place a few weeks after that to see a for sale sign in Annie's lawn. Every day she sat quietly in their front parlor and watched real estate brokers come and go from the home as she convalesced. Then one day, a post card was delivered. It was from New Zealand. The front of the card had dolphins jumping out of the sea and on the back of the card was written, *Having a great time, wish you were here,* in Annie's unmistakable scrawl.

Sally, on the other hand, was only too happy to return to daily work. She delighted in the daily minutia. It was dull, predictable, and most of all, safe. The postcard from New Zealand was familiar to her when she arrived home one day to see it sitting on the coffee table. She took it into the kitchen, steamed the edge, pealed the card apart, and handed it back to Lorna. The inside of the card read, *I hope you understand. I have a purpose now and am relatively happy. But I miss my friend.* Sally held her tight as Lorna finally broke down and cried for a long time. She mourned the loss of friendship, of the promise she had for their new home, and of her family. But would it would clear the way to let the healing and processing begin.

Roberta, after seeing Lorna in such a physically diminished state, had taken it upon herself to "fatten Lorna up". Roberta and Lorna had always had a somewhat thorny relationship but Sally was grateful for the relief Roberta brought to her. Of all the people on the island Lorna had dealings with, it bemused Sally that it was Roberta whom Lorna could truly count on. Eventually Roberta began talking through various cases she had and those visits are what finally brought Lorna back around emotionally.

Sally's heart leapt one day when she walked onto the front porch and could see in from the window the outline of two familiar figures sitting on the couch. It was Mrs. Strangler and Roberta. Lorna walked into the room with a tray of beverages. When Sally first let herself into the front door she didn't hear the hum of the sound scrambler but as the laughter died down she gave Lorna a quizzical look and point her index finger up.

Lorna came over to her smiling and gave her a peck on the cheek, "I'm sorry, we should have waited for you."

"Lorna's giving us the play by play," Roberta said.

Sally's mouth fell open and she looked at Lorna, "Should you be doing this?"

"I didn't sign any kind of secrets act or some shit," Lorna raised her eyebrows.

Sally blinked, "No, you didn't," and smiled.

Lorna's retelling took on a much more humorous air than Sally remembered the events being. But it didn't matter now and Sally joined in the folly of recounting the events to their friends. It felt so healthy for Sally to be talking openly about this, making light of Lorna's determination, and laughing at her self. Afterward, as she bid goodnight to Roberta and Mrs. Strangler, she felt physically drained as if she had run a marathon. That night she slept soundly for the first time in a year.

~~~

It was a full six months after they had returned when Lorna was coming home from her morning *power walk,* as she called it, with Burt and Ernie, when she saw Annie sitting on the front porch. The dogs must have seen or sensed Annie first because they tugged at their leashes so hard Lorna had to let them go several yards away from the house.

She stopped a few feet from the porch and smiled. "Lunch?"

"I would love some." Annie said as she hugged the dogs and let them lick her face.

The two women shuffled about the kitchen as if their routine of having lunch together nearly every day hadn't changed. But neither woman wanted to go back to that old life now, they had seen and done too much. Working from home, to those who go into an office everyday, may seem like heaven. But it had trappings office workers could never understand, isolation being the worst of all. And without even knowing it, they had both been a salvation to each other in that respect. These lunches had become the structure in which many of their workdays operated around.

"How was New Zealand?" Lorna asked over a

steaming bowl of tomato soup.

"It's beautiful," Annie said with a new glow. "How are the new neighbors?"

"Weird," Lorna answered. "A couple of not very friendly yuppies. A lot has changed in the last couple of months. New mayor."

"New President."

"That's true," Lorna nodded taking a bite of her sandwich. "And a minority at that."

"Things are changing hopefully." Annie blew on her soup and scraped her spoon on the side of her bowl. She cleared her throat.

"I miss this," Lorna said. "Kinda like old times for us."

Annie cocked her head to the side, "No. It feels weird being here."

"Does it?"

"It's like an out of body experience." Annie paused and swallowed a bite of her sandwich. "So what's going on, any more of your little adventures in social anarchy?"

Lorna shook her head, no.

"Oh come on, I don't believe it." Annie rebuked her.

"No, really, I don't get involved in the community these days." Lorna shrugged reluctantly, "It sucks."

"I'm surprised."

"Well, Roberta comes by from time to time to talk through a case or something, but that's about it."

"Right. But well, we can't go back to how it was. I can't."

"No." Lorna agreed.

"How's your healing? Are you drug free and," Annie moved her shoulder up and down, "hearts all good?"

"Like a clock. How's your healing?" Lorna countered.

"Oh, well, I'm nuts. I just spent several months in New Zealand with Lek and Ivy. Hey, what happened with

Tessa and Quill?"

"They are on a need to know basis still. And I don't feel any need for them to know anything."

"Well, they just didn't give you any choice, did they?" Annie said.

Lorna shook her head, no. And slurped some soup. "*I* would have never guessed it."

"You've heard nothing from them, no apologies? Nothing?"

"Nope. It's been six months."

"Over six months!" Annie corrected her with astonishment. "I *really* didn't see that coming."

Lorna nodded. "Yeah. How hard is it to say, 'I'm sorry. I was wrong.' I do it all the time."

"No you don't," Annie chided her playfully.

"Because I'm never wrong," Lorna laughed and took a big bite of sandwich.

They ate in comfortable silence for a few minutes.

"Oh," Lorna remembered something. "We do have some news or future news, we're moving back to the east coast. New York or maybe Vermont."

Annie was not surprised and nodded as she swallowed, "I think you'll be happier."

"Yeah, there's been too much water under this bridge. We had some good times though."

"We did," Annie agreed. "When do you move?"

"Not until next summer at least, maybe fall. Sally's waiting for an opening in one of the eastern offices, she said there were some retirements in the summer. So we'll put the house up for sale in April."

"Well, mine went really fast. So keep that in mind."

"Can I ask you one question?" Lorna said, lowering her voice again.

Annie nodded, leaning in over her soup.

"Did your trip to *New Zealand* have anything to do

with a *new job*?"

"You mean was I influenced by my hosts? Yes. I'm going to be doing travel writing. Adventure travel."

"Really? Sounds exciting. Do they train you for that?"

"Oh sure. A couple months at training facility, and then you get a mentor. Learn the ropes, how to work out deals with local businesses."

"Huh," Lorna said sitting back. "Will you be stationed any one place or like on a continent somewhere?"

"I don't know," Annie said cagily. "We'll see."

"Can I ask if your new bosses name starts with a C?"

Annie laughed and dropped her spoon. "Yes. It does. She's awesome. She visited us in New Zealand. But I think she really just wanted to hang out with Lek and Ivy."

"Okay," Lorna put her hand out and mimed zipping her mouth shut.

"It's okay, it's part of why I'm here, actually. I need a next of kin and there is some paperwork. I was hoping, if you wouldn't mind, I mean it would make sense since you guys are like the only ones who know what's going on with me-" Annie fumbled.

Lorna put her spoon down. "Annie. Are you sure? I mean." Lorna pursed her lips together in a worried frown.

"Yes. I feel like I need to do this."

"But, now listen to me. You are my friend and I love you and want the best for you. But you can't let tragedy define you. Going forward ya' know - it was an event. Well, several events really. But they were events that just happened. Not events because-"

Annie cut her off, "I know. Please, Ivy's like the Dr. Joyce Brothers down under. But I realized it's interesting work. And you know what? Those two put me through my paces, taught me things only experience can teach and I can carry that on, you know?"

"Okay, right on. If this is what you want," Lorna nodded. "Just, don't tell Sally."

Annie furrowed her brow.

"It's just that Sally's so happy now - you know how boring she likes her life. I don't think she's ever been happier than when I was on the mend. And she deserves that."

"She deserves to be boring?" Annie asked.

"Yes. That woman went to the wall for me. She sacrificed everything she wanted for herself and she never once, not once, mentioned my family's betrayal or blamed me for it, she never complained when I was sick, and she always put me first. So if she wants to go around taking her pictures or digging in the boring dirt on the weekends. If that makes her happy, so be it."

Annie was at a loss for words.

Lorna didn't miss a beat, "Are you staying a while?"

"If you don't mind, just overnight." Annie said.

"Good. I think it'll be fine, of course. But take it easy when you ask her. Like don't leave anything out."

"Like what?" Annie asked.

"Like if it's going to be linking her to her parents somehow-" Lorna started to explain.

"No, no, nothing like that. I just need to have a next of kin notification and an executer for my will, stuff like that. I'm not asking her to be covert or anything exciting."

"Oh, good. That's fine then. By the way, what happened to Michael? I'm assuming Christy filled you in."

"Oh yes. Poor Michael. Well not really, he's happily back in the IT department. He got a promotion and I think Christy taps him from time to time when she needs something." Annie explained.

"I'm glad really. Nice guy but-"

"Almost got us killed? Yeah. You know he only trained like one day. I'm going in for at least a month. Depending on how I do on my tests. And that's not even counting the time I've spent in New Zealand and then time with my mentor. That sorta tells you all you need to know."

"What about The Nurse?" Lorna was getting to the crux of the matter.

"She was captured. The Russians were going to send her back for a trial but she didn't make it."

"The Russians got her?" Lorna was astounded.

"No, but she ended up in Russia. How she ended up there, no one knows for certain, but she died there. Hung herself."

"Really. Are they sure she's dead?" Lorna wanted to know.

"Oh yeah." Annie said definitely. "I saw the pictures."

Lorna nodded solemnly. There didn't seem to be any more to say.

ABOUT THE AUTHOR

M. Saylor Billings is the author of The O Line Mystery series, which includes *Saint Charles Place*, *The Disaster Relief Club*, *The Rot is Deep*, and *Red, White, and Scotch*; *The O Line Mystery Shorts*, dramatized audio books, available on Audible; and *Nobody, Really, Likes You*. She lives with her family in Northern California. She is a producer for Billibatt Productions.

www.ingramcontent.com/pod-product-compliance
Lightning Source LLC
Chambersburg PA
CBHW071135170626
46809CB00002B/627